For Better,

For Worse

Caryl Rivers and Alan Lupo

Summit Books

NEW YORK

To Steven and Alyssa
To Max and Esther and to
the memory of Helen and Hugh

Contents

CONTENTS

Foreword

A Love Story

She was a convent girl from the suburbs who kept her Catholic Youth Organization All-Star basketball jacket lovingly wrapped in tissue paper and who liked to commune with nature. He was a Jewish kid from the city who got separation anxiety when he got 500 yards away from concrete and whose idea of a sporting afternoon was a fast game of pool in a smoke-filled room.

She thought he was terribly exotic because he bought her meat knishes, taught her to say "schmuck" and said it was a fact that nuns ate babies. He thought she was wonderfully exotic because she was blond and she said that you would know when the end of the world was near because all the Jews would convert right before the second coming.

They met at the Columbia Graduate School of Journalism, making a documentary on rats. They crouched in fetid alleys while he held a camera and did poor imitations of the mating calls of rodents and she gripped a light meter and called softly, "Here ratty, nice ratty," thinking of *The Wind in the Willows*. One day, in a particularly rancid alleyway, he looked deep into her eyes, and she looked deep into his eyes, and she said, "Jeez, hit the lights, there goes one of the little buggers now."

From there it was only a short step to love among the roaches in his basement apartment on 113th Street. The cries and whispers were due partly to passion and partly to the three-inch nail sticking up out of the bedframe.

Hand-in-hand they walked off together into the brave new world of Journalism. On a small paper in New York State, they wrote of the great events of the day.

She was nearly bludgeoned to death by a band of irate Polish onion farmers, when she covered their meeting on the very day her paper had editorialized that a jetport should be plonked down right on top of their furrows. "But I love onions! I live on Big Macs!" she screamed as they chased her through the parking lot with hoes and pitchforks.

He covered the seamy world of crime in the Catskills. He looked on in transfixed horror as Chief Carl Shapiro (Fallsburgh, pop. 2,004) gave hot pursuit—along with Nero the police dog and the PR man from Mandelbaum's International Hotel—in a golf cart, chasing a felon who had been stealing the flags from the 18th hole at Mandelbaum's. The cart hit a sandtrap, sending the chief and the PR man flying in one direction and Nero the police dog sailing in another. "There are 2,004 stories in the Naked Township," he wrote, "and this has been one of them."

They lived in sin, more or less, in an apartment which had a three-quarter bed with a big grease stain on the wall above it and a couch covered with itchy green upholstery on which it was impossible to stretch out full length. They tried sleeping two in the bed but one of them always crashed to the floor at some point in the middle of the night. They took to arm-wrestling for the bed; the loser got the couch. They decided to a) junk the couch, before they were both permanently crippled, and b) buy a bigger bed. Having made that investment, they figured they might as well get married.

They decided they would have a family, have their careers, have their cake and eat it too and go 50-50 on cleaning up the crumbs.

Today, they have two children, a cat and a dog, and a rambling old Victorian house designed by a deranged monk. After years of marriage the earth still moves for them—but, since they live 3,000 feet from runway 15-22 at Logan International Airport, they are never sure if it's ecstasy or the TWA Super-Saver to Dallas. He still tells her she is a fine writer and has great legs. She tells him the same thing. He is her best friend and vice versa. People think they are weird because they are married and they like each other.

They have two children, Steven and Alyssa, who also like each other, except for those times when they karate chop each other, mouthing invectives they learned in school. At such times, sailors would have a hard time keeping up with the vocabulary.

The children give their parents love and laughs. Thus encouraged, their parents soldier on, trying to manage jobs, kinder, animals and the vagaries of modern life—and doing it with roughly the same skill as the guys who planned Custer's Last Stand. But they try. God knows, they try! Here, in their own well-chosen few thousand words, is how it's going.

Part One

Side by Side

Caryl

Ode to a Liberated Man

THE YEAR our daughter entered kindergarten was the year of the Big Switch: role reversal, the sociologists call it. Alan had just remarked to the publisher of a magazine he was editing that said publisher could take the magazine and shove it—not the sort of constructive criticism that endears one to the heart of management.

I had been doing the major part of the child care for the past few years, since my schedule as a writer was more flexible than his. I also had a part-time teaching job. When Alan walked out of the magazine, that meant we had three-quarters of a job between us. Even with my lousy math, I knew *that* wouldn't keep us in Spaghetti-O's. So, we decided that I would take on a full-time university appointment, and he would write a book and take care of things on the home front for two years. Our son, Steven, was in school all day, but Alyssa only went to kindergarten in the afternoons. So Alan would make Alyssa's lunch, get her ready for school, and drive her there. On many days, he would also pick up Steven and Alyssa when school was out and drive them home. The rest of the time was blocked out for work on the book. A snap, he figured. I knew better but kept my trap shut. I took notes. Here is how it went on one day in the life of a liberated man:

6:30 A.M.: The alarm rings. Alan leaps out of bed and gets to the bathroom first. He always gets to the bathroom first since all I do when I hear the alarm is moan and pull the covers over my head. He finishes in the bathroom and walks the dog and comes back and screams at the rest of us until we crawl out into the daylight. He organizes breakfast while I wander about in a fog, seeing my family through a glass darkly. Alan leaves to do the elementary school car pool while I take a whack at Alyssa's ponytail. In the mornings, Alan starts on a schedule that requires the split-second timing of a tailback. He stays on it right through the day.

8:15 A.M.: Having deposited Steven at the local elementary school, Alan drives back and toots the horn outside the house. Alyssa and I dash out for the drive to Boston University. We are on the road for all of twelve seconds when Alyssa announces: "We are all going to play puppet hands."

Alan moans, audibly. I groan.

Alyssa ignores us. "We are going to play puppet hands," she says brightly.

"Alyssa," Alan says, "puppet hands is driving me bananas."

"We're going to play puppet hands, aren't we?" she asks, a slight tremolo in her voice. Alan caves in.

Puppet hands is a game she invented all by herself. Her hands become characters. "Cowey" is her right hand and "Horsey" is her left hand. Cowey and Horsey converse to each other in a screechy falsetto that would quickly drive a saint to screaming heresy. But it does not stop there. She has created other dramatic personae as well. My right hand is Frog and my left hand is Phyllis Frog. Alan's right hand is Fishy and his left is Elephant. Elephant is a morose sort, doesn't say much, but Fishy has been too engaging for his own good. So now Alyssa chirps away in the back seat, "Fishy. Fishy. Where are you, Fishy?"

Alan narrowly avoids a car that is switching lanes without a signal.

"Fishhhy. *Fisssshhhhyyyy!* Where are you, Fishy?"

A blue VW cuts us off. Alan rains contumely over his ancestors seven generations back.

"Fishy. Fishy. Say something, Fishy!"

"Fishy is undergoing analysis. Don't bug him," Alan snaps.

Fishy's "father" has tried to get rid of him. He recently claimed that Fishy had been caught by a Russian trawler and would never be heard from again. But then he made the mistake of having Fishy reappear to do a chorus of "Burger Czar" in pidgin Russian—"Piroski pickle, piroski lettuce . . ."—and now Alyssa keeps nagging Fishy to do "Burger Czar." This morning, as we pull up to a bigger tangle of cars than usual at the entrance to the Sumner Tunnel, Cowey is insisting that Fishy is a girl, not a boy. (She is an unrepentant female chauvinist.) She created Fishy, ergo Fishy is a girl. And Fishy must wear a dress. Alan is arguing that Fishy is his hand, therefore Fishy is a boy and he will not wear a dress.

"Fishy is a boy," says Alan.

"She is not! She's a girl!"

"Boy."

"She's a girl!" Alyssa says, her jaw squaring off, "and she has to wear a dress."

"He isn't and he won't!"

"Yes she will!" (All of her rapier thrusts of debate are made in Cowey's trill.)

"No he won't!"

"Yes she will!"

"Stick it in your ear, Cowey!"

We are inching toward the tollbooth at a snail's pace. Alan asks the green-uniformed guard what has happened. The guard hears but stares impassively into space with well-honed civil service arrogance.

Alan glares at him. "I vas on ze Russian front. I know nothing!" he says, so the guard can hear. In the back seat, Cowey and Horsey are punching each other. Cowey starts to cry, a sound that is akin to the bleat of a stuck pig.

Through the tunnel, up Storrow Drive, through Kenmore Square, Alyssa does puppet hands. My teeth are on edge. But dare I discourage her? If I tell Cowey and Horsey to can it, will I be destroying the Lillian Hellman of 1984? Alan drops me off at the university. Alyssa waves good-bye and I hear her saying, "Fishy, will you do 'Burger Czar'?" as they drive off. Alan's knuckles, where he grips the wheel, are turning white.

9:45 A.M.: Alan and Alyssa arrive home, and Alan goes up to the attic-turned-office to work on his book. He has been hard at work for twenty-three minutes when he senses peculiar smells, accompanied by peculiar sounds, drifting up the stairs.

He descends to the first floor to discover Jane, the family dog, having an attack of diarrhea on the dining-room rug. Alan drags Jane into the kitchen and starts to swab her off when he notices a huge red mass about to emerge from the rectum. He feels a stab of panic. Is the beloved dog hemorrhaging, about to expire on the spot?

He holds his nose and looks closer. It is one of my lipsticks Jane has eaten, which is now emerging intact out the other end. He wipes that off, too. Alyssa wanders into the kitchen, wrinkles her nose, and says, "I hate that smell. I think I am going to throw up!"

He hustles her up the stairs, cleans the rug, and locks the dog in the kitchen. Back to the book for another twelve minutes. He washes his hands five times before the odor completely disappears. Then Alyssa calls and says she has made a do-do but can't get it all wiped off. He cleans her up, sniffs his hands. The odor is back. He picks up the Johnson's baby powder, shakes it too vigorously, gets it all over Alyssa and his last clean pair of pants. He has an interview for his book with the mayor tonight. Hizzoner will inhale a strange mixture of smells.

12:00 noon: Alan makes lunch and takes Alyssa to school. He has two and a half hours to work, interrupted only by two wrong numbers, the gas man, and the Jehovah's Witnesses.

2:30 P.M.: Time to pick up the children. Alan arrives at the school. He picks up Steven and Alyssa—plus Steven's cronies Joey, Jonathan, Chris, and Michael. Alan tries to ignore the conversation coming from the back seat. Third-grade repartee is cheerfully, relentlessly anal. It is full of poetic onomatopoeia, one of the great favorites being to blow into the crook of the arm to produce a sound that exactly duplicates the expulsion of gas from the rectum. Punch lines involving excrement of any variety, however lacking in wit, produce gales of laughter. As they drive home, Alan attempts to block out the cackling, punching, and assorted animal sounds in the back seat.

3:15 P.M.: Alan goes up to his office. He types vigorously for thirteen minutes and eight seconds when he suddenly becomes aware of eyes boring into his back. They belong to Deanna, age three, who lives down the block.

"Awan," she says (her version of his name), "can I kiss Jane? Does Jane have *jorms?*"

She is inquiring about germs. Alan had to ask her to leave his bedroom once when he had the flu and, ever since, Deanna has been very cautious about *jorms.*

"You can kiss Jane. She hasn't got *jorms.* I mean germs."

"But will I get a cold if I kiss Jane, Awan? Does she have *jorms?*"

"She hasn't got *jorms.*"

"Do you have *jorms,* Awan?"

"No."

"Does Alyssa have *jorms?*"

"No."

"Does Steven have *jorms?*"

"No! Nobody has *jorms!*"

"Awan, there's a pigeon. He has *jorms.* He sick. He dead. Can you fix him, Awan?"

Steven and Joey come charging in. There is indeed a pigeon with a broken wing hobbling across the front lawn. Alan is called on a mission of mercy. He looks at the pigeon and the list of communicable diseases runs through his mind: hepatitis, influenza, rabies, whooping cough, VD—who knows what pigeons carry. He calls the dog officer and waits on the lawn to make sure the kids don't touch the pigeon and that the pigeon does not wander into the street and get hit by a car, which would upset the kids. He stands by the street corner and yells, "Back, pigeon, back" at the bird. Finally, the dog officer comes and carries away the pigeon.

4:45 P.M.: Alan returns to the typewriter. He stares at it for five minutes. Nothing comes. The muse has vanished, eaten up, perhaps, by a cloud of pigeon *jorms* attacking the brain. The phone rings. It is I, his loving wife.

"Are you having a nice day, dear?" I ask.

Alan

Letter to My President

It's CLEAR I can't handle this situation alone, that I need help. I'm too old to stomp and yell and too young to apply for home-care visits. You can't call cops to help clean dog crap off the rug, and shrinks are too expensive. There's only one person who can help me, a fellow American.

Dear Mr. President:

A long time ago, you showed up in my state, and you attended the town meeting in Clinton, Mass., which, by the way, you should do more often, because when they called the next town meeting they couldn't get a quorum and everybody had to go home. As is your folksy style, you stayed at a private home with real Americans, as opposed to some motel with room service and color TV. Ever since your stay, I've been thinking about what your host and hostess said of you. They said you were very neat, meaning tidy, and you made your own bed. Apparently, they didn't even have to say, as I do, "For the fifth and last time, Jimmy boy, make your bed!" Except that I don't say "Jimmy."

This shows me that you understand the nature of the U.S. presidency, and this should convince the Harvards who worry about the Imperial Presidency. You understand that we broke away from England because King George rarely made his own bed, and when he did, it was frankly a sloppy job, and you couldn't bounce a ha'penny on it.

I have figured out a way in which you can help us, and by doing so, you can really get close to the people and get your hands dirty with at least the gritty, if not the nitty. We are hereby extending you an invitation to stay at our home, and we don't mean overnight only. We are talking about a commitment.

My wife is a great wife, mother, writer, and teacher, and what with both of us working, we don't get our living room picture taken often for the Sunday supplements. We need somebody here who will make a bed, do a little dusting, some vacuuming, nothing heavy.

Before you start in with why you cannot consider this, let me appeal to your now famous down-home nature and explain the dimensions of the problem we have got here. My wife's answer to cleaning the house is to go out and buy $80 worth of lumber and spend two weeks building another shelf.

"Why," I ask her, "don't we just clean the stuff off the stairs?"

"Look," she says, "you clean it off one day, and it comes back the next. This way, we'll have a place for it."

"Who needs a place for dust?"

"You want to walk in it all the time?"

We now have, by the last count, and I have not been home since this morning, twenty homemade shelves, not counting the already built, ready-to-clutter-up-with-stuff you get at the suburban discount stores, and you still can't walk through a room without tripping over things. I do not remove these things, as I know how important they are to have around.

"Don't throw out the bag," says my daughter, Alyssa, holding a small brown bag which recently carried her now half-eaten meatball sub.

"Why not?"

"I like it."

You get the point? The bag is small, greasy, and useless, but what am I gonna do, hurt a child?

You think you can hold a family together these days without a French flag stolen from a Paris building in 1957? How do you go from a Monday to a Tuesday without a nun's habit, worn by Ms. Rivers when she played that role in high school, a habit autographed by the Class of 1955, Academy of the Holy Name?

Some women bring dowries. She brought me pillows from the

Chesapeake and Ohio Railroad. They are signed by members of the Catholic Students Mission Crusade of 1951.

We have important stuff here. We have, for example, Jane the Dog. She sheds daily and at night. She has been shedding for seven years. She is seven years old. By now, she should have disappeared. You could take what this dog sheds and weave yourself a whole new dog.

You're beginning to get the picture, a sense of crisis? It's worse than you think.

Where we live is windy. The wind comes off Boston Harbor and moans. You open up the back door, and the wind blows up the refuse in the house. This house is the only place east of Oklahoma with dust storms.

Where we live is full of kids. I legitimately claim two of them as heirs. The others belong to other people. But they like coming here. What kid doesn't like playing in junk? Sometimes we lose a few here and there. Their parents come over, and we search for them. Sometimes we find them. Sometimes we don't. Maybe you'll stumble across a couple. They're old enough now to vote; they've been lost a long time. They'll remember you in November.

Your services are needed. Don't worry about how it will look if you're not in the White House. There is plenty of precedent for this. FDR had his retreat. Truman often returned to Missouri to work. LBJ had the ranch. Nixon certainly got a lot done in San Clemente. Grant had his tomb in New York City, very roomy with a nice view.

You could get the basic cleaning done by 11 A.M.; make yourself a cup of coffee and you've got the rest of the day to work on nuclear disarmament, national health insurance, whatever. You can even bring your presidential papers and stuff. We'll make room. My wife is putting up more shelves.

Yours sincerely,
Alan Lupo

Caryl

The Odd Couple

As you can see, Alan and I have deep philosophical differences—not about religion, that's a snap—but about dust balls. He believes they are carriers of typhus and should be disposed of at once, preferably buried in a deep underground pit in Nevada.

I am convinced that dust balls are an act of God, not to be disturbed without filing an environmental impact statement. This difference has caused us some minor contention over the years (screams, threats, attempted murder) but we have come to something resembling détente on the matter. He no longer says I could take lessons in housekeeping from a bag lady; I no longer call him a Nixon anal compulsive who was toilet trained too soon. At least, not very often. We do have some conversations about it. Alan will point to a sink with a slight gray film around it and declaim, in Patrick Henry tones, "Germs!"

I peer at the sink. "Probably. Germs are our friends. I was reading this science fiction story about an astronaut who lived in a sterile environment on a space trip and when he came back to earth he choked and died because he had been without germs too long. His immunological system got weak."

"Didn't you ever hear of the Black Death?" Alan says. "What do you think wiped out half of Europe, unsightly dandruff?"

"Rats. Bad rat germs. There are good germs and bad germs. It is written."

Alan mutters that's what you get marrying a Catholic with a college degree, Jesuitical cunning and a theological approach to dirt.

"The house is not dirty," I reply. "It is simply a bit cluttered."

I suppose I must admit that housekeeping is not my forte, although I always maintain that there is basic cleanliness underneath the litter. The day of my wedding, when I was sharing a hotel room with my mother, she got out of bed and looked at the state of my belongings, scattered about as if they had been ground zero for a thermonuclear device.

"I can't believe you're getting married today and you never learned to clean up your room," she sighed.

But Alan knew about this when he married me. At the time we were first engaged, we were toiling in separate vineyards. I was writing features about teenage rock singers and Hadassah vice-presidents for a newspaper on Long Island, and he was a member of the Second Army television team at Fort Knox, Kentucky. He was making a vital contribution to national defense by producing "hometown specials," video-tapes in which a tank would roll up to the camera, the hatch would fly open, and a pimply seventeen-year-old would pop up and announce, "Hi, Mom. Hi, Dad. I'm having lots of fun in the Army."

I wanted Alan to meet my parents, so we arranged a rendezvous at the family home in Silver Spring, Maryland, at Christmastime. He got a ride with two RA's—a four-hour brush with death careening across back roads in West Virginia in a blizzard. Understandably, he was a bit shaken when he finally made his way up the front steps of the Rivers home.

And there I was, his beloved, his fragile flower, waiting with open arms.

"Hi," I said. "Choke me."

"I beg your pardon?"

"Choke me."

Thinking this might be some odd rite of the Catholic religion, a celebration of homecoming, he obliged. Then he screamed in pain as I bent his little fingers back.

"Isn't that neat? I'm learning judo and self-defense. I did a feature on this lady singer who has a black belt and her husband has a dog act. I'm taking judo lessons at her house. It's sort of noisy with the dogs playing the piano all the time, but it's fun. Want to see how I can throw you?"

"Could I please have a drink first?"

"Oh, sure."

I fixed him a Scotch and water. Then I nagged my brother until he agreed to a hip throw. Except I didn't do it very well and I threw him right into Alan, whose drink spilled all over his one clean uniform.

"Gee," I said, "I guess I need more practice on that one."

Alan wiped himself off with a towel, his eyes darting about. Clearly he had wandered beyond the pale of settlement, and what was he doing with this deranged *shiksa* who was walking around the kitchen going "huh-huh-huh-huh" and chopping at the doors of the cabinets?

He settled down during dinner, because he found he liked my parents and they did not say he killed Christ. But after dinner, he watched as the meat scraps were cut up, placed on one of the dinner dishes and set down for the dog. He stared in horror as the dog lapped up the meal.

He pulled me aside and whispered, "The dog is eating off a plate!"

"Sure. He's a high-class dog."

"But it's one of *your* plates. It's not a dog dish. It's a people dish."

"Sure."

"Dogs have strange germs. They foam at the mouth."

"Only when they have rabies. Tippy doesn't have rabies. Besides, the dishwasher sterilizes the dishes."

"Does he always do that?"

"Eat off a plate? Yeah, usually."

"The plate I just ate off. The dog ate off that?"

"Probably."

"Oh God!" He staggered slightly, his eyes glazed. They warned him about *goyim*, but he didn't listen.

"Didn't your dog ever eat off the plates?"

"Who had a dog? Cossacks have dogs."

"Your eyes look funny. I think you're coming down with the flu."

"My tongue is turning black. Foam, can you see foam?"

Eventually, he was seduced by Tippy to the point where he spoke proudly of "my dog-in-law." By the time we got Jane he had become an unreconstructed dogophile. But even Jane is not permitted to eat off the people plates. Alan does not believe me about the sanitizing powers of the dishwasher. In fact, he is very critical of all my efforts with the dishwasher. He says I wash dishes wrong.

"What do you mean, wrong? I put the dishes in the thing and I push the button. How could that be wrong?"

"You put the dishes in the wrong position."

"What do you mean, wrong position? This is a KitchenAid, not a Kama-Sutra."

"You leave the salad bowls turned too much. They get filled up with water. They sit there with old water in them."

"Germs, right?"

He also does not like my refrigerator policy, *Et Cannus Therin Lyum* (Let Sleeping Dogs Lie). Periodically, he attacks the refrigerator with boiling water and Ajax. He drags out jars and bowls from the back of the fridge and demands that I come in and inspect them. They look like the rejects from a recombinant DNA lab. Greenish, bluish, and yellowish slime creeps across the surfaces of what used to be edible substances. I peer at them with interest.

"Penicillin is made from mold, you know. I bet if we applied some of this stuff to an open sore we'd see some amazing cures."

The look he gives me clearly indicates that the only open sore to which he wants to apply the refrigerator crud is my mouth.

Alan also fights an unending war against clutter. He is the only one who does. He is frequently seen bending down to pick up sneakers, old homework papers, gum wrappers and various items of clothing, often belonging to children not his own. He does so much stoop labor that Cesar Chavez once showed up at the front door trying to organize him. Now and then he reaches the breaking point. When this happens he stands up straight and screams:

"THIS HOUSE IS A PIGPEN. I WANT THIS HOUSE CLEANED UP RIGHT NOW!"

Steven and Alyssa and I, feeling pangs of guilt, dash about removing the top layer of our possessions and hustling them out of sight. Remorse lasts, on the average, forty-five minutes. Then the kids go back to leaving their sneakers on the couch and I hang my bras on the towel rack again.

But Alan does not give up. Surrounded by slovens, he battles for order on land, sea, and air. Especially the latter. Alan has a sense of smell that makes the average bloodhound look like a little old lady with a head cold. Alan no sooner enters the house than his nose starts to quiver.

"Garbage. I smell garbage. Or maybe it's dog-doo. Quick, Steven, check the living room."

Alan sniffs around like the lady in the Lysol commercial who gets her jollies by inhaling the fumes from the kitchen sink. "Can't you smell it?" he rails at us, and when we shake our heads he says we must all be defective in the nasal regions. He identifies most bad odors as belonging to three categories:

1. Dog-doo—garbage
2. Dirty laundry
3. Feet

The children go off on a search-and-destroy mission for dog excrement, but none is found. Alan is sure it is there, wafting deadly bacteria through the air.

Alan is a one-man olfactory KGB. The family will be settled on the sofa, watching TV, when suddenly Alan's nose will begin to vibrate like a tuning fork. He suddenly barks, "Whose feet smell?"

I, knowing that I will be the number-one suspect because of the $3.99 shoes I buy at Third World Oppressed Workers Discount Outlet, am prepared. I have showered, washed my feet, and dusted them with so much talcum powder that from the knees down I look like the Abominable Snowman. Steven sticks out his feet to display fresh athletic sox. Alyssa still has her sneakers on.

"It's Jane," Steven says.

Alyssa and I nod in agreement. It must be Jane whose four feet are smelly. We do not, of course, examine further the question of how Jane's feet could ever get dirty enough to smell—since Jane rarely deigns to place a paw on any surface not covered by wall-to-wall carpeting.

Alan

Sick, at Home

I COULD deal with odors by washing the dog, but I am not a kamikaze warrior. I could, on the other hand, wash the house, but my boss won't give me the three-year leave of absence I need. I've found that one of the most effective ways of dealing with house odors is to hide behind blocked sinuses. I don't use this method often, because I'm normal enough not to like colds and because my parents impose guilt on me when I get colds. "You're sick again?" they ask, in a tone of voice used by a magistrate confronting an incorrigible repeater.

Colds, however, have a bright side. When sick, I catch up on my reading. It takes my mind off the rawness in the throat, the throbbing behind the left eyeball, the two hands that hang from the wrists like barbells. My favorite book is *The Baseball Encyclopedia*, which lists more than ten thousand professional ballplayers and tells me when they played, and for whom and how.

It is a veritable fount of wisdom in an age that treats history as a collection of irrelevant details. It has taught me that indeed there was a pitcher named Egyptian Healy and a third baseman called Walter "Arlie" (The Freshest Man on Earth) Latham. I am getting to know that baseball book the way Jimmy Carter's reborn sister knows her Bible, and maybe that's why neither of us gets invited to many parties.

After a while, however, even the minute reading of the nomadic career of Bobo Newsom pales, and I look elsewhere. Near the bed, within crawling distance, is a magazine.

It's one of those house-beautiful-redecorating-town-and-country-squire magazines. It is one of about 150 that Caryl has collected, figuring that if she ever inherits a mansion on the Hudson, she'll know how to decorate it. These magazines are boring, but boring is not why I don't like them. I don't like them because in every edition there is at least one story on a couple our age who, working every Saturday for three weekends, have managed to convert a Vermont outhouse into a solar-heated, 76-room weekend retreat with natural oak ceilings, a sunken bathtub, a hall of mirrors and a Kung-Fu demonstration room.

It makes me jealous to know how Sven Virile, a lawyer, heart-transplant specialist, tennis pro, and Army general during the week, likes to relax on weekends either by flying to Taiwan, where he coaches a championship Little League team, or just by puttering around the backyard. Here's Sven in his backyard with his prize forty-two-pound, seven-foot-long zucchini and a nuclear submarine which he built from old spare refrigerator parts.

Mrs. Virile, who looks like Candice Bergen, is shown in a shimmering strapless gown, hoisting a twelve-foot-long two-by-four up six flights of stairs and into her sculpture studio, from which she emerges in the next frame with a precisely carved bas-relief of Napoleon's retreat from Moscow.

Why, I ask myself feverishly, don't those magazines visit our house?

> Lupo, a part-time writer, *mal vivant*, and a famed mechanical incompetent, likes to relax on his weekends by hiding from the rest of the family in one of the three closets in the spacious Lupo household. With his own hands and nothing to guide him but instinct, he is shown here leafing through the pages of his baseball encyclopedia. "I'm up to Reynolds, Danny (Squirrel), 1945, Cubs, 72 at bats, 12 hits . . ."
>
> Not one to rush into anything gaudy or extravagant, Lupo has opted for sporadic house improvements, which he subtly calls "tasteful, yet cheaperooney." He is especially proud of the tin mailbox, which he nailed to the front porch three years ago (as good as new) and the homemade wire-hanger loop he uses to clean out the bathtub drain.
>
> The next project, he says, is the expansive backyard, now tastefully spotted hither and yon with dog droppings. As he puts it quaintly in his slow New England Yankee drawl, "I'm gonna pave over the #$%*!# grass and let the bugs suck a little cement."

Meanwhile, Mrs. Lupo points out the little oddities: the toaster, which, if plugged in when the oven is operating, blows out half the lights; the clothes dryer, which takes in wet clothes and dispenses same one hour later; her collection of Aztec folk art death masks that she has nailed all over the bathroom walls, thereby scaring the children.

This last picture shows Mr. Lupo lying on the floor and hugging the leg of our photographer in an attempt to sell the house. "Airport? What airport? There's no airport out there! It's a wall mural. What my wife can do with water colors, boy . . ."

Caryl

The Penicillin Connection

ALAN AND I have two distinct personal styles in coping with illness. His method harks back to an honored tradition that may have begun in the age of Euripides. Alan believes that sinus congestion is, quite simply, the curse of some malevolent deity. Whom the gods would destroy, he believes, they first give blocked nasal passages or bad reactions to ragweed.

He believes that if fate were just, flu symptoms would be a direct result of *hubris*. When he gets sick, Alan wallows about like a wounded bull with a spear in its side, bellowing, "Why me? I am a good person. Why am I being made sick?"

It is impossible to reason with him at such times, to explain the randomness of the universe of germs. He will have none of it. Instead, he recites chapter and verse of his virtues—he never parks free at a broken meter, pays the gas bill on time and reports to the IRS his twenty-five-dollar honorarium for speaking to the Jaycees. To such a man, God should send the heartbreak of stuffy nose? A *shanda!*

One cannot explain to him that God does not mess around with minor ailments. When He gets mad at you, He sends a plague of frogs, which clog the transmission of your car with their little green bodies and eat the shrubbery. Or He makes all the faucets run blood, which is not great for instant coffee. God does not waste his time on penny-ante ailments. Would God have told Moses to announce to Pharaoh: "Let my people go or thy entire nation shall suffer from the occasional stiffness of minor arthritis pain?" Would He have boomed in a stentorian voice from the burning bush: "Do not have false gods before Me or I shall smite thee with acid indigestion"?

Alan will not be mollified. He rages at the fates, at times assaulting inanimate objects such as bedposts. I try to assure him that no one in medical history had ever expired from clogged nasal passages, but he insists that in Vladmirvolinsk in 1732 a peasant named Chaim was struck, in the midst of the rutabaga harvest, with such a severe attack of stuffy nose that he let out a shriek and fell down dead.

I remind Alan that Chaim did not have, on his dresser, a vial of nasal spray so powerful it could defoliate half of Yonkers.

He ignores me and declaims: "God should not make me sick."

I, on the other hand, like to think of myself as something of a stoic, the sort, who, while the Godless Atheistic Communists were holding lighted matches to my feet, would be chatting blithely about the weather. (In parochial school, we were told the Godless Atheistic Communists wiled away their afternoons torturing little Catholic schoolchildren, trying to get them to renounce the Baltimore Catechism.) I feel that sickness can be conquered by an act of will, that if I ignore the microbes long enough, they will, like spurned relatives, march away in a huff.

I think I know where this personality trait comes from. It is certainly not from the Irish side of the family; the common cold encourages the Irish to indulge in drink or bad poetry. It's not the English genes—the English have enough sense to wrap up in a blanket with a slug of stout when they feel the germs advancing. It's the damn Germans. My German grandmother was a stoic of the first rank; she never took to her bed until she was on the verge of falling over. This sort of foolish behavior comes from having ancestors named Wooden and Nooden who painted themselves blue and rolled naked in the snow—after which they contracted lumbar pneumonia and departed shortly for Valhalla. The Great God Thor would look on with a sigh, saying, "Not another schmuck who rolled bare-assed in the snow. When will these clowns learn that the Ruhr valley in January ain't the Club Med?"

I am prone to several types of maladies—stomach virus and bursitis. The latter I blame on Spiro T. Agnew.

Perhaps I had better explain that one. In the days before Agnew became a household word, he was running for governor of Maryland. Alan was working at the *Baltimore Sun* at the time, and Agnew was regarded as the liberal candidate by the press and public. This was so because he was running against a man who spent most of his time in a sound truck that blared a song called, "Your Home Is Your Castle, Protect It, Defend It," a musical comment on the state's proposed Fair Housing Act.

Now, this candidate, George P. Mahoney, wasn't any Cole Porter, but his lyrics did remind white voters that black folks could indeed tote that bale—as long as it wasn't filled with topsoil for the lawn of a duplex in Baltimore county. Give a black man a mortgage and he'll strew watermelon rinds in your black-topped driveway and want to marry your daughter.

Agnew looked pretty good next to Mahoney and his racist rhapsodies, so Spiro got elected. From then on it was all downhill for Spiro, all the way to the unindicted coconspirator we all came to know and love. As the 1968 GOP convention drew near, the big joke in the *Sun* city room was that Agnew would get nominated for veep. Ho, ho, ho.

The reporter who covered the convention for the *Sun* that year spent the usual busy days and sleepless nights, and when everything was all wrapped up but the veep nomination, he called his city desk to say he was going to get some sleep, let the wire services handle the veep story. "Don't call me, Ernie," he said to the city editor, "unless, of course, it's Agnew. Ho, ho, ho."

A few hours later, sleeping the sleep of the just, the reporter heard a faint ringing sound. He staggered to the phone to hear the voice of the deskman back in Baltimore.

"Phil, Phil, this is Ernie. Phil, it's Agnew!"

"That's a rotten joke, Ernie. Fourteen hours straight I didn't get any sleep. You guys think you're funny. SCREW YOU, ERNIE!" And he slammed down the phone.

Meanwhile, I, who had been sick in bed with a stomach virus that day, had moved the TV set onto the floor near my bed so I could watch the convention. I saw a familiar image flash on the screen as the new vice-president-to-be was announced.

"Oh my God, it's Spiro Agnew," I said. I leaned over to gape, fell out of bed on my shoulder, and got bursitis.

Bursitis, unfortunately, does not respond to penicillin. It is, I believe, the one chronic ailment I possess which cannot be cured by the Wonder Drug. I have the same sort of faith in penicillin that my mother-in-law reserves for chicken soup. I take it for everything, from athlete's foot to the common cold. Never mind that the doctors say it doesn't work on anything viral—viral, shmiral, it works on me. But since it's a prescription drug, I am not always able to get it when I need it. I sock it away for times of crisis. Sometimes I even shave on the four teaspoons a day I am supposed to give the children when their tonsils are covered with gunk. A drop or two skimmed, how could it hurt them?

Or so I reason, with the logic of an alcoholic seasoned at hiding the stuff in the Windex bottle. I stash the old bottles in the back of the refrigerator until a fine sediment settles on top. I skim off the sediment and swill down the rest of the stuff, whenever I feel a twinge in throat or tummy. Penicillin keeps me on my feet. What I need, I know, is a penicillin connection.

There I would be, walking carefully, collar turned up, down a dark alley in a sleazy part of town. He would sidle out of a side door and I would sigh with relief.

"Needles, did you get the stuff?"

"Well, there's been a problem."

"Don't con me. You promised. One bottle of the real stuff, cherry flavored."

"The cherry-flavored is hot, the feds just picked up a whole boatload on its way in from Tijuana."

"Orange?"

"I got some real good Erythromycin."

"Needles, have a heart! My throat is pounding and I have to get to the Brownie bake sale and a TV panel show on nuclear power."

"I can let you have some Pen-Vee K capsules, but they'll cost."

"Not the damn stuff you cut with cornstarch. You can't dump that stuff on me, Needles!"

"Don't get tough with me, you crummy junkie! I'll cut you off so fast you won't be able to get Flintstones vitamins. Not even a jar of Vicks VapoRub."

"No, Needles, not cold turkey!"

"OK. The stuff I got is flavored pistachio-butter walnut."

"Where am I, Howard Johnson's?"

"Take it or leave it."

"You got a deal!"

Penicillin does strange things to me, however. Whenever I take it, the intensity of my dreams seems to increase tenfold; I get the PT's, you might say. Not long ago I had such a rotten bug that all I could do was lie under the covers and shake. All night long I kept dozing off to sleep and waking up again, feeling rotten. I wasn't sure which was worse, waking or sleeping. I may have been miserable with my eyes open, but in my sleep I was negotiating the Zimbabwe-Rhodesia peace treaty. Let me tell you, it was rough going. Mr. Mugabe, Bishop Muzorewa and Mrs. Thatcher kept yelling at each other and I had to tell them to can it and get down to serious business. I must have been pretty loud about it because I kept waking Alan up.

"Would you settle for fifteen seats in Parliament with free tickets to the next Muhammad Ali fight thrown in?"

"What?" Alan mumbled, turning over in the bed.

"And no messing around with Mozambique."

"Caryl, will you shut up and go to sleep, please?"

"You drive a hard bargain, Mrs. Thatcher."

Things got even worse, because as it turned out, not only did I have to chair the peace talks, but vacuum the rug as well. Mrs. Thatcher kept dropping cigar ashes on the rug. I told her it was a filthy habit for a well-bred prime minister. She told me I could bloody well stuff it, and then, as I remember, she hit Mr. Mugabe with a lime pie in the face. Things got a little fuzzy after that.

Alan

Guess Who's Not Coming to Dinner?

I HATE when people drop over to the house when either or both of us is sick. My eyes are rheumy; I can barely speak; I haven't shaved in a week, and I'm sniffling, and a visitor says, "Hey, how are ya?" If Caryl's sick, she says, "Fine, how are you?" She's so damn polite. If she had just undergone a day of brutality in the Spanish Inquisition and someone had asked how she was doing, she'd say, "Fine, how are you?" Not me, boy. People ask me how I feel, I tell them. Everything. "I feel lousy. I have a rotten cold. I've had it for a week. I'm all stuffed up. The medicine is making me sick. I got a headache. My back feels funny. In the mornings . . ." By this time, the visitor is backing out of the front door. Good riddance. Who asked you to come over when I'm sick? I even have reservations about people coming over when I'm healthy.

"Let's plan to have some people over for dinner," Caryl says every once in a while.

"Why?" is my triggerlike response.

"It'll be nice," she says. Her tone is polite; her answer reasonable on the face of it.

"Who needs it?" is my repartee.

"Loop," she says, now with some impatience, no, more like disbelief, as if I had just emerged from a life in the Australian outback and she were teaching me the rules of civilized behavior. "Loop, it's normal. Friends have each other over for dinner. People invite us for dinner. We never invite anyone over for dinner!"

"We *had* people over for dinner," I insist.

"That was almost three years ago," she says.

"Yeah, and the dishes are still in the sink."

That's the nub of it. When noted journalist Caryl Rivers cooks dinner, Alan Lupo, noted busboy, goes into hard labor. "Caryl," her father (may he rest in peace) once said, as he looked with disbelief at the state of our kitchen, "you're a wonderful cook, but you sure do leave a mess."

He was polite. What she leaves resembles Berlin in April 1945. Counters, floors, tables and walls are spattered with globules of food and gravy; filthy utensils are strewn about in a fashion that would turn the stomach of the poorest vagrant in Calcutta. Standing open and getting warm are cartons of milk and containers of sour cream. Closed up and replaced in the refrigerator are empty cartons of milk and bottles that once held soda.

Two rooms away, in yet another littered area which she has the temerity to call our dining room, guests are politely staring at one another after she has heaped a ton of slop on their plates. She is making conversation, oblivious to the absence of any forks on the table. Nor are there any forks in the drawer in the kitchen. I am in the kitchen, however. I am reaching under the garbage she has left to find all the forks I can lay my hands on and wash them with steel wool. I usually find one fewer than what I need. I don't give her one. That'll teach her. I give forks to the others, who smile with some relief, maybe pity. She never notices. She will eat with whatever utensil happens to be nearby—a spoon, a knife, a can opener, a straw, a guest's fork.

Her cooking is excellent. She makes great beef dishes with rice and almonds and frozen veggies and garlic bread. She throws them all on one plate. The bread bobs up and down as it floats upon the gravy from pea to almond to rice grain to meat chunk. Once, a guest got seasick watching his own little piece of bread.

The conversation is scintillating. At least, it sounds that way from the kitchen, where I am. I'm there for a variety of reasons. I'm there trying to get from the wine bottle the half of a cork she has left in the nozzle when she tried to open it. I'm there washing some of the dishes from breakfast so we can put the dessert on something other than the hands of the guests. I'm there listening as one of the mice places a phone call to the local health inspector.

Sometimes I'm there because I can't sit for more than a half hour in one chair, unless I'm at the movies or a ball game. I don't care how fascinating the company is, I can't sit that long. My rear end hurts. I have to move around. It comes from hanging around on corners as a kid. You don't just stand or sit; you keep moving around, even in a small space. Also, the conversation sometimes gets too deep for me. If they talk about anything beyond politics, baseball, jazz, and ethnic hatreds, I'm lost. On top of all that, I get tired. I get tired sometimes at 9:30 P.M., which can be a problem when Igor the Monster Chef hasn't quite timed things and the beef is still bleeding at 9:25 P.M. like Billy Conn in a fight with Joe Louis.

I like our friends, those few we haven't alienated by never inviting anybody over, but I just don't like working that hard on Saturday nights. I'd rather eat at their houses, so I don't have to work that hard, so I can get up and carry a few dishes into their usually sparkling kitchens and hear them tell Caryl how nice it is that I am not a chauvinist piggy. Better yet, I like to meet them in a restaurant and let someone else worry about what's going on in the kitchen.

The only people I really want visiting are Italian families, big ones with lots of uncles. Sometimes the uncles don't even like one another, but they all come, and they bring their own food. They also bring their own tools. You get a solid Italian-American family over for dinner and by dessert, they've already added three rooms and a bath to your house. All in tile.

But even they are not perfect. You've got to watch them. One of them will say something like, "Uncle Cheech will fix your lawn."

"But we don't have a lawn."

"That's why Cheech is gonna fix it."

By the time they all leave, you've lost your sidewalk and driveway. Instead, you've got two acres of fresh green grass, each blade evenly cut, a row of hedges, a tomato patch and a vineyard. If Cheech is really good, he will have also built a porcelain black or white jockey holding a saddle strap around the neck of a pink flamingo, which is staring at a statue of the Madonna and Child.

"But I'm Jewish!" you scream.

Cheech has figured that into his initial estimates. He presses a button in the jockey's head, and a tape cassette inside the flamingo, which is looking at the Madonna, begins playing "Mein Yiddishe Momma."

But at least these people clean up afterward, which is more than I can say for Caryl the Cook and Journalist. At the end of one of her evenings with guests, she looks at the kitchen, which, if it were a municipal landfill, would be closed by the authorities, and says, "I'm too tired to wash these. I'll get them in the morning."

This, from a person who moments ago was telling jokes, making party conversation, regaling a half dozen people with clever stories, while I yawned and kept whispering, "It's late. I'm tired. Enough fun already."

"You can't leave it for morning," I tell her. "By then, it will have crawled upstairs and eaten us and the kids. You're dealing here with the kind of stuff they use to make horror movies, 'The Leftovers That Ate Tokyo!'"

So, at 2 A.M. on a Sunday we are cleaning the house. And three years later, she's got the gall to want guests *again,* without so much as a break?

Caryl

Intemperate Zones

ANOTHER REASON we don't have guests a lot is because Alan likes to greet them in his undershirt, looking like he is ready to do Stanley in *Streetcar*. He claims this is a protest against my desire to re-create the South Pacific in the rooms of our home. How two people, presumably of the same species, can react so differently to a scientific fact like the temperature of the air at any given moment is hard for me to fathom. We sit watching TV, with Alan peeled down to slightly more than what a male stripper could get away with, while I am wrapped in a quilt. He claims there is something wrong with me. I say it is hormones, or something, and began with Adam and Eve. I know just how it went.

God finished mucking about with a lump of clay and commanded it to speak. Adam stood up, looked around, and right away started to sweat.

"Jeez, it must be eighty-five degrees around here. You call this place *paradise*? Jersey City in August is cooler. You could have put me anyplace you wanted to, so why did I get stuck in a sweat-box? Why don't you do a little more creating and get me an air-conditioned high rise?"

Beginning to wonder about what He had wrought, God cast the lout into a deep sleep, peeled off a rib and started on a new improved model. When the work was finished, she dusted herself off and immediately started to shiver.

"My God, I haven't got any clothes on. Is this the Garden of Eden or the centerfold at *Penthouse?* What kind of a Divine Plan do you call this, creating a person and leaving her out in the wind freezing her tail off? If you had to create *him* first, couldn't you have managed Halston or Givenchy? Either I get some woolies, fast, or I'm leaving right now for St. Croix."

Alan does not buy my theory. He insists that if I had willpower and lived clean, I would not be cold. As a couple, we are the mating of a Russian peasant who likes rolling naked in the snow to one of Tennessee Williams's dipsomaniac southern belles. Alan *likes* the cold. Worse than that, he likes all varieties of it; but most of all he likes weather that can only be described as clammy. Weather that makes most people want to huddle by the hearth with a hot bowl of soup brings out the Marlboro Man in him. He is the only person I know who rushes outside to stand around in the fog. A cold, steady drizzle makes him want to fling open the windows and inhale. He took a stroll on one of the bridges across the Charles River one night when the wind-chill factor was forty-five below. He said the night was "bracing" and got a frostbitten ear.

I, on the other hand, like the sort of day when one can languish on the veranda with a mint julep and a wet cloth pressed gently against the forehead. I do not think it all implausible that Daisy Miller died from the evil vapors in the night air in Rome. My voice slides into a syrupy drawl whenever I start to speak of a person's constitutional right to warm air. Alan is quick to point out that my native land, a suburb of Washington, D.C., is not exactly the heart of Dixie and that in the fragility department, I have more in common with Bronko Nagurski than Blanche Du Bois. I retort that when he recited his Hebrew name during our wedding ceremony, I had no idea it translated as Nanook of the North.

It is at bedtime when the issue arises most heatedly. I drift toward the connubial bed, a vision in coffee-brown lace with cleavage down to *there.* His eyes light up until his gaze rests on the green wooly socks I have placed upon my feet. The fact that they are *his* socks (I refuse to buy wooly socks when his fit me just fine) seems to heighten his displeasure, which he vents in a subtle manner.

"Blaugh. You have socks on!"

He says that I remind him of the Polish farm ladies he used to see lugging bags of wash to the laundromat when he went to college in western Massachusetts. He wonders aloud why it is that I can wander about with nothing but a thin film of lace standing between me and a chest cold while my feet are swaddled like I was about to join Amundsen at the Pole.

I retort that I do not get chilly in the cleavage, but my feet are different. They are very sensitive and prone to the faintest of chills. I feel solicitous of them.

"Nobody's feet are so cold that they have to wear wooly socks under one blanket and two quilts."

I peel off a sock and stick out a foot. "Feel!" I command.

He places his sweaty palm against my toe and recoils in horror.

"Christ, it's like a block of ice. I must have married The Thing."

I pull my wooly sock back on and smile from the pure sensual pleasure as my feet warm up. Alan mutters something about mental cruelty. He knows that the worst is yet to come. For, as I huddle under a pile of covers, body heat gradually begins to do its work and turns the whole area into a nice, warm burrow. I am nearly asleep by this time, and my feet begin to get a tad too warm. So I peel off the socks one at a time and fling them out into the darkness. This is a habit that disgusts Alan totally. The only thing he finds more revolting than socks on my person is socks off my person, lying crumpled in various parts of the room. He says it is a loathsome habit. I begin to get annoyed.

"Do I complain when you wear two pairs of pajama pants because one is ripped in the seat and the other is ripped in the crotch and that is the only way you can avoid a draft? Do I complain when you make sounds like a rocket launcher or utter sentence fragments in your sleep? One bad habit I have, flinging socks, and you make a federal case out of it."

At this point, he counterattacks. "You leave your bras on the towel rack."

"Not always."

"Most of the time. I wash my face and grab for a towel and wipe my skin with this stringy thing that feels like a spider. Yuk. Mental cruelty."

"Minor flaws in an otherwise admirable character."

"You undress in the bathroom. You undress in the bathroom and wear socks to bed because the nuns told you to."

"Oh, sure. The nuns always said when you go to bed in a brown lace nightie cut so low it makes Gypsy Rose Lee's pasties look like a turtleneck, wear socks. Bonnie Doons are better than a chastity belt."

"You do undress in the bathroom."

"I undress in the bathroom because, as you may have noticed, the weather stripping on the windows is shot to hell. Every night when I go to bed I feel like Napoleon retreating from Moscow. I figure if frostbite doesn't get me a Cossack will."

Throughout the winter, our private cold war rages on. In the evenings, after work, I pick Alan up for the ride home. No one can say the romance has gone out of our marriage. As we drive along the river, the lights softly twinkling on the opposite shore, his hand tenderly meets mine—on the knob of the heater. I have shoved it all the way over to Bake. He yanks it toward Freeze.

I whine—piteously and shamelessly—that I am blue with cold. He cannot stand to hear me whine, and so he retreats. Brute force is not his style. He prefers theatrics. The heat filters through the car, and I smile and wiggle my toes. He begins the death scene from *Camille*. First, he starts to gasp. Then a little rhythmic panting as he tugs at his collar, yanking it open. Then he emits a few low moans. I start to feel guilty.

"OK, I'll turn the fan down to low."

It is still nice and cozy in the car, even with the fan on low. Suddenly there is a blast of cold air on the back of my neck. I let out a shriek. I turn to him. He is smiling. The window is open.

"Pneumonia!" I scream. "Cold air on the back of the neck. Pneumonia in ten seconds flat. You will have to wait on me hand and foot, I will develop a racking cough and I will go to the sanitarium. The children will cry."

He rolls up the window. I turn up the fan. In a minute he is gasping. He peels off his coat. Then his sweater. Outside it is twelve degrees. Inside, it is eighty. He puts his hand to his throat and starts to gag. He is really pouring it on now, Laurence Olivier doing heat prostration.

"I'm going to throw up. Just watch me. I'm going to throw up right now if you don't turn that fan off."

It is the ultimate threat. Throwing up is his ace-in-the-hole. He knows that I am not really sure. I think it is all acting, but it is possible that one of these days he just might do it.

"Oh, all right," I say.

"The fan all the way off. Not low. All the way off!"

"My toes will turn blue. They will have to amputate."

"Ten, nine, eight, seven, six . . ."

"Oh, all right."

I acquiesce, but not for long. When he is not looking, I slyly nudge the fan with my hand, at the same time flipping the radio on to mask the sound. The air begins to heat up again. Suddenly, Alan screams, in panic, "LOOK OUT! LOOK OUT FOR THAT GUY ON YOUR RIGHT!"

I jerk the wheel to the left. "What guy, where, what's the matter?"

"There he goes, over the hill. He must have been going eighty. Lucky I saw him. He could have killed us all."

"I didn't even see him."

"Speed-crazy kids. No one under thirty should be allowed to drive."

As we enter the Callahan tunnel, I notice there is something wrong with my feet. They are numb to the ankle. How can that be? The fan is still on. I reach down and put my hand under the blower. It feels like it is blasting straight from a Siberian labor camp. While I was looking wildly to my right, Alan had craftily turned the heat control to cold, leaving the blower on high.

"You rat! There wasn't any car going eighty! That was just to get my eyes away from the heater. You rotten fink, how could you!"

He chuckles, a throaty, private-eye chuckle, and he says, "It was easy."

When we get home, the whole theater of operations changes complexion. It used to be a fairly equal contest, but then Jimmy Carter came on TV in his damn cardigan and said that no loyal American would turn the thermostat higher than sixty-five. I can shiver, moan, whine, curse, all to no avail. Alan simply looks at me and says, "Moral equivalent of war" and starts humming "Remember Pearl Harbor." He strides to the thermostat as forcefully as Patton racing to Bastogne. He sets it at sixty-five, commanding, "Nobody touch this dial."

I bundle up and try to function. It is difficult. I really have yet to get the hang of making tacos while wrapped in a blanket. I start to grumble. I am Ruth amid the alien corn. My husband has taken me from a land of milk and honey (swamp fever and muggings, Alan would say) to the frozen wastes of the north, and now I am denied the right to be warm in my own home. My spirit rebels. Am I going to stand here and shiver as Mobil Oil takes out ads in the *Times* saying that a 70 percent profit is not enough to keep its derricks dusted? Am I going to put my upper respiratory tract at risk so some sheikh can buy up another five blocks of Dallas? Ruth turns into Patrick Henry. "Give me seventy degrees or give me death." Better hot lead than cold feet. But the forces arrayed against me are formidable, from the chief executive on down to Alan. I cannot risk open confrontation. I must stage a guerrilla operation.

I have gotten very good at covert operations. I strike when least expected, a one-woman Entebbe. When Alan is busy trying to figure out the new math with Alyssa, I engage in a lightning raid on the living room, seize the objective, and fall back to the family room. Often, it is hours before my maneuver is discovered. Alan snaps the thermostat back to 65 and yells, "Who turned up the heat?"

I keep my face expressionless, my eyes wide and innocent. The Geneva convention says all he is entitled to is name, rank, and serial number. This is war. He interrogates the kids, then Jane and Kitty Widdums. Finally he comes to me. I meet his steely gaze head on. I do not flinch. I resort to the standard CIA maneuver, bald-faced lying.

"Certainly," I say haughtily, "you cannot think it was I!"

Alan

Dial M for Murder

THE REASON marriages lasted longer in the old days was because there were fewer mechanical things to argue over. There were no cars, so there were no car heaters or fans. There were houses, but no thermostats. Heaving another log on the fire was hardly an act that could be carried out covertly. The lack of central heating made for more open marriages, more honesty. People dealing with people are all right; it's the machinery that's fouling up life. Thermostat arguments, for example, are skirmishes, compared to the global wars over Mr. Bell's insidious invention.

"Hi, were there any messages, any phone calls?" I always ask, in the vain hope that (a) there were none, because I hate to return phone calls and (b) that if there were any, she might remember, so at least I can return them if I choose.

Usually, when prompted like this, my wife the journalist, the impeccable recorder of cosmic phenomena and pithy detail, will look up from some vital reading ("How the Amish Weave Doormats"), stare at the ceiling for a while with her mouth open like a guppy begging for fishfeed, and hum at the back of her throat, "Errrhhhhhh." This is called the process of total recall. It is also called irritating.

"Ohhhhh!" she usually says, as if a little electric bulb had just turned on in her brain. "John called."

Now, John is a friend. Along with that, he is a source of useful information. There are two good reasons right there for wishing to know that John called.

"Good. When did he call?"

"Monday."

"This is Friday!"

"I'm really sorry." (She always says that.) "I meant to tell you. It must have slipped my mind." (She always says that, too.)

I do not listen to the utterings subsequent to "Monday." By then, I am into my biweekly attack on her integrity, loyalty, mental agility. "Why the hell didn't you tell me Monday? Or even Tuesday? Wednesday would have been nice. Even Thursday was an option. Are you saving the news until next Monday, like an anniversary, so that you can say to me, 'Loop, one week ago today, John called. Exactly one week ago today. Gee, how time flies.' What good is screaming at the kids to write down messages when their mother doesn't write down messages? I write down all your messages, including all the stinking, useless, unimportant messages about tennis matches. But not anymore. No way. Screw tennis. Next time you've got a match and you don't show up call Billie Jean King, ask her for your appointments, because old dependable Daddy is retiring."

She has turned the page of her magazine and is now reading, "Memoirs of Picket Duty with the Bulgarian Screenwriters' Guild in the Tepid Summer of 1924."

"What if it was something important? What if somebody calls me and has a *story*? You remember stories, don't you? The things you used to write, when you were a reporter instead of now, when you are a writer? People call with stories, you know, with information that maybe is crucial to the stories?"

She looks up. "If it's important, they call back."

"Yeah, well what about courtesy?"

"What about courtesy?"

"People call and talk to you, and they think you're gonna tell me they called, and you don't tell me, so I don't return the calls, so they think I don't care."

"But you don't *like* to return calls."

"But life is not doing what you like. Life is returning phone calls."

"If they're your friends, they'll understand."

"I don't *have* that many friends!"

"If you keep screaming, you're going to lose another one."

Sooner or later, it's going to happen. Either New York is going to call with the Pulitzer or Stockholm with the Nobel and she will forget to tell me, and four months later I'll be watching the news, and the reporter will be doing a voice-over videotape of luminaries getting their prizes in Stockholm: "The Excellence in All Walks of Life Prize was going to Alan Lupo, of Winthrop, Massachusetts, U.S.A., but he apparently wasn't interested in it, so instead, it is being given to Dmitri Warmongerovich, of Kiev."

She remains placid, unperturbed. She's now reading "Will the Mount St. Helens Eruptions Discolor Saturn's Rings?" Nothing will change around here. But it could have been worse. She could have taken a message the way she usually does: "Irvink Brchsgtzch—20 Lakeside—$2 each—bring own trowel—Saturday latest—Dog was out, but no doodoo—Love, Caryl."

When I see these messages, written either in the margins of the previous day's newspaper or on small scraps of paper cleverly hidden in a room that I'm least likely to visit during the course of a week, I try not to anger quickly. I try to figure out the message.

Clearly, at some point, a guy named Irving called me, not Irvink. It had to take place after June 1968, because that's when we moved to this house. That narrows it down. Brchsgtzch is probably a gentile spelling for Berkowitz; Lakeside is undoubtedly the name of the street. It has the sound of a suburb, so we've got to run a check on suburbs with Jewish residents. Not more than a year's work there. It seems this man is having some kind of party, probably a pool party, which would account for the towel, unless he really said trowel, which means we might have to build the pool first. The $2 a head could be to cover the cost of catering or cement, and our dog is constipated.

When she arrives home, I try to make her feel guilty. "This is what you call a message? I'm supposed to understand this? I'm supposed to respond intelligently to this? Can you remember enough about this to tell me what in hell this could possibly mean? Your adult-ed courses in Albanian have certainly paid off."

She happily takes the note. "Sure. Irving Berkowitz is having a pool party at 20 Lakeside Road, and all we have to bring is $2 each and a towel and let him know by Saturday at the latest whether we're going. Also, I took the dog out, but she didn't go." She passes it back to me. "What's so hard about that?"

She's right. It wasn't hard. I had figured it out myself. But I can't let on, or else there'll be no chance of improving the message system around here. "Aha! But *where* is Lakeside Road, hah? Where? Is it in Montana? Honduras? Which hemisphere is Lakeside Road?"

"It's in Newton." Newton is, indeed, a suburb just across the city from us. A fair number of Jewish people live there. I had been in the ball park all along. "Anyway, I remembered that part. And I got everything else right. I even got Berkowitz."

"You call Brchsgtzch a Berkowitz?" She's winning this one. I'm reduced to sniping at tanks from stone barricades now. It's only a matter of time before my position falls, and I sulk. Suddenly, she gives me an opening.

"Who is he, anyway?" she asks.

"What's that? Who is he? You take a message from somebody, and you don't know who the somebody is?"

"I thought *you* knew him. He asked for you."

"You can't assume I know everybody who calls here. I never *heard* of Irving Berkowitz."

"Well, how am I supposed to know that you didn't know a guy who calls you and asks us to a party at his house? What am I supposed to say, 'Oh, thank you very much. By the way, who in hell are you, anyway?'"

I'm beaten, and I know it. "Well, what are we gonna do now?"

"The towels are in the laundry," she says. "You got four singles?"

"No way. I'm not going all of a sudden to a pool party at somebody's house I don't even know, because you didn't have the guts to ask him who he is."

It's sulking time. I grab angrily for a magazine. It's the one she's been reading. I go into seclusion, where nobody will bother me, and I begin reading: "Communication—the Key to an Enduring Marriage."

Caryl

Begin the Benign (Neglect)

IT's NOT that I don't try to remember phone messages; it's just that my brain is so crowded with more urgent items that sometimes the details get lost. Anyhow, I figure that if it's important, they'll call back. Phone messages fall into an area I define as "slippage"—nonessential items where there is room for error. My slippage area is roughly the size of the Houston Astrodome.

I have discovered, you see, that the only way to get everything done is not to do a lot of it. Now and then people ask me how I do it all—"all" presumably meaning the running of a house, the raising of children and a career. My answer is simple. I don't do it all. In fact, I do as little as I can get away with on every front. But kids have a way of making sure they get theirs, editors can be nasty about deadlines, and bosses like you to show up for work, so it's in the "running of the house" category where most of the slippage occurs.

I have a theory about household management. I call it (with apologies to Pat Moynihan) Benign Neglect. A house, after all, needs some time to do its own thing—settle, chip, molder, and peel. Long ago I gave up the notion that I could be Superwoman. Too much efficiency is bad for one's health; over-organization, I am convinced, gives you hemorrhoids. So, to implement my policy of Benign Neglect, I have drawn up a list of things I do not do:

Ironing: I am proud to state that in fifteen years of marriage I have never ironed anything. Nothing, zero, zip—not so much as a lousy handkerchief. Now and then I do take out my steam iron, fill it up and watch it hiss. The way Alan hates to travel, I figure it's as close as I'll get to Old Faithful in Yellowstone.

Have you ever really taken any time to think about ironing? A person, usually female, stands in front of a board which is set at just the right height to ensure long-term problems in the lumbar region, gripping a heavy object which is spouting steam and waves of heat into her face. She proceeds to push the hot, heavy object repeatedly up and down across endless lengths of wrinkled cloth to make it straight. After one wearing, the cloth becomes wrinkled once again, and it's back to push, shove, and sweat. If Dante had had any imagination at all, he would have dreamed it up for the Inferno. He would have had all the people who cheated on their wives or their income tax standing down in the ninth circle of hell, ironing.

Actually, I do have some historical information on the person who invented ironing. It was Torquemada the Inquisitor, who used it to make heretics recant. One day in 1485 the Inquisition police picked up a guy who was clearly a heretic—he was handing out Scientology pamphlets on the steps of the cathedral. They said to him, "Don Carlo, we are going to make you see the error of your ways. We are thinking of putting you in thumbscrews for six months."

"You can't break me. I'm not one of those lousy TM finks who cracks after one turn of the rack."

"Possibly we might use 500-pound boulders on your solar plexus while you recite the corporal works of mercy."

"I'm sticking to L. Ron Hubbard and his engrams. Do your worst!"

"Then again, we might make you iron 5,000 white shirts, all cotton, lightly starched, with button-down collars."

"No, no, anything but that! Mercy! Please, mercy! I never thought much of Scientology anyhow. The pamphlets are boring."

It has long been my opinion that the person who invented Permanent Press and thus made ironing obsolete should get the Nobel Prize for chemistry. I personally will not purchase any item of clothing that does not bear those magic words, *tumble dry*.

Polishing: Anything: I have a great affection for the fine dull glint of stainless steel. I don't want to see my face in anything except mirrors, and then, only dimly. Good luck to anybody who tries to see his reflection in my everyday china. He'd do better peering into the waters of the Great Dismal Swamp. If you want glitter, go to a rock concert.

Unfortunately, we do own several silver bowls, thanks to some awards Alan and I have won. Press associations seem enamored of little silver bowls; chintzy fake plastic gilt would be more appropriate to the profession, but even reporters feel the urge to be grand once in a while. My strategy is to place them out in plain view and forget them. A peculiar thing soon starts to happen. They develop an odd, mottled surface, growing more encrusted the longer they sit. Before long they look exactly like the primitive pottery I like to collect. At that point I simply tell guests that they are pre-Columbian artifacts. Now and then someone picks one up, peering intently at the surface.

"I think I see an inscription. It seems to say P-R-E-S-S. It seems to say Press Club."

"Oh yeah, that's an ancient piece, very valuable. It was presented to Quezaquetzel, editor of the Itachel Times in 50 B.C. He wrote a piece saying it wasn't right to cut people's hearts out in sacrifice to the sun god when the spleen was perfectly adequate. They called him the Ed Murrow of the Yucatán."

Writing Letters: Since I have unusual dexterity in my index finger, allowing me to dial ten-digit numbers with relative ease, I do not communicate via the U.S. mail. I worry about this a bit, because what will happen if I become a famous literary figure? Years hence, a professor of literature at Yale will have to be content with editing a volume of my correspondence called *The Long Distance Phone Calls of Caryl Rivers.* If Virginia Woolf had used my system all posterity would have is a collection of itemized bills that read: May 10, '37, London, 35 min.

I do have some correspondence lying around, but I have a suspicion it would not set the Cambridge literary world aflame to read:

"Dear Mrs. Cohen: Please excuse Alyssa's absence yesterday as she was suffering from severe diarrhea"; or "To Jordan Marsh Company: We do not understand why your delivery man left us twelve guppies and an Eames chair when all we ordered was a set of sheets."

Washing Windows: The care and cleaning of windows has become tedious work ever since the invention of storm windows. It is harder—and more hazardous to one's health—to dismantle and clean a storm window than it is to do the same to an M-16 rifle. Given the air pollution these days, a person could get cancer just from inhaling the gunk cleaned off the windows. I therefore avoid washing windows for sound environmental reasons. I find this course of action has psychological benefits as well. A fine gray sediment settles on the windows, giving the interior of the house the constant atmosphere of a comfy London fog. It might be the blaze of noon outside, but inside it's always dusk on the Thames. In these times of change, this constancy is reassuring. The pace of the modern world is too swift. To have to watch the sun go up and down, up and down all the time is unsettling. In our home, the perpetual twilight is more calming than 1,000 grams of Valium.

Trimming the Shrubbery: When we bought our house ten years ago, it was surrounded by abundant greenery of an anonymous nature. Today, the shrubbery is still anonymous, but quite a bit more abundant. I like to think of it as romantic excess, the sort of place where Lady Chatterley and her gamekeeper would have dallied, or as a pleasant home for Heathcliff and Cathy when they got tired of roaming the moors. The neighbors tend to think more in terms of the castle of Vlad the Impaler.

The front of the house has more or less disappeared in a riot of omniverous greenery. The way the plants strangle each other and gasp for air is very entertaining. The children can learn about Darwin's survival of the fittest just by sitting on the porch and watching the bushes go at each other. There are rumors around the neighborhood that we are growing man-eating plants in the tangled underbrush. This is nonsense. I have been grabbed a few times but easily managed to struggle free. I did hear the mailman shrieking once and had to cut him out of the forsythia with a hacksaw. The forsythia can get a bit hostile once in a while, but I explained to the mailman that if he didn't show fear he would be all right. It certainly has cut down on the volume of our junk mail.

Alan

The Money Game

ONE OBVIOUS antidote to the results of Caryl's do-nothing approach to housecleaning would be hired help. We generally have been unable to hire hired help because they insist on being paid. Rather than employing someone to show up regularly, Caryl once resorted to one of those housecleaning outfits who show up in battalion strength to clean and wax everything in sight.

It was a frightening experience, as vans pulled up into the neighborhood, vans full of men and women and strange-looking equipment. They came in both sexes, all kinds of shapes, white, black, and brown and in a variety of nationalities—black guys who did rugs, Hispanic guys who did kitchens, a Jewish couple who did windows. A truly democratic experience. Everybody was a specialist. As soon as one group would leave, another would show up, each careful not to tread on another's turf.

When they departed, they left behind a home none of us recognized. The familiar odor of old dirt had been replaced by the aseptic stench of ammonia. Dry, dirty rugs were now wet and clean. "Don't step on the rugs for about fourteen years," they had warned us, after shampooing them. The dog, not knowing better, stepped on one and almost drowned. They also left a bill. We looked at the bill and clung to each other like boat people with no hope of rescue. I was upset, because I was angry. Caryl was upset, because she was surprised—my goodness, we're being charged for this!

Caryl seems sincerely shocked when presented with a bill for any-thing. Her jaw drops open, her eyes widen, and she stares at whoever is nearby with an expression suggesting something between pain and the demise of innocence. After all her years on earth, she can't get used to the capitalist notion that when you buy something you must pay for it. Caryl is such a nice person; she doesn't understand why anyone would want to charge her for, say, dinner or a department store purchase. The recurring shock of this experience, however, has not prevented her from buying more things or planning to buy more things.

This tends to conflict with my attitude toward money. To me, credit, stocks, bonds, commodities, minerals and investments are capitalist plots to steal my hard-earned cash and shove it into a slush fund for oil exploration in the Gulf of Oman or into condos in Houston. No, I want my money, such as it is, near me. If I can't keep it under the bed —the cat will pee on it—I must keep it in local banks. I go in weekly to check on it. I drive by almost daily to make sure the banks haven't burned down or been robbed or relocated.

Caryl's attitude is that money is a fast moving commodity to be parlayed into instant debt in order to have any intrinsic value. She reads a menu. The menu says lamb chops cost $8.50. She orders lamb chops, along with various vegetables, salad, bread and, for a fee clearly dis-played on the same menu, a glass of wine. Having eaten this, she gets the check. It indicates she owes $8.50 for lamb chops, $1.25 for a drink and some tax. She is shocked. But she never asks a waiter if the bill is correct. "Is that right!" she asks me incredulously. "That couldn't be right. They must have made a mistake."

"Why?"

"The last time I had lamb chops, it was much less."

She's right. The last time she had lamb chops, she was seven years old and eating them free in the officers' club family mess at Barin Field, Alabama, where her father was stationed during World War II. Since then, prices have risen somewhat. Caryl has not noticed.

My fixation with the value of money may have begun when my mother entrusted me with $15 one day a month, when the rent was due. My job was to carry the $15 to the landlord, a very responsible and scary task. What if a bigger kid jumped me and took my family's hard-earned $15? What if I tripped and fell on the $15 and tore the bucks beyond recognition? What if the money blew out of my hand? It was, after all, sixteen steps down to the landlord's apartment, all inside. Who knew what could happen?

We did not worship money, but we held an abiding respect for its awesome power. Nobody I knew talked about investments or tax shelters. What you did with money then was you put it in an envelope and deposited it in two places. The biggest chunk went into the checking account, and the smaller bit went into the savings bank or credit union, which was a storefront place between the Jewish Community Center on one corner and the Roosevelt Beauty Shoppe and Al's Kosher Meat Market on the other. This is what you did if you had any money left over. There were times for a lot of us when leftover was not an operative word. The presence of any naked money lying around—a penny stuck in the tar, a nickel in the gutter—aroused the kind of passions previously seen only on Wall Street on Black Friday.

Caryl's family was not rich, but it was suburban and basically comfortable. As a child, Caryl asked only for the basics—her own horse, a swimming pool. These were promptly denied. Caryl did not pout. She never looked down, always up. She never worried about the possibility that she would not have access to money. Even when she became a journalist and knew that trade paid zilch, she never worried. Even when she married a journalist, who has made a career of making zilch, she hasn't worried. She's right. My mother worried if she was one day late paying the utility bills. Caryl figures the utilities will outlast all of us. The utilities appear to be proving her correct. A couple of times, during major blizzards, my mother was a day late getting the utility bill to the drugstore four blocks away where you could pay it. I have noticed that the drugstore has closed, my mother has grown older, and the utilities are wealthier.

Caryl's blasé attitude toward cash keeps her emotionally healthy. What it has done to me is not so healthy. Marriage is a see-saw. If one mate is not going to worry herself/himself sick about things like money, the see-saw is imbalanced. The other mate has to worry not only for himself/herself but also for the non-worrying partner. While I no longer worry about a bigger kid jumping me for the mortgage money (having officially become middle class, mortgage money has replaced rent money), I still worry about bigger-kid symbols. I'm convinced that on a given day, representatives from the gas company, the phone company, the electric company, the bank holding the mortgage, the town tax collector, two downtown department stores, one suburban shopping center, the car insurance company, the life insurance company, the home insurance company, all magazines to which we subscribe, the local gas station, the fuel-oil dealer, the milkman, the credit-card conglomerate, and assorted others will coordinate their watches and collectively mug us.

The phones will go dead; the lights will go out; the gas will be turned off; a summons will be served for late payment of real estate and excise taxes; all credit will be canceled; the furniture, animals, and kids will be repossessed. I'll be sitting frightened and alone with Caryl in a dark, cold house, listening to the demolition crew remove the basement, and Caryl will say, "Loop, you know, there's a sale this Saturday on Russo-Finnish-War surplus snow boots. I think I'll go downtown and get four pair, one for each of us."

Caryl happily lets me balance the checkbook, because she too harbors a sixth sense of impending disaster if good old dependable Alan doesn't fulfill the role of family tightwad. Caryl once took a shot at handling the checkbook. It was an exercise in new math. She managed to subtract from a $116 balance a bill of $96 and end up with a new balance of $349.

"It's wrong," I told her.

"Wrong is one way to put it," she said. "I think we should regard it as found money."

"The American financial community, along with its varied law enforcement arms, regard it as illegal, not as found money."

I repossessed the checkbook before the bank could move to repossess my few worldly goods. But that deals with only a small part of the problem. To understand Caryl's moves with money, one must picture a guerrilla war, the classic kind. I am the establishment army. I take over a checkbook, which is the capital city. But she, the guerrilla army, appears and reappears without warning or fear of effective retaliation. I may temporarily control the checkbook, but she travels at will through the countryside of cash. When the adult cash runs out, there is Steven's cash he gets for certain household chores. When that runs out, there is Alyssa's cash, which she has hoarded ever since her first nickel collected at age four. As I move hard against her cash reserves, flushing them out of the bush, she turns to the ultimate guerrilla weapon, the credit card.

Some people have been impressed by the invention of the steam engine, others by the discovery of atomic power. Caryl Rivers thinks the Nobel Prize for science and the advancement of mankind should go to the inventors of credit cards. With credit cards, she has rented hotel rooms, bought clothes, dined at restaurants, purchased cans of fruit salad, and obtained shoelaces. She wanted to know if rabies shots could be paid for with a credit card. She was ready once to offer a credit card to the toll keeper at a tunnel exit because she couldn't find a quarter. She can't understand why the Girl Scouts of America will not accept a Sears, Roebuck credit card for the purchase of a box of Do-Si-Do cookies.

I believe history will show there were only two other instances in

America that outranked Caryl's financial manipulations. One was the Teapot Dome scandal; the other, the issuing of useless specie by the Continental Congress to pay farmers for feeding Washington's hungry army. Right now, Confederate currency is worth more on the open market than Caryl's credit.

Steven has inherited Caryl's attitude. If he makes five bucks, he rushes out of the house with an energy not in evidence previously in the day and crashes through the door of the nearest hobby or sports shop. "Another street-hockey stick?" I ask. "You have eight street-hockey sticks. You have only two arms and one set of teeth, which means you can't possibly use more than three sticks at once. You now have a surplus of six such sticks. When I was your age, I didn't throw my money out on such things."

"When you were my age, they didn't invent street hockey," he says.

"When Daddy was your age, they hadn't invented streets," Caryl says, to the amusement of our children.

Alyssa has copied my attitude toward money. She has more than copied it. She will not keep the change from her lunch money; she returns it to me. She will not spend her own dough except at Christmas. Money, she reasons, is for dumping in piles on the rug and counting. This kid spends so much time counting change we're worried she's going to miss school days. "Dear principal, sir, Alyssa Lupo was not in school last week because she was locked in her room counting her money. She has, however, done all her homework, because her brother, Mister Big, bought copies of finished assignments from her classmates."

The living memorial to Caryl's profligacy is the unfinished finished basement. This proved to be yet another in a series of failed programs to beautify urban America. The basement is very strong, which is to say, it was built at the turn of the century with big, ugly rocks. It is a living testimonial to Edgar Allan Poe's powers of description. It is, in a word, dank. The ceiling is made up of scores of pipes containing a variety of waters, gases and electrical conduits and resembling, in all, the innards of a U-boat. At some point one of the windows slipped open a notch, and the occupant stuffed the hole with a newspaper, which is now very yellow and tends to flake upon being touched. I don't know when the incident occurred, but there's a news analysis on the page visible that urges Gentleman Johnny Burgoyne to adopt Indian tactics if he intends to fight "their" kind of war.

I'm sure the basement is not a total waste of space and that it has some use beyond storage and the housing of washer, dryer, and heating units. The old fellow hanging by his wrists on one of the walls says if you pace your breathing just right, you can last down there for years. Anyway, Caryl decided we should convert part of said basement into a "playroom." That's like suggesting that a good interior decorator could wallpaper the Khyber Pass.

"John L. Lewis wouldn't have allowed his mineworkers down there for time-and-a-half, and you're going to make it into a playroom?"

She said the pitted stone floor could be covered easily by the right kind of rug; that a drop ceiling could be installed to cover aged beams and rusty pipes; that wooden supports could be nailed to the right places and that plywood or Sheetrock, in turn, could be nailed to the supports. She herself would paint the jagged rock walls. The other stuff she had mentioned would be contracted out. After all, she asked, how much could it cost?

"A couple of thou," she was told, minimum. A few hundred just to insure the lives of the workmen who go down there, not to mention labor, materials, memorial services for the laborers who don't return, and what have you."

"So?" she asked. "Don't you want a place where the children can play?"

"We got a place the children can play in. It's called the house. When I was a kid we had a little apartment, and I had a room to play in. Why do these kids need the King Ranch?"

"But this is some place they can go with their friends and make noise, and they won't disturb us."

"This is middle-class crap. In the old days, if you made noise when you were playing, somebody would yell, 'Shaddup!' and that was the end of the noise. It saved a lot of money. You didn't need playrooms. What we need in this family is money, and we don't have enough of it, much less any to build a playroom."

"You forget," she reminded me, "that I've written a piece for *The Saturday Review*. And I'm getting paid soon, about a thousand or more. So we're not paying for this room; *The Saturday Review* is paying for this room."

For the next few weeks, as Caryl hand painted the stalagmites and gorges, a variety of workmen—beam specialists, rug layers, dropped-ceiling experts, electricians, and such—wended their way warily in and out of the cellar. Each had a different task, and each looked and talked differently, and each was his own man, but they all had one thing in common—an immediate need to be paid on the spot. They did not wish to hear that *The Saturday Review* check hadn't shown up yet, nor did they display any great interest in *The Saturday Review*'s circulation figures or in its influence upon people in power.

So we paid them, each and every one of them, all of them, on time, on the spot. It all cost a few hundred more than Caryl's promised incoming check, but she said we could swallow that, given the bargain we were getting. Then, two things happened.

The first thing that happened was the mushrooms. I ventured down to the new playroom after a rainstorm and noticed that the rug was very squishy. I also noticed the mushrooms. They were growing between the edge of the rug and the hand-painted walls. A few days later, the mushrooms developed a bad case of mildew and began to croak. We now had a drop ceiling overlooking a flood plain area with endangered mushrooms. Our kids' friends said they didn't want to visit anymore because the mean old Lupos wanted them to play in a scary, wet cellar, and they were afraid of drowning or getting lost.

The second thing that happened was *The Saturday Review* folded. It folded before it paid Caryl. A few years later she got a letter from a lawyer announcing that bankruptcy proceedings had ended and enclosed was her share of what could be salvaged—$40. *The Saturday Review* was later resurrected, but too late for the playroom.

The Saturday Review Memorial Playroom now stands quiet and deserted, like a forgotten marshland in some untraveled southern bayou. Occasionally I think I hear hooting and chirping from the general direction of the playroom. In the dead of night, I have told Caryl, I can hear moaning. It seems to be saying, "*Saaaaave yourrrrrr moneeeeee. Saaaaave yourrrrrr moneeeeee.*"

"That's nonsense," she assures me.

"You mean the moaning?"

"No, what he's saying."

Caryl

The Graying of America

ALAN DOES not understand about money. Now and then I catch him stuffing dollar bills into socks and hiding them under the mattress where he thinks Jane can't get them. I try to tell him banks are safe these days. He shakes his head.

"Banks will fail."

"But they are insured by the government."

"The government will fail."

"Then the only safe thing to do is to buy gold and lug it to a cave in the Sierra Nevada and spend our lives sitting on it."

"Damn, why didn't I think of that!"

Buying things makes him break out in a rash. My buying things makes him break out in a rash. It is not as if I am swathing myself in mink. He casts a hard eye on utilitarian items—laundry hampers being a case in point.

Laundry hampers, in fact, bring all the incompatibilities in our psyches to the fore. Alan has very straightforward views about laundry. He takes the Teddy Roosevelt charge-right-up-San-Juan-Hill approach to dirty clothes. He believes they should be washed forthwith, with dispatch and no dithering about.

I, however, take a more modern geopolitical approach. I believe one must keep a tight rein on the flow of laundered clothes. A glut of clean laundry creates chaos in the space-time continuum: clean socks bulge out of drawers, the hanger supply is quickly exhausted. I advocate the commodity-management style of laundry maintenance. I model my actions after the Secretary of Agriculture. He buys grain silos to store surplus soybeans; I procure laundry hampers to deal with the proliferation of washables.

As I lug my newest purchase, a pink wicker model, up the stairs to the second floor, Alan looks at me with dismay.

"Christ, another hamper?"

"Actually, there's two. Sears had them on sale for a mere $19.99 each in Tahiti coral or Polynesian pink. The coral was just a shade too intense, but the pink ones—"

"We already have more hampers up here than the laundry room of the Chicago Hilton. Why do we need more?"

"The towel hamper in the bathroom has been running at overcapacity. The bottom fell out of the one for the tennis wash, and it's time to break out an auxiliary sheet hamper."

"How could we possibly need an auxiliary sheet hamper? We have had the same sheets on the bed for a month."

"Correct."

"By the way, why have we had the same sheets on the bed for a month?"

"We shower every night, so how dirty could we get the sheets?"

"Then why in God's name do we need an auxiliary sheet hamper?"

"Sheets have a very low priority number for access to our limited washing apparatus. Changing sheets means four sheets per month, twelve times a year; forty-eight sheets, not to mention Steven and Alyssa's sheets and the ones for the new room. That means there are approximately sixty-seven sheets in the holding area at any given time."

"Why don't we just wash them?"

"Washing all the sheets at one time would not only severely tax the labor allocations of the household—we would not, for example, have time to eat—but it would create a crisis of unprecedented proportions in the space-priority system in our household excess-commodity storage spaces."

"We haven't got room for all the goddamn sheets."

"Correct. Not when they are clean. When they are dirty we have lots of room, now that I have the auxiliary sheet hamper."

"Why don't we get rid of some of the sheets?"

"What if there is a fire and we have to make a rope of sheets to escape?"

"We have enough sheets to get down from The Towering Inferno. Besides, if the room was filled with smoke we would get the wrong hamper and we'd be trying to tie square knots in your tennis panties."

"It is a crime to throw away designer sheets. God would get us for throwing an Yves St. Laurent in the trash."

"What about the ones the dog bled all over when she cut her nose?"

"Oh, yes, the blue-and-white counterpane. Bill Blass. No problem. I just stick the part with the dog blood on it at the end of the bed where it gets tucked in."

At this point Alan wanders away, mumbling incoherently to himself. I drag up the second hamper, pleased with my purchase. The auxiliary sheet hamper will be the solution to an environmental eyesore, the sheet pile in the basement. When the sheet hamper got full, I had no alternative but to pile the sheets in the basement next to the washing machine. Due to their low-priority number in my laundry master plan, they tended to stay there. The sheet pile grew, over the years, until it became a synthetic mountain—a Dacron Matterhorn. A Sears repairman came in to fix the washer one day and vanished from the face of the earth. We fear he may have fallen into the sheet pile. His remains are probably moldering away under there right now. Alan is certain that the Sears man will go the way of the Heap, the venerable World War I comic book character. The Heap was a French aviator who crashed in a swamp but didn't die—a spark of life remained. He lay there for a while, merging with the swamp grass and slime, and then he lumbered out of the swamp to terrify the kids of America. Alan swears he hears grunts and burbles out of the sheet pile; he has nightmares about the day the basement door will swing open and a monstrous blob of pastel polyester will come lurching out. When I hear Alan gagging in his sleep I know he's at the point in the dream where his throat is being gripped by large white hands dotted with Marimekko carnations.

So Alan stays away from doing the sheets, which is understandable. Towels, however, have become his specialty. I used to do them, but sometimes I would forget, and Alan did not like having to dry off after a shower with Kleenex. The only problem with towels is that they get heavy when wet and overtax the simple brain of the washing machine. So the cycle knob sticks, and the machine just sits there and hops up and down in distress, bleating. You have to kick it to get it to flip to spin. When this happens, Alan curses in several languages and rushes downstairs to punt. I suggest he think of it as therapy. Kicking the hell out of a washing machine gets rid of more hostility than an hour of meditation.

Alan also hates to put socks away. He claims he is too color blind to match them right. So after he washes them and gets them out of the dryer he leaves them in green trash bags (we have been using them for laundry bags ever since Jane ate the real one). More often than not, they multiply.

"Have you noticed," he says to me, "those green mounds you have been stepping over for two weeks?"

"Oh, those. They look nice."

"They look *nice?*"

"A touch of greenery in our otherwise sterile environment. Greenery is big in home decorating these days. Mark Hampton uses it. So does Angelo Donghia."

"Angelo Whatshisface puts trash bags full of socks in people's living rooms?"

"Not exactly, but you may have started a new trend. Ficus Gladbagus. Never has to be watered and for $5.99 you can have more greenery in your home than the Ho Chi Minh Trail. You could be the Johnny Appleseed of polyurethane. Make a thousand flowers bloom."

"*Will you please match my socks?*"

"OK, kick away a great career for a few crummy pairs of socks, see if I care."

But my greatest triumph in the whole field of laundry is the creative use of hot water and detergent to create new and subtle color combinations. Throwing caution to the winds, I ignore the instructions on the back of the box about what to wash with what. The things that emerge from the washer are a constant source of wonder and amazement to my family.

Steven wandered out of his room one morning and announced: "Ma made my underwear pink."

Alan stared at the item of clothing Steven was holding aloft. "The Andy Warhol of wash-and-wear strikes again."

Steven protested, "I can't wear this to school. The kids would laugh at me."

"Pete Rose wouldn't," I said.

"Pete Rose wears pink underwear?"

"Paisley. He posed for a jockey shorts ad wearing paisley. Besides, this isn't pink, it's pale mauve."

Alan snorted. "You want to send this kid off to the Albert Capone Memorial Junior High School in pale mauve underwear?"

"Why can't I just have white underwear like everybody else?" Steven moaned.

I examined the shorts. "White I won't be able to manage. How about I throw them in with your dress socks and they will come out navy—or perhaps a very fine eggshell gray?"

His face brightened. "Oh, thanks, Ma."

Alan, meanwhile, was pulling on his eggshell gray T-shirt. He likes gray. Next to brown, it's his favorite color. Alyssa's knee socks are a bit deeper, more the color of pussy willows in the spring.

And, as for me, I am the only person at the tennis club who can execute a perfect overhead smash—in dazzling tennis grays.

Part Two

Planned Parenthood

Alan

Birthday

IF SHE wishes to be blasé about the laundry, I can live with that. I do not live so easily with her equally easygoing attitude about those who must wear the laundry, i.e., people, us. She cannot understand that nothing must be left to chance, that life must be well ordered and *planned*. And should there be any disruption of the planned order of things, then we must engage in crisis management. I have not cottoned easily or gracefully to disruption.

"Whatsamatter, whatsamatter?" I muttered, and rightfully so, given the sudden commotion in the middle of the night, when sane people tend to sleep.

"My water broke," she said. She said it with the same degree of passion and excitement displayed by the weather lady on the telephone, when she notes, "Some cloudiness, with mild temperatures."

"What plumber is gonna show up at this hour?" I wondered.

"You'd better get ready," she said.

I had told her a hundred times I was no good at fixing things. I could make a snake out of a clothes hanger and unplug a stuffed drain, but if the water broke, that meant the pipes broke, and that meant a plumber. It was hard enough getting one in the daytime, much less the middle of the night. I began to stir. I pushed myself up on one elbow. We were living in a duplex apartment. If there was a big leak in the bathroom, that meant the water could seep through the floor and down into the small kitchen.

"Towels!" I yelled. "Put towels on the floor." I stumbled out into the hallway and saw her standing in the bathroom in a pile of towels. "Good work," I thought. "Fast thinking for a sleepy time of day." I asked, "What broke?"

"My water broke. We'd better get going soon."

Suddenly, I knew what she meant. *The* water didn't break. Pipes break. Water doesn't know how to break, not running water, that is, or rainwater, or water lying around in a puddle or a pond. *Her* water broke. Inside her, that water. The months of self-discipline and training now took command of the situation. Now, in her ninth month of pregnancy, my wife was to have a baby, our first baby, and I, her husband, was going to deal with it competently, intelligently, calmly.

"*Ohmigod! Jesus! Oy vei es meir!*"

She stood there quietly, while calmly applying the last touches of makeup to her eyelids.

"What do you need that for?" I yelled. "We going dancing between pains?"

She led me firmly downstairs, so I wouldn't fall.

"How could it be?" I asked. "It's only been nine months. Are you sure?"

"I'm sure," she said, standing there, now dressed to the nines.

"Pains, you're supposed to be having pains. Did you time the pains?"

"No. Don't worry about pains. They'll come later. If the water breaks, that means I'm about ready."

"But I'm not ready," I whimpered, as she led me to the car.

The car. The car meant driving. That's what you did with cars. You drove them. It meant getting the key, turning the ignition, steering, accelerating, braking, shifting gears, hoh boy.

"OK," I said, getting settled behind the wheel. "OK. Right. OK." I didn't seem to be doing much of anything. "OK. Right. All right now."

"Do you mind if I don't drive?" she asked.

"What are you, crazy? You think I would make you drive? I can handle this situation. I'm calm. I'm all right." I tried forcing the key into the cigarette lighter. She looked at me with some question.

"Wanna smoke, baby?" I tried to recoup.

"Neither of us smokes," she said.

"Good, good. Just testing your reflexes. Making sure your memory's okay, no delusions, no vertigo, no senility."

I found the ignition. The engine turned over. It seemed to make an awesome noise. What noise was that anyway? How did the keys get into the ignition? That's an interesting word, *ignition*. I wondered about that. And why was it dark? Why was it the only thing I could remember was the date the Braves left Boston for Milwaukee? I drove off in the general direction of a main road. We lived only a few miles from the Beth Israel Hospital. I had even driven the route, a dry run, so that there would be absolutely no mistakes, no delays. Besides, I had lived most of my life in the area. I felt suddenly strong, in charge. I was driving through no-man's-land, casually guiding my commanding officer and a very important pouch through enemy minefields. I was a cocky pilot, maneuvering my P-40 through heavy ack-ack. I peeked out from under my jauntily worn flight cap at my copilot. "You okay?"

"Fine." She smiled.

"Radio tower. We're comin' in on a wing and a prayer."

"What?" she asked, looking at me strangely again. I understood. These new kids were cocky and gutsy, but they just didn't have the training.

"Roger. Rosie O'Grady, this is Able Baker Niner. I'll guide this baby through."

She just shook her head.

I seemed to be driving in the right direction. So far, everything was where it was supposed to be. I hoped nobody had started any major urban renewal project in the last couple of days. I found the side street that would take me directly to Brookline Avenue and the hospital. I patted the dashboard. "C'mon, baby. C'mon, shweetheart. We're almost home."

I hooked a left. Yessir, I was OK, A-OK, Number One, all right, hum chuck. I was frigging lost is what I was. "Oh, shit," I said quietly so as not to disturb my copilot, my wife, whoever that woman was in the car. "Oh, shit, shit, shitshitshitshit."

"Why are you whispering 'shit' to yourself," the lady asked me.

"Don't panic!" I screamed at her. Who was she anyway, asking inane questions, while my wife was having a baby? "Just don't panic, all right? I know this is hard to believe, but we're lost. I've lost the damn hospital! It's not here anymore. It used to be over there, on my right, but it's not there anymore. Goddamn urban renewal, nothing's sacred anymore. All the old landmarks are gone. All the swing bands. And then in 1953, the Braves. We're destroying our past. How you doing?" I remembered to ask, praying there were no pains yet.

"Fine." She smiled, but the smile didn't seem as strong as the last smile when she had said "fine." Was she losing faith in me? In my ability to lead men? How would it look for the upcoming kid to be born at a moment when the wife might not be thinking highly of the husband? *Born. Baby.* What if the *baby* was *born* in the car? It was cold. It was early on the morning of November 1 in New England. Babies shouldn't be born in cars. They should be born in hospitals. Hospital. Caryl had remembered to call before we left so they were waiting for me and her and the towels at the hospital. Maybe they got sick of waiting. Maybe they thought it was a prank. Sure, a prank. Why not a prank? It was just after Halloween, right? People on Halloween probably call the hospitals all the time. "Hello, City Hospital? I'm about to do an emergency appendectomy in my kitchen, and I'd like to know if I have to wash both hands." I'd have to get to the hospital in time to catch them before they disappeared. You can't just drive up to a hospital and have a baby. Hospitals have sections. They have tonsil sections, fainting-spell sections, ear-eye-nose-'n'-throat sections, and baby sections. Every hospital has four sections. How was I going to find the right section? Good, I was beginning to come to, beginning to make some sense. Find the baby section. And to find the baby section, I must first do something. What was it? It was there, stuck in a small corner of my mind. Haa! Right. Find the hospital. Find it, find it quickly and find it without upsetting Caryl.

"Of all the times you pick to have a kid!" I yelled at her. "You don't have kids at night. You have them in the daylight, when you can see things, like buildings and signs and streets. Everything you save for the last minute! Nine months, and you have to wait for the last minute."

"For God's sakes," she yelled back, "stop the car, and I'll get a cab."

"Cute. Even in the midst of child bearing, it's cute how you throw little darts of guilt around. You wait until the last minute to have our first kid, and then you blame me. Cute. You know what the problem is? The problem is that there's nobody to ask, because nobody but winos and perverts are out at this hour, winos and perverts and us."

She pointed to a truck. "Ask the truck driver. Truck drivers have a good sense of direction."

I pulled up alongside the truck and began blowing the horn. I forced the truck over to the curb. Not bad. I calmly got out of the car, sauntered over to his cab, moved my lips and jaw about as if I were chewing a piece of straw and asked in a calm shriek, "The hospital! I lost the hospital. My wife's having a baby! The Beth Israel Hospital? Everybody here knows it. You must know it." On the truck was a license plate, and on the plate it said, "West Virginia." The driver smiled. "Aah thank it's ovuh theah," he said, pointing a half block up the street at a big illuminated sign that said: "Beth Israel Hospital." It was true. These men have a finely honed sense of direction. They know everything. God bless the Teamsters Union. God bless West Virginia. God bless Burt Reynolds who hadn't even been invented yet.

"OK, Caryl," I said, driving the car into the parking lot, marked

"Parking." I urged her not to panic. "We're almost there, honey. We're home free." She was yawning. I stopped short, jumped out of the car, grabbed a suitcase from the back and ran to the door. Then I turned around and ran back to the car, where I had left the one who was pregnant. "No problem, no problem. Where the hell is everyone? It's deserted here. Where are the cops? Where are the doctors? No paramedics, no nurses, no attendants, what the hell! Everybody on a coffee break? Damn unions. They're probably in the Teamsters, damn Teamsters. Sure, what do they care? They're not pregnant. You call, and nobody shows up."

A nurse was staring at me. "Maternity?" she asked. She was smiling. "Right," Caryl answered. She too was smiling.

"We're having a baby," I yelled. I was not smiling. "Any minute now." I rushed past her and jumped into a wheelchair.

It was 1 A.M. Steven Lupo was born at 6:30 A.M.

Caryl

Birthday

I DON'T know why Alan was so upset when the water broke. I was quite calm. I had things all planned. I marched to the bathroom, piled up the towels, and right away grabbed for the mascara. That was step one in my plan for glamorous motherhood.

In the movies, mothers were always smiling, wearing lipstick and perfect pageboy hairdos as they gazed raptly at their babies. The only time that *didn't* happen was in the Western epics where they gave birth under covered wagons with the Indians attacking. But even then, their false eyelashes didn't slip off.

After I finished with the mascara, I got out my $49.95 genuine Dynel thirty-six-inch fall, wound it into a chignon and started attaching it with forty-seven bobby pins. By this time Alan had come fully awake and started to panic. I had to shut the bathroom door to keep him from clutching my knees.

"*What are you doing in there!*" he screamed as I put in bobby pin number forty-eight.

"I'm fixing my hair."

"Oh my God, she's fixing her hair."

"Then I have to find my eye shadow."

"*Vei es meir*, eye shadow!"

He was pounding on the door with his fists as I lightly dusted it on my lids. By the time I got to the blusher I could hear him sobbing as his fingernails scraped down the outside of the door. Actually, he had bitten off his fingernails and it was the raw skin rubbing up against the pine. I figured it was time to go.

After our interesting ride to the hospital, a nurse ushered us into a small room and told Alan to time my contractions. We did this for a while—ten minutes, five minutes, twelve minutes, eighteen minutes.

"Why are we doing this?" Alan asked.

"Beats the hell out of me. Maybe we are playing 'Beat the Clock.' "

"You're supposed to know about these things. Haven't you been doing any reading?"

"Yeah, I just finished *Tender Is the Night*. It's about this lady who goes crazy and her husband . . ."

"*Books about babies. Having babies. Did you read them?*"

"Um-hum, I just got through one by Margaret Mead about this tribe of Fiji islanders. When a woman is about to have a baby she goes into a special hut made out of banana leaves while the husband takes part in a special birthing rite where he walks around with a large boulder between his legs and hums a droning chant about fertility and next year's harvest. The rest of the men do this wonderful dance . . ."

"*Screw the Fiji islanders. Modern books, for chrissake. Didn't you read any modern books?*"

"No, I figured I'd wing it. All that breathing and panting looked boring."

The blood seemed to drain out of his face and I thought he was going to faint. He went back to timing contractions. A nurse came in and I asked her about the strange sounds from across the room. "Why is that lady yelling?"

"Oh, she's really not in pain. It's just the drugs."

A likely story, I thought. The Godless atheistic materialistic communists had her and were sticking pins in her toes, demanding she renounce her faith in transubstantiation.

We kept timing, and finally the nurse said nothing was going to happen before morning so I should get some sleep and Alan could go home and collapse. I went into this little room and a nurse came in and asked me if I had a hairpiece on. Like a fool, I admitted it. She said it had to come off. I asked why, and she didn't give me a reason, but insisted it had to come off. I said that while I was aware that Athena sprang full-blown from the forehead of Zeus, I didn't think my delivery was going to be like that. Forehead births have not been big in the past 5,000 years.

"It could get in the doctor's way," she said.

"What's he giving me, a shampoo and set?"

In the end, she won. She even took my rings.

I wished then that I had read the panting and breathing books so I could threaten to take my business out to the parking lot. Glamorous motherhood was down the tubes (no pun intended). I was sure the baby would enter the world, take one look at the rat's nest that had been my hairdo, and think that he had fallen into the clutches of Medusa.

So there I was, scruffy haired, wearing a hospital johnny and not having a clue as to what was going on. To make matters worse, it was like Saturday night at the station house. It was the busy season for babies; stretcher wheels clattered down the halls, babies wailed, voices droned. I lay there, noticing that the contractions seemed to be getting closer and closer. Nothing to scream about, however, so I thought it wasn't much. I tried to sleep, except my stomach kept hopping around. I thought I'd better ask someone.

"Excuse me," I called out softly. Nobody heard. "I hate to bother you, I know you're busy." The well-behaved little parochial school girl didn't want to make a fuss. Suddenly my stomach churned and there went dinner, over the rail.

A resident happened to be walking by and came in.

"Oh, I'm really sorry about that," I said. "If you've got a towel I'll clean it up, maybe the sour cream I used was bad."

"Oh, my God," he said. "You're four centimeters dilated."

"I haven't gone metric yet. What on earth are you talking about?"

"You're going to have a baby."

"No kidding. And I thought this was the gall bladder ward."

"No, I mean you're going to have a baby any second."

"Now? Right now? Aaaarrrggghhh!"

The obstetrician came running in, still buttoning his shirt. We rolled at what seemed like excessive speed down the corridor to the delivery room. All of a sudden, my stomach started going whang! whang! whang! so I guessed they must be right. Whoever was inside was ready to launch. Someone said to me, "Arch your back like a cat," and I thought, "Terrific, they've made a mistake and sent me to the Joy of Movement Center." Then someone stuck me with a needle and things got hazy and the next thing I knew I was holding this very small person who was all pink and white and perfect. I had been prepared for something red and wrinkled, but Steven was plump and gorgeous, with a lovely head of dark brown hair.

He opened his eyes and looked me right in the face. While I was admiring his lovely, soft hair, his gaze moved upward to mine, which looked, at this point, like it had spent twelve seconds in the food processor on "puree." I could have sworn I heard him say to the nurse who came to bathe him, "Jeez, Mr. Kenneth is really coming up with some weird ones these days."

Alan

Wheels

I CONTINUED to drive with trauma, constantly worried that I'd jam on the brakes and Alyssa, the baby, or Steven, the toddler, would hurtle out of the back seat and crash into Caryl's neck. How would it look in court for a mother to sue her two little kids for whiplash? I figured the nervousness would disappear as my kids grew older. I didn't know that the only thing that threatened to disappear was my sanity.

"Who is this kid?"

The years pass quickly, and I can't remember the kid's name or even what he looked like. All I remember is what he did to me, and when he grows up, I want it to happen to him once. It was raining, and not just raining, mind you, but raining in the New England sense, which is clammy and relentless. Alan, the nice daddy who runs the elementary school complex car pool, had arrived at same to pick up children, of most of whom he is neither the parent nor legal guardian.

Life around the old elementary school complex gets a little hairy in the rain. Parents and grandparents who were never driven anywhere and learned how to walk to dangerous places like stores and schools now apparently believe that we must give our children rides. I am one of the worst offenders. I have inherited the "what if" theory of life from my parents. "What if one of those chlorine gas trucks on its way to the sewage-treatment plant explodes, and what if, in the confusion, some inmates from the nearby prison steal away unnoticed, and what if one of them takes a car, and what if the police begin chasing him, and what if he should panic and suddenly careen insanely through the center of town, and what if the cops should be firing at him, and what if one of the bullets should strike the curbstone, and what if, Godforbid, one of the chips of stone should fly up and hit the kids in the head, hah? You can't be too careful, they should look both ways."

So, along with assorted mothers, grandmothers, grandfathers, and guys who work the late shift, I used to be a regular at the fast-food-restaurant parking lot. I would stand with the rest of them in front of the fast-food restaurant and peer across the street at the 835 kids who came out every afternoon in the only school district in America that refused to practice birth control.

The winters were the worst. Everybody wore snorkels, boys and girls, K through six, tall, fat, short, skinny, everyone wore the same kind of coat with a hood. Now, in your higher-class suburbs, which have bus service or which have among their residents people who think yelling is barbaric, you get these mothers with chiseled features and very straight teeth who look across seven acres, spot their kid, and say quietly with teeth clenched, "Charrrrles," and the kid comes, like a missile to the heat of a jet fighter's engine.

In our community, many of us are the descendants of people who yelled their way out of the old country, yelled over the noise of elevated trains, yelled from one apartment house to another. In fact, a lot of that last action still goes on. So you should hear what goes on when the 835 kids used to come out all at once—"Kevin . . . Anthony . . . Daaaavid . . . Sean. . . ." As a sidelight, you could always tell which mothers had been taken in by soap operas—"Kimberly . . . Stacy . . . Tracy . . ."

My problem was that I was there to pick up and account for those who had left with me in the morning. I had a long yelling list. "Steven . . . Alyssa . . . Joey . . . Thi . . . Amy . . . Michelle . . . David. . . ." Deep down inside, I just wanted to yell, "Alleee, alleeee infreee, dis is Dadeeeee!"

It was bad enough not to find my own kid or kids, but terror struck when I couldn't find somebody else's kid. Then I felt like the soldier assigned to tell a family that their son is missing in action. I would stand, hat in hand, nervously shuffling my feet on the stairs of the presumably bereaved mother's house, and mumble, "I, uh, I'm really, uh, sorry, but I couldn't find —— (fill in the blank), and, honest to God, I looked, and I sent Steven to look, and I asked the girls if they saw her, and they said they didn't, and . . ."

And the mother would stand there, smiling. I finally figured it out. They knew the kid was walking home. Do you know what that means

to an average mother? You take your normal first grader and have him
or her walk home, say eight blocks. That's good for a half-hour minimum, maybe even an overnighter. That's at least thirty minutes more
of sanity and quiet in the house.

But knowledge of this didn't stay my guilt. On this particular rainy
day I felt pretty good, for I seemed to have accounted for all my
charges. I knew what the ride home would be like. You get seven kids
in a car, ranging from age five to eleven, you've got yourself a verbal
prescription for Valium. But I was a veteran at this. I could figure out
their battle plans, and as they charged into the front and back seats
with their incessant giggling and yelling and shoving and such, I stood
in the rain and yelled, "Hurry up, or you'll get sick, and your mother
will get angry. No, we ain't stopping for gum, candy, or anything. No, I
can't take anybody to the library. Reading is bad for your eyes. No, you
can't watch the dumb cartoons on TV when you get home. TV is bad
for your eyes. I got cupcakes for a snack. Yes, if your mothers let you,
you can play over and have cupcakes, but you gotta call first, and who is
this kid?"

He was a stranger. He was sitting in the front seat, next to the pas-
senger door. He had appeared from nowhere. "That's ——— (whoever
it was)," yelled his contemporaries.

"That's nice. Why is he in my car?"

"It's raining," two of them yelled at once. "He needs a ride home,"
Alyssa screeched. "He'll get wet," concluded another.

"But maybe somebody's coming to pick him up," I yelled. I was pan-
icking. I was okay for the regular shift. I could handle their noise, their
questions, their fake farting, their punching, kicking, shoving, yelling,
but I couldn't handle the unexpected. That "what if" philosophy was
manifesting itself. Those plagued with it are unable to make command
decisions. They make great monks and Talmudic scholars but lousy platoon leaders.

"What if," I thought to myself, "somebody comes for the kid and
the kid isn't here? Then, I'm driving around town with an extra kid,
and somebody is driving around town with one less kid, and how are we
gonna know each other? And if they see me with their kid, they're
gonna yell, 'Hey, you, whaddya doin' with my kid? Are you some kinda
pervert? Did he touch you, honey? Did the big fat man put his hand on
your pee-pee?' "

Meanwhile, the regulars in my car pool were yelling for action. The
kid is OK, they told me. One of the boys. A real regular guy. Somebody
you can put your trust in.

"All right, already. We'll take you home first. Where do you live?"

"In Winthrop."

"That's a good beginning. That's where we all live. That's the name of the town, Winthrop." There are 21,000 persons living in Winthrop, all in one square mile. In other words, a lot of houses and apartments.

"Now, what street do you live on?"

"It's near here."

"It's near here? Near the school?"

"Yeah." Good. The kid is bright. I like that in kids. A little self-reliance in an age of car pools. This kid is gonna go places. Except home. That's one place it looked like this kid wasn't going to go.

"Go up here," he said. I took a right and went up the street to an intersection.

"Now go there," he said.

From the back seat came screeching and yelling and laughing. Each kid yelled a different direction. "No, he means the other way!" one yelled. I was in an intersection. There are four ways, right, left, straight, and back. "Which other way?" I yelled. A car began honking. Massachusetts drivers, famous for their courtesy and patience, do not cotton easily to motorists who stop for more than ten seconds at an intersection. The voices from the back were coming in like shot and shell. "This way . . . no, the other way . . . no, that way . . . no, straight ahead . . . no, left, I mean right . . . no . . . ."

The older ones were yelling at the younger ones. The older ones had recently learned left from right. There's nobody more hotheaded than a recent convert. "Ya stupid, ya don't know right from left. Cheez. They don't know right from left. Wassamattah, kid, don't you even know what street you live on, huh? Awww, shaddup . . . He does too . . . He does not . . . Honk, honk, honk, honk. . . . The other way . . . Which way? . . . This way . . . That way . . . Beep, beep, beep, beep. . . ."

The hell with it, I figured. I turned right, just as the kid said, and as I did it, the kid said, "I think it was the other way." That started it again.

"Which other way?" I said, my voice breaking as if to cry.

"Seeee," yelled the vindicated ones from the back. "Seee, I toldja, I toldja. Nyaaaaahhh! . . . Honk, honk . . . Which way is the other way? . . . I don't believe this kid, he doesn't know where he lives."

"I do too!" the kid yelled back.

"Good, maybe you'll be kind enough to tell me."

The kid smiled at me. A very nice kid. He stared at me.

"Look, kid, don't look at me. Look at the street. Look at the houses. See if you can recognize where you live."

"Okay." He began staring intently at the houses. Every few seconds, he'd say, "Wait a minute, I think it's that one . . . nope, nope, it's not that one. Wait a minute, it's after that one, nope, nope, it's not that one."

Every time he said wait a minute, I slowed down. Every time he said nope, the occupants of said vehicle roared with laughter. This was a wonderful afternoon. If you were under the age of twelve, this was a very funny thing. I was past twelve. We got to the end of the street, which meant we were now at the intersection of a main street.

"Go there," the kid said with enthusiasm. Aha, the scent of the hunted, I thought. "I think," he added quietly.

"You think? Whaddya mean, you *think*?" Hold it, Al, I told myself. This is combat. Stay calm. Don't yell at other people's kids. We drove for a while.

Up and down streets we drove. The traffic was easing up, which meant most people had brought their charges home safely. We kept driving. The rain was getting worse. The kid was trying hard to keep up my spirits.

"I think it's this way," he said. He said that on every turn we made and every street we drove up or down.

"Look, I'm going back to the school, and we're gonna start all over again, except this time, we'll take a left out of McDonald's instead of a right."

"Yaaaay," they yelled, "McDonald's!"

"No. No, we aren't gonna eat there. We're gonna start out from there."

Heavy groaning. "We're hungry," they yelled.

Who could blame them? A few more minutes and it would be time for supper.

I made a rare command decision. "I'm takin' all the other kids home first, because your mommies are gonna worry, and then we'll figure out where you live." This met with great disappointment. The kids were looking forward to Alan further making a fool of himself. "In fact, I'm gonna ask each mother where you live until I get the right answer."

As I approached the corner of my own street and another, the kid came to life. "Up there," he shouted, "up there," pointing up my street.

My eyes narrowed. I took a deep breath and said quietly, with a degree of self-control, "You . . . live . . . up . . . *this* . . . street?"

He smiled and nodded. So, what the hell, so I had been driving all over town for a half hour, when I could have just driven back to my own neighborhood. What am I gonna do, I thought, take it out on this sweet little innocent first grader?

"Hokayyy," I said with renewed confidence. "This is called Court Road. Now, the next time you get a ride home, and somebody says where do you live, you'll know what to tell them. Right?"

"Right."

"Good, what's the number of your house?"

"I don't know."

"What?"

"I don't know."

"You don't know." I rolled down the window and looked up to the heavens. "Okay, God, enough already. I apologize. I don't know what I did, but I'm sorry." It rained all over my face.

"It's a blue house."

My prayers were being answered. I turned to the kid. My face could not conceal the small glimmer of hope, despite the encroaching darkness of evening. "You live in a blue house?"

"Yup, and it's on this side."

Hey, a double. I hit the daily double. The kid knew the color of his house and the side of the street it was on. We were almost home free. I slowed down, and we peered through the rain-soaked windows.

We peered and peered and peered.

"Kid, we are almost done with Court Road. Pretty soon, there will be no more Court Road, and I don't see a blue house."

"It's coming," he said.

I had to go to the bathroom. "Soon?" I asked.

"There it is," he said. I pulled up short. The brakes squealed.

"No, not that one."

"Which one?"

"*That* one," he said, pointing two houses down to a brown house. "The blue one."

I drove up to the brown house. "This is not a *blue* house. This is what you call a *brown* house. Didn't you have colors yet in school? Are you sure you live here?"

The kid was getting out of the car. He looked at me with disgust. "I live here. This is my house."

I waited until he knocked on the door. A lady came out. She smiled. I got out of the car and stood in the rain. "He didn't know his address," I yelled, a sick smile on my face.

She was very kind. She smiled and thanked me. She said it was very nice of me to bring him home. They went inside the brown house, but not before the kid yelled, "Seeee, I toldja I knew where I lived."

Caryl

The Liberation of Dawn

ALAN GOT the car pool assignment because of his experience in the tank corps. It takes the same kind of nerves of steel to make the six-block run to the school complex as it did to make the breakthrough to Bastogne. I am assigned the shopping detail, because Alan claims it is against his religion to buy retail. He is never confident, however, about my command abilities in this area. He always asks, nervously, as I set off with Steven and Alyssa in tow, "You won't leave the children in the store, will you?"

I reply, "In fact, I am meeting a pair of white slavers in the Tots department at Filenes at 11:30 to trade the kids for three camels and a string of glass beads. *Why do you always ask me that? For twelve years you have been asking me that and I haven't lost a kid yet!*"

The shopping detail, in fact, involves the sort of moral decision-making absent in car pooling. It is I who must be the fortification against the onslaught of commercial America; I who is supposed to say no to all the things kids want in stores and should not be allowed to have. Unfortunately, moral decision-making is not my strong point.

A while ago Alyssa received a small check in the mail from some relatives. Off we marched, she and I, to the five-and-ten to spend her newly acquired windfall with wisdom and sobriety. I had laid down the rules: no candy, no breakable plastic junk. I watched as she wandered down the toy aisle, wrestling with the decision, and suddenly she brightened and came back with a small box in her hands. "This!" she announced triumphantly.

I groaned. She had followed all the rules. It wasn't candy and it wasn't breakable. It was Dawn.

Dawn, for those of you who don't know about such things, is a smaller cousin of the Great Earth Mother Barbie, the Eve of a whole race of plastic dolls. Barbie begat Dusty who begat Tuesday Taylor who begat Cher who begat Farrah who begat Kelly, according to the word of the Great God Mattel. There is also, of course, Growing-Up Skipper, a teenager who magically sprouts a pair of budlike breasts when you twist her arm. (Where this will all end, I am reluctant to speculate. I have visions of the Kama Sutra Barbie and Ken, whose movable parts can be maneuvered into 127 positions.)

Alyssa handed me the box containing the doll, and Dawn looked up at me through her fake eyelashes, and I knew it was the moment of truth. Not only did I harbor a virulent dislike for the entire Barbie tribe, but I had spoken publicly against it. As a commentator for the public TV station in Boston, I gave Barbie the award for the Most Atrocious Toy of the Year. I expressed my opinion that Barbie trained little girls to be mindless consumers of fashion, nagging their mothers to buy Barbie outfits at $4.98 a shot, as well as such other products as Barbie Thunderbirds, Barbie town houses, and Barbie beauty kits. One viewer wrote in saying, "Thanks for socking it to Barbie, the All-American plastic tart."

I looked at Dawn, and the hussy stared right back. She had the air of a very high-class call girl, a Playboy Bunny tired of living off tips. She was wearing a blue silk halter (no bra), a frilly miniskirt, and tiny blue high-heeled shoes. Her long hair was the shade of blond that only comes from a bottle.

"Sweetheart," I said to Alyssa, "why don't you look for something else?"

"I want *her!*"

"Get something else, sweetie."

She clutched Dawn to her chest and looked up at me, stricken. Two big tears welled up in those baby blue eyes.

"I love her, Mommy!"

I wish I could report that I snatched the sexy wench from the hands of my innocent child and stood as firm as Susan B. Anthony. Alas (I ask God for Her forgiveness), like any weak-kneed, overpermissive, Spock-reading modern mommy, I caved in. *Mea culpa.* I grabbed Dawn and threw her into the bottom of the shopping bag. Dawn came to live with us.

When I took her out of the bag at home, Alan stared at it. "What's that?"

"It's Dawn. Alyssa bought her."

"That doll is stacked. Look at those . . ."

"I know, I know, don't remind me."

From that day on, Dawn became Alyssa's constant companion. The doll was just the right size for clutching in a childish hand. In the process, Dawn got somewhat shopworn, aging fast, as is customary in her business. Little did I know she was about to become a major political embarrassment.

The next weekend I was scheduled to attend a Women in Politics conference at a university some distance away from home. Those were the early, heady days of the women's movement, and the uniform of the time was old dungarees, combat boots, and not a trace of makeup. The sessions got pretty heated at times—one woman nearly got trampled by two dozen pairs of boots by making the mistake of referring to her female friends as "girls." It was just as the meeting was ending that Alan arrived—with Steven and Alyssa in tow—to give me a ride home. Clutched in Alyssa's hand—looking as much like a sex bomb as ever—was Dawn.

"Omigod!" I said, making a lunge for Dawn. I snatched her away from Alyssa and tried to cover her lascivious little body with my hands.

"Hold this!" I said to a friend. "I've got to find my pocketbook." I thrust Dawn into the hands of my friend, whose feminist credentials were impeccable. My friend looked down at the item she had been handed.

"Aaarrrrggghhh!" she said, shoving Dawn at the woman next to her. Dawn kept going from hand to hand like a hot potato until I could safely get her under wraps in my pocketbook.

So Dawn came back home with us again. There were slight rips in her halter now and one eyelash was askew. Alyssa loved her as dearly as ever. One day Alyssa stuck Dawn's leg in the cap of a ballpoint pen, thought that was hilarious, and came running to show us.

"Look, Dawn's in the pen!"

"What did she get, three to five for soliciting?" Alan asked.

I thought the whole problem was solved when Dawn disappeared a few days later. Alyssa looked high and low, but no Dawn. However, the next week Alan found Dawn under the couch. The silk halter was pulled down to the waist and her hand was resting lasciviously on the knee of a pink plastic elephant. Alan brought her to me and I repaired the dishabille, while he suggested that, given Dawn's obvious taste for kinky sex, he would offer to fix her up with the Tyrannosaurus rex from Steven's dinosaur collection.

Alyssa was overjoyed that her friend had been found. I resigned myself to life with Dawn. After all, I reasoned, how much evil influence could she have in a home with a liberated mommy and daddy? Alan and Alyssa had already argued about her future. She said she wanted to be a nurse and he said she should be a doctor so she could invest in condominiums where her aged parents could live rent-free.

The problem of Dawn was finally solved by Alyssa herself. Dawn had her consciousness raised.

I came into Alyssa's room one day. Dawn as usual was clutched in my daughter's hand. But Dawn looked different. Her blond hair was no longer neatly groomed but flew off in all directions. One of her little blue shoes was missing. Dawn was socking stuffed animals around the room. Sock! Pow! Biff!

"Alyssa, what are you doing with Dawn?"

"Her name isn't Dawn anymore."

"It isn't?"

"No."

"What is it?"

"It's Supergirl, and she's beating up bad guys."

Biff! Pow! Sock!

Dawn gave a karate chop right in the snout to a blue (male chauvinist?) pig. I'd swear she was smiling.

Alan

Animal House

THE BLUE pig is not a nightclub. It's one of approximately eighty stuffed animals of varying breeds, sexes, sizes, and colors who have joined our family since I purchased a floppy-eared stuffed dog about one month before Steven's birth. For a month, I would go two or three times a day into what was to be his room and stare at the little dog standing on the dresser and fantasize about how he'd come home from the hospital ward at the age of four days and turn to me and say, "I will call him Bozo, Father." It took more than a month for Steven to acknowledge the dog's presence and once having done so, he tried to eat it.

These animals have been good companions all. They have put up with outrageous treatment. They have been stuffed into cardboard boxes, which are shoved down a flight of stairs in my direction. They have been flung through the air from second-story bunk beds, also in my direction. With such a large and pliant cast of pigs, elephants, tigers, dogs, monkeys, porpoises, and such, no adult or kid in the house has ever lacked for company. The stuffed animals have been great bit players. They have been set against one another in mock wars and thrust into one another's arms or paws or fins in vaudeville dance routines.

Either despite or because of these inanimate animals, three-fourths of the human members of my family kept voting sporadically to get live animals, the real thing that pishes on your leg and eats your underwear. Caryl pretended for a long time that she also did not want, as I did not want, the trouble of raising something like a dog. Deep down, she wanted a dog as much as the kids did. "You know, it probably wouldn't be much trouble," she informed me. "We always had dogs. I never found them any trouble."

"You never took care of them. Your parents took care of them."

They took good care of them, in fact. Tippy, my dog-in-law, was seventeen when he finally died, and he was alleged to have had an active sex life until the very end. And do you know who helped care for Tippy? Alan is who. The whole time we lived with Caryl's parents, I never saw her walk the dog. You had to tell her when to scratch the dog. The only thing Caryl ever did for the dog was occasionally turn to it and say, "Ooooohhhh, poooocheeee wooocheeee mooochies." Even while doing this, she didn't exactly strain herself. She could continue to read, write, or stare off into space and not miss a beat on a single "mooochie."

We never had any dogs when I was growing up. When you totaled up a lack of working capital, a lack of apartment space and, on the part of us Jewish folk, a lack of trust in a canine's attitude toward people whose parents had been hunted by same, you did not end up with a lot of dogs. What you ended up with was irrational fear of dogs, which was not mollified when a Great Dane lived at one end of the street and a snarling, yapping bulldog at the other. How did I know the large, throaty "Rooof, rooof!" of Roma the Great Dane was a sign of friendship?

Tippy enabled me to lose my fear of dogs. When I first met him, he slobbered all over my face. I have in my house pictures of Tippy and miss him. I can't remember my first date, but I remember the first dog who treated me like a human being.

Steven began early beating the drums for a living dog. He conned Caryl into it the day he appeared downstairs with a little cardboard box filled with cotton. It was, he said, a little bed for one of the mice taking up residence with us. "He will be my pet, because I can't have a dog. I will leave food for the mouse, and I will leave this bed. Maybe I will never see him, but he'll be my pet, and I'll love him." She cracked immediately, clasped him to her bosom and swore, "Sweetheart, of course you may have a dog!"

It was only then that she noticed that look in his eye, the kind of look you get from the itinerant workmen who blacktop your driveway for a hundred bucks less than the reputable firm and, unknown to you, have used marshmallow fluff dyed with licorice juice. The gleam in the eye was followed by a large grin. "Okay," he told her in a voice that had changed from one of self-pity to one of business-as-usual, "I'll tell the dog officer we'll take one of the puppies they found in the back seat of a car. He brought them to the room yesterday in school. Thanks, Ma." I came home from work one winter day to discover a house that now smelled like a kennel and my daughter, carrying a spoonful of baby food and toddling after this thing, urging it to, "Eat. Eat." The thing had baby food on its nose. When it spotted me, it crawled under the kitchen table and cried.

"Eat!" Alyssa shouted, happy to have someone around that she could command.

"This is our dog," Steven yelled, as he arrived downstairs.

"Meet Jane," said my wife from behind a door, where I couldn't slug her.

"Jane?"

"It was gonna be Ralph or George, until I turned it over. So, it's Jane."

"Hi, Jane," I said in what I thought was a comforting voice.

She attacked my hand and peed on the floor.

At this writing, Jane has been with us about seven years. We counted up the other day how many human beings she likes. We didn't reach twenty. She has tried often to kill the milkman and mailman by eating her way through the front door. She chased the best friend I have in the neighborhood back to his house. My father is convinced she's anti-Semitic.

She weighs about seventy or eighty pounds. She is alleged to be part collie and part German shepherd. She is all mutt. Her coat cannot be groomed, anymore than her temper can be controlled. She is, like me, a thing of emotional peaks and little moderation. For those she loves, she is outrageous in her licking, slobbering, running in circles, jumping, sitting on top of, sticking wet nose under covers and all that. She has since been joined by a gray and white cat, one Kitty Widdums, rescued by Steven from a pool of water and oil under a car. These two animals share at least two traits—they started out free of charge and have since cost more than I make in a year, and they can't stand each other.

To keep them apart, we have devised what Caryl calls the "airlock" system, patterned after what submarine crews do to keep the water where it belongs, the air where it belongs, and the humans where they belong. During the night, Jane has the run of the house, except the kitchen, where, behind a closed door, is Kitty Widdums. In the morning, I walk Jane, and then send her to our bedroom, where we shut the door. I run back downstairs to open the kitchen door, and let Kitty

Widdums out of the house. Then I run back upstairs and let Jane out of the bedroom, but I have to cover the kitty litter or else Jane will, ugh, eat the stuff. In the afternoon, Steven walks the dog and then coaxes her into our bedroom and shuts the door, so the cat can have the run of the house. The cat immediately runs upstairs and sits in front of the bedroom door so that she can drive the dog a little nutso. In the evening, the cat is dragged off Alyssa's top bunk and sent down to the kitchen, where the litter box is uncovered and she is fed. Bang, that door is shut, and I run upstairs to free the dog, who runs downstairs and sniffs at the kitchen door to scare the hell out of the cat on the other side.

It has not been easy to live totally without tension under such circumstances. But with enough practice drills and dry runs, we have mastered it. I have learned how to deal with a cat who stands in my gravy and stares at me eating, and with an uncoordinated dog who regularly whonks her head on doors and walls and nearby people. They have come to be my friends. They are loyal little folks, and most of the time, I can deal with them. There are times, however, when I do not deal very well.

In winter, for example. Winter is the pits. Kitty Widdums, being fairly independent, manages pretty well in the cold weather. Jane is another story. In the summer, the fall, the spring, and some other in-between seasons that the federal government hasn't named yet—but which they have in New England anyway—it is a piece of cake. I put Crazy Dog (our affectionate nickname for her) on a leash or vice versa, and I take her out, and she does what dogs do when you take dogs out to do it. But winter is not so good.

That is because—and now there should be music, not so much to introduce but to wash over what I'm going to tell you, as it is embarrassing—I make toilets for the dog.

Out in the deep snows of the tundra, which otherwise serves as a backyard, just before dawn so as few neighbors as possible can see or hear me, I hold Crazy Dog by the leash in one hand, use my other hand to maintain my balance, and do a Bolshoi ballet with my feet. Like a Cossack gone mad alone on the steppes, my feet thrash about, kicking blocks of ice and clumps of snow about while the dog looks away (even the dog is embarrassed) and my head jerks about, my eyes darting from house to house in hopes that I won't see anybody. On a good morning, if there isn't too much drifting, I can even hit a spot of grass. That's the end of Phase One.

Phase Two is more complex. Phase Two is less physical, more psychological. In Phase Two, I coax the dog. I start out quietly, syrup dripping from my voice. "Okay, Jane. C'mon, Jane. Here we go. Here's a good spot." At this point, I have the dog's attention. At least, she is looking at me. She is looking at me as if I were a maniac. And that's all she does. She stands there, the wind blowing her curly brown hair in all seventeen directions in which it naturally grows, her Fu Manchu beard bristling wet, and she looks. That's when Phase Two gets a little rough. I start yelling.

"Fa Chrissakes, go areddy! Whadda we standing here for? We're taking a cruise on a luxury liner? We're waiting for Simon Says? For brunch? Go. Bend down. Do it, baby. Like yesterday."

Remember, in the old days, when the kid was constipated, the mother would put the kid on the seat, and the mother would tighten her hands and scrunch down, and her face would get red, and she'd strain and grunt, "C'mon, darling, unh, unh, unh, unh," like the kid was stupid and didn't know how to use his own bowels? Remember that foolishness? I am a second generation American, and I would never do that with a child.

Only with a dog.

"C'mon, you dumb bastard, unh, unh, unh, unh." Nothing.

I point to the small patch of bare ground. "Hey, look, look what I made for you, hah? Ground, like in the summer." Nothing. Begin Phase Three.

This is called outlasting the enemy at his/her own game. The dog stands; I stand. The dog begins to wander; nothing doing. I'm still standing. I'm rooted to the spot. The dog strains at the leash. Strain all you want, I'm staying. The wind-chill factor is thirty below, the harbor is half-frozen, but I shall not move, or, better, to reverse the strategy of Verdun, "She Will Pass." The dog begins to grasp the point. It's going to happen. She starts pacing. I got a dog that paces. Back and forth. She looks like a guy outside a hospital delivery room. Then she goes faster and faster, her rushing back and forth occasionally interrupted by a test squat. To the left, squat, to the right, to the left, to the right, squat, to the left. I professionally shift the leash leather from hand to hand. That's all I move. I am a study in casual dogmanship.

Crazy Dog is going slowly mad. The pressures of the intestines are overcoming her inclination not to get her rear end wet in the snows of New England when there are so many available rugs in that nice house a few yards away. Finally, nature takes its course. What must be, must be. God did not give man a brain to be ruled by the whims of dogs.

Yessir, boy, and it took only about twenty minutes, and my hands are freezing, along with my face, and there is snow down my overshoes, and my socks are wet, and I am sniffling, and back at the house everybody thinks Daddy has run away with Jane, and they are beginning to get anxious because they miss their dog, and they may be late for school, and I may be late for work, and I am so stupid that I think I have won and the dog has lost, whereas, in fact, when all is said and done, I, Alan I. Lupo, of sound mind and body, do, in the dead of winter, before the sun riseth, with knowledge aforethought, make toilets for a dog.

Caryl

Homework

Not only does Alan attend to Jane's bodily functions, but this grown man, who has engaged in debate, flinty eyed, with governors, mayors and recalcitrant bureaucrats, has been seen kneeling down looking into the limpid brown eyes of a dog, babbling baby talk. Sometimes he says to me, accusingly, that I have not kissed Jane lately, which means I don't love her. The children chorus, "Mommy hates Jane! Mommy hates Jane!" I have to go over and kiss stupid Jane on the forehead so they don't fink on me to the ASPCA.

The problem is that Alan is one of those men who Never Had a Dog As a Child and they become the most obnoxious dogophiles in adulthood. They think dogs are people—except finer, more sensitive ones. Alan worries about traumatizing Jane's psyche by leaving her home alone, which is ridiculous, because Jane is clearly psychotic anyhow. She hurls herself, fangs bared, at the panes of glass in the front door every time someone she doesn't know rings the bell. He hates to go on vacation because Jane will be lonely in the kennel. I suggest we check her into the local house of correction for a week. A little solitary, a few workings over with a rubber hose might improve her disposition.

Jane has only one great advantage, in my eyes. She does not take part in any organized activity, and she does not need to be driven anyplace except once a year to the clinic to get her rabies shot. That does not hold true for the rest of us.

We are all involved in so many things that our daily family schedule offers logistics only slightly less complicated than the plans for D-day. J. Alfred Prufrock had a life that was measured out in coffee spoons, T. S. Eliot once wrote. Our lives are marked by the little black lines in the sort of appointment books given out free by insurance agents and realtors. Alan and I thumb through our daily calendars the way a Talmudic scholar fingers the Holy Book. Things do not always run smoothly.

"Brownie fly-up," Alan says one day as he leafs through his book. "Is that something we have to go to or a new kind of grass?"

"Uh-oh," I reply.

"What's uh-oh? I don't like the sound of that."

"I was planning to go to the Brownie fly-up but I have an important faculty meeting. They are having elections to the faculty council."

"So?"

"If I don't go I will get elected and have to go to boring meetings every week. People who don't go to the election meeting always get elected."

"I have an interview with the director of Massport at noon. If I do it fast, I could get home."

"Good. How do you feel about carnations? No, I think it's gardenias."

"You are trying to tell me something. I am not going to like it."

"Oh, it's nothing, really. It's just that it would be nice if you like gardenias, because Alyssa is going to pin a corsage on you. All the mommies get one."

"I am going to have to stand there with a bunch of women and get a corsage pinned on me? What do I look like, the queen of the junior prom?"

"Do it for Alyssa. Besides, you'll look adorable in gardenias."

"I'll get you for this one."

"OK, I'll take the midget hockey game on Saturday. *There's* a sacrifice for you. All you get is a few minutes of humiliation, but I have to sit there for two hours watching little blue Quasimodos with big white heads skating around trying to brain each other with big long sticks. It looks to me like H. G. Wells meets the Ice Follies. I sit there freezing my butt while people mumble strange incantations I don't understand, like 'hat trick' and 'icing.' My idea of hell is an endless midget hockey game."

And so the deal is struck. Our system, as intricate as the Houston Oilers' platoon system, works pretty well, with the services of a teenage sitter and Alan's mother as emergency backup. At least, it works when everyone is healthy. The chinks in the master plan really appear when one of the children wakes up with red eyes, aching tummy, and fevered brow. One morning Steven tries to get out of bed and says he is too dizzy to walk. Who will dispense tender, loving care? Alan and I go into a huddle.

Phase one is comparison of schedules. Escalation is the main tactic.

"What's your schedule?" Alan asks.

"Let's see," I say, pretending to thumb through my calendar. "I am having lunch with Charles de Gaulle to prepare an article on the future of the European alliance."

"Charles de Gaulle is dead. He has been dead for the last ten years."

"Maybe that's why he didn't RSVP. What's your schedule?"

"The mayor asked me to have lunch to advise him on policy matters."

"The mayor is in St. Thomas."

"It'll be a long lunch."

We go into Steven's room to investigate his condition and find him crawling along on his back, firing a Space 1999 ray gun. He says he is doing this because he is too dizzy to fire standing up.

It is decided that Steven is not sick enough for one of us to stay home—Childhood Ailment Plan A. Plan B goes into effect. He will go to work with me. He is a bit too sick to go to Alan's office (Plan C) where there is a Nerf basketball hoop and he can play with the phones.

In my office there is a couch. Well, not exactly *in* my office. The couch is actually in a faculty lounge across the hall, which means I have to go in and commandeer it, then tip it on its side so I can shove it through the door. If there are people on the couch I dump them off, mumbling something barely audible like "Dean-needs-this-for-an-urgent-meeting." After much pulling and hauling I get the couch into my office, where it takes up every available inch of floor space, so that anyone who has to meet with me has to climb over both the edge of a couch and a coughing child.

On this particular morning, I tuck Steven under a blanket and prop a pillow under his head. It is soon time for me to go to class, and I look down at him, pale and wan on the couch. I feel a stab of guilt for leaving my poor, suffering child.

"Sweetums, are you sure you're going to be all right?" I ask anxiously. He nods, giving me his best good-little-soldier smile and I leave, feeling like a rotten mommy.

The minute I disappear around the corner, Steven rifles through my desk and comes up with a rubber band and a supply of paper clips. He jumps off the couch and hotfoots it into the corridor, where he takes up a strategic position in the hall. There, he can fire directly into the student mailboxes. He keeps up a steady barrage, winging two freshmen, a professor emeritus and an associate dean.

But at least now I *have* an office. There was a time a few years back when I thought I could get away with working at home. Since the children were very young, I decided it was time to give up daily journalism to get rich and famous writing magazine articles. I envisioned myself lunching with Mailer and the editor of *The New Yorker*, while the latter begged me to sell him my scribblings for fabulous sums. As it turned out, I was nibbling on the crusts of the kids' uneaten cheese sandwiches while trying to wheedle a hundred dollars via the telephone out of some newspaper Sunday editor for the story I'd just spent a month slaving over. The money I made was barely enough to keep me in nice, grandmotherly ladies who would baby-sit while I went out and researched my stories. Because I wasn't making any money to speak of, I felt I couldn't spend money on my professional endeavors. I could not, for example, buy a desk.

Alan had a desk. In fact, *I* insisted he buy a desk. If I had said to him, "I need a desk," he would have said, "Go buy one." But I did not believe I *deserved* a desk. Despite the fact that I had earned my living as a writer for nine years, had covered presidents and prime ministers, I was acting just like any other housewife trying to write around the kids. This is a very female way of thinking. A man in my position would not only have bought a desk, but a swivel chair and a push-button phone as well. I took four books of green stamps and bought myself a metal typing table.

This table was made of the scrap metal we sent to Japan, generously laced with cardboard. Not only did it wobble outrageously, but it had two really major drawbacks. First, the little metal flaps on which you were supposed to place the material you were typing kept falling off, usually in the middle of crucial sentences. Once, a typed manuscript page fell on the floor and Jane ate it, which did not improve her disposition. (Mine either, for that matter.) But even more distracting was the fact that this typing table seemed designed for midgets, since I could not find a chair low enough to keep the metal edges of the table from digging into the top of my thighs. If it's true that one can work off time in purgatory by self-mortification, I earned more brownie points in the course of typing one manuscript than a whole abbey full of self-flagellating monks.

Working at home never did live up to my expectations. I had a vision of myself pounding away at the typewriter while my angelic little *Kinder* played quietly at my knee. When the phone rang, I would say to them, "Now, dears, you must be very quiet because Mommy is going to be on the phone to an editor in New York, and if he hears the sound of children in the background he will write Mommy off as a housewife with a mail-order degree from Famous Writers' School who writes her stories in longhand on the back of shopping bags."

And the children would chirp, "Oh, we will be very quiet, Mommy dear."

Somehow, it didn't quite work out that way. Any sound connected with the telephone produced an almost chemical effect on Steven and Alyssa. On mornings when they were so quiet they seemed almost comatose, and so good to each other it was hard to believe they were siblings, I would sneak away to make a phone call to an editor. Somehow they could hear the sound of dialing from two rooms away, and the sound hit them like a shot of adrenaline. They would immediately begin to shriek, assault each other with criminal intent, and head straight for the lamps, mayhem in mind. One day, I had to make a call to a particularly elitist editor in New York, the kind that thought having kids was the worst sort of unprofessional behavior. If I missed a deadline with him, I'd as soon say I was falling-down drunk than admit I was taking care of a kid with the flu.

I barricaded myself in the bedroom, having told Steven and Alyssa that they were not to come near the bedroom unless they looked out the living-room window and saw a mushroom-shaped cloud—and even then, not unless it was 100 megatons or more. I called the editor, and things were going very well. I was congratulating myself on my crisp, professional tone when there was a click on the line. My stomach lurched. I had forgotten about the kitchen extension.

"Mommy," came Alyssa's wet little voice, "Steven said *fuck*."

"Sweetheart, I'm on the phone."

"But he said *fuck*. You said he shouldn't say *fuck*."

"Alyssa, dear, hang up the phone."

"He said it a lot. He said *fuck fuck fuck fuck fuck*."

"HANG UP THE PHONE!"

Click.

The editor's voice turned frosty. I could hear the thin edge of contempt in his voice for a writer who could do something so tacky as *reproduce*. Did he want a mother soiling the prestigious pages of his magazine? But I was cool under fire. I kept right on with the summary of my proposed article, listing the major points as if there had been no interruption at all.

It seemed to be working. His tone began to mellow. By George, I thought, I've got him! The assignment was nearly mine.

Then the line clicked again. This time it was Steven.

"I didn't say *fuck* a lot. Alyssa is a liar. But I think I have diarrhea and it's dripping all over the rug."

Alan

Guilt Trips

CARYL MANAGES to put in whole days like that, accomplish absolutely nothing that she started out to do, and feel no guilt whatsoever. I, on the other hand, do all that I am supposed to do out of a sense of guilt and rarely with any sense of enjoyment. I didn't do my homework regularly because I wanted to learn; I did it regularly because I wanted to avoid guilt. I don't write so much because I wish to write or even like to write; I write because I am *supposed* to write. Sometimes, people try to figure out why they feel guilty about such things. We have laid out Jewish guilt, Roman Catholic guilt, Calvinist guilt, Puritan guilt, blame-your-parents guilt and all the other theories one comes up with when one is drinking. My theory is that guilt, for me, anyway, and maybe for our whole generation with the exception of Caryl, springs from food.

I remember a time when fat was good, as opposed to the current era, in which fat is said to be bad. It was fun getting fat in those days, because we were still eating the heavy, old-country food. Unlike today, when we are instructed to sanitize our living spaces with ozone-destroying sprays, we used to bask in the smells of whatever was on the stove. Nobody felt demeaned socially if a neighbor, passing by, began sniffing like a beagle at whatever aroma was drifting through an open window or down the stairs into the hallways.

The old houses preserved the aromas, so that on a Thursday, say, you could walk into a friend's apartment and tell him, "You had kasha varnishkes for dinner Sunday." Nobody would even be surprised that you knew. Certainly nobody would feel guilty that you had smelled the evidence, though his mother would feel guilty that there were no left-overs to offer.

The smelling was nothing, compared to the eating. Shoveling in goulash and kasha or great globs of pasta was fun. What was not fun were the veggies, or certain stray and mongrel specialties like fish loaf. These were the necessary accoutrements to the stuff you really wanted to eat. American nutritionists, cleverly using the public schools as a front, had convinced our parents, often with the use of charts with colored pictures of very red carrots and very green spinach, that the old-country foods just weren't good enough for a well-rounded American child. Gravy globs were for Bolsheviks.

There was a problem. The only thing American children of my generation hated more than school and cleanliness was the U.S. vegetable. The spinach tasted raw. The stringbeans were stringy, ergo the name. Carrots were bland. Turnips induced vomiting.

To compromise, parents tried drowning the zucchini in tomato sauce, burying the radishes and celery under sour cream, hiding the lima beans behind pot-roasted meatballs. But the nutritionists were implacable. No, they insisted, these running-dog descendants of Puritans, with their penchant for suffering, the veggies must be right out there on the plate, visible, naked, with maybe some salt if necessary. Parents complied. They would do anything to prove their loyalty to America, even to the point of making their kids barf.

So, games were instituted. "This is the train," the mother would announce, lifting a forkful of glop. "Now, open your mouth, and the train will come into the station." This was not much of an impetus for kids over the age of five. Those young enough to fall for the train gambit once rarely did again. Sometimes, a kid, angered over being conned, would spit the train right back at the old station master/mother. The train would be all over mommy's face and housedress. Was this any way to run a railroad?

Obviously not. The way to deal with us was not through our mouths but through our hearts. Millions of Armenians were starving, we were told, so eat. There were some flaws inherent in that one. What had happened to the Armenians had taken place sometime before this rationale was presented to us, and starvation had been only part of it. History was the first casualty in this trick. Reason was next. There being no Armenian Americans in the neighborhood, we had no clear concept of what a starving one was. Nor did those who exhorted us explain which Armenians were starving, where, why, or how our eating could possibly help them.

World War II buttressed the plight of the Armenians. Now, our parents could point to almost any nationality and prefix it with the adjective, "starving." We were told how lucky we were to have cauliflower, while kids in Italy were begging for food. The Movietone News showed kids in Italy begging for food. The same newsreels also showed GIs giving the same kids chocolate bars, and we were getting stringbeans. We developed some fast responses to this new tack. One was, "I wish I was one-a those kids in Italy gettin' the chocolate." Another was, "Can we send this stuff to the Japanese and make them sick?"

Parents were getting desperate. Their sense of guilt had been roused by the goody-goodies who were in charge of ensuring that whatever foodstuffs America produced were damn well going to be eaten. They were talking big agribucks. Guilt-ridden parents were moved to great cruelties.

- "Your nana was lucky to get a cold potato in Sligo, God knows, and you're sitting there with your lips zipped together like some corpse, which, God help us, you'll be, if you don't open your trap and chew."
- "You will sit here until you eat those peas. I don't care if they are cold, and I don't care if you're all alone, and I don't care if you are here all night and all day tomorrow, and I'm leaving the kitchen now and shutting off the light."
- "Uncle Angelo asked me today if Guido was a good boy, and I told Unkie Angie that Guido was a very good boy, and now the same Guido sits here with his hand in front of his mouth, making his mommy look like a liar. I'm gonna call Uncle Angelo right now and tell him Guido is no longer a good little boy and that he shouldn't give you the Lionel train set he told me the secret about."
- "You know when you're leaving the table, Mortie? When Momma and Poppa both drop dead, Morton, that's when you're leaving, over our dead bodies."
- "If you do not eat by yourself, we'll hold your head back and force supper down your throat."
- "Eat your carrots, or go away forever."

Given that parents who normally did not behave that way were screaming such things, kids finally got the idea that veggies might not be good, but they were *important*. Once having been trained to believe that vegetables were *important*, one no longer questioned why.

I vowed, as did the other "enlightened" members of my generation, never to worry the food into my kids' guts. If they ate what they ate, then they ate, and if they didn't eat, then their body metabolisms were simply sending them a message that they were full. Why mess with nature? Besides, watching them gum the baby food veggies and then spray the stuff all over Caryl was fun. I didn't know that the childhood experiences had created for me and others a religious aura about food and the eating of such. Much like those trained in the ceremonies of a religion without knowing why they do what they do, I held certain rules sacrosanct. Deviation was heresy.

The catechism said there were three meals a day: breakfast, lunch, and supper. Breakfast should not be eaten after 8:45 A.M. Lunch should be at noon. Supper began at 5 or 6 P.M. There was no such observance as dinner. Rich people ate dinner. There was nothing in our scrolls relating to the practice of brunch. Beatniks and Druids ate brunch. Vegetables were to be eaten regularly and never cooked in anything to disguise their flavor, or give them any flavor. All the blood should be broiled out of steaks. One was to continually shove fruit at people until they either ate it or ran out of the house. Women who couldn't cook flanken and lima beans were to be driven from the house. Women whose idea of cooking soup was to open a can of stuff and pour it into a pot were to be exorcised. Anyone who served pizza as a meal as opposed to pizza as a rare treat was a barbarian. To defrost a frozen dinner was to defrock a priest. To allow the eating of instant food was to deny the Commandments. Deviation from any and all rules of eating, as I had set them down in my subconscious, was cause for guilt and responsive reading.

"Caryl bought mashed-potato mix.

"Bless us, Father, for we have sinned.

"Caryl spreads mayonnaise on corned beef.

"Save us, Father, else we upchuck.

"Caryl buys the kids McDonald's.

"Dissuade us, Father, from the golden arches of idolatry.

"Caryl, an adult, does not eat veggies.

"Smote her with warts, Father, that her negligence shall set an example for the children and generations to come.

"Caryl, a mother, does not force our children to eat veggies.

"Give unto us new devices, Father, as I am sorely tired of the choo-choo-train gambit.

"Caryl, the consumer, buys packages of food without looking at the labels to determine what kinds of chemicals have been inserted by those who wish to sap our precious bodily fluids.

"Open our eyes, Father, that we may read and understand, that we may follow in the guilt trip of our parents and according to the dictates of our grade-school nutritionists, that we may not again disgrace ourselves before others by so arguing in the aisles of local supermarkets.

"'Hey, Riv, don't you read the damn cans? Look at the label. Look at this. Hydrosulphuridical glocamoramin. They put it in canned corn. God only knows what it'll do to the kids. Look at there—cutum verminosum.'

'Loop, everything has some kind of chemical in it.'

'So you're gonna feed this corn to the kids?'

'For God's sakes, my grandmother used to eat this corn.'

'Right! And she's dead!'

'Loop, she was in her eighties when she died.'

'The prime of life.'

'Loop . . .'

'Cut down before her time by unknown chemicals.'

"Oh, yea, but I have strayed greatly from mine upbringing. I have partaken of soup of the can, yea, and I have eaten of the jiffy burgers. And I have known pizza for dinner, and I have gone a whole supper without veggies, forsooth. I have partaken of the heathen brunches and have fallen out of faith, for I no longer call supper by its rightful name, but call it instead the heathen dinner."

But there is one thing I shall do, and, by God, I intend to do it to my last breath. I force my kids to eat vegetables. It's what I said I wouldn't do, but I do it. You just can't totally abandon everything you ever believed in.

When Steven turned thirteen and Alyssa became ten, they asked if I'd be kind enough to stop playing "here comes the train" with utensils full of food. They had held off asking me all those years because they figured I liked the game. Left without my primary means of forcing vegetables and other good nutrients into their systems, I decided not to fall back on the unsophisticated arguments of my parents' generation, but to explain in clear Keynesian econometrics the reasons for domestic consumption of certain basic foodstuffs as a protest on behalf of the small, independent truck farmer against the ravages of agricultural conglomerates. Once having done this, I then calmly concluded that if they did not eat what was on their respective plates, they would destroy the subtle balance of nature, and I would, of course, be forced to hold their heads back and force the food down their throats.

Caryl

The Forest Primeval

THERE ARE actually two kinds of guilt blooming in our household. Alan's brand is Urban Jewish Guilt, which, as you have seen, usually centers on the digestive tract. He watches me like a hawk. He is sure that whenever he spends a night away from home I am shoving Coke, Twinkies, and Doritos down the kids' throats. I on the other hand, suffer from a more suburban malady: Activities Guilt. I am certain that any child who does not take tap dancing and tennis lessons will end up in analysis. As a result, I shove the kids into more self-improvement activities than the children of Grace and Rainier had to endure. Alan does not understand how important this is to the children's enrichment. He wants to spend money on dumb things like good shoes and well-trimmed brisket when I know what the kids really need are cross-country skis. He thinks activities are things that are intrinsically cheap and faintly sleazy. I watch him like a hawk; left to his own devices, he would take the children to pool halls and teach them to run numbers.

My activities guilt makes me a patsy for a request by the children to participate in any and all extracurricular events. They don't even ask me if I *want* to go anymore—they just count me in.

I missed the Whale Watch with Steven's class because I had to work. It sounded like fun. The boat hit a storm and the whales got to watch 200 seventh graders puking over the rail. But I had no excuse the day Alyssa announced, "We're having a Brownie overnight and I said you could be a chaperone."

Panic clutched at my entrails. Alyssa's baby-blue eyes looked up, hopefully. How could I say no? After all, I had propagandized her all these years with jolly stories of my own camping days at Camp Mayflather, learning to chant like an Indian and freezing in a mountain stream. "Camping is fun!" I always said to my daughter.

I was not lying—exactly. Camping is fun when you are ten years old. But my notions of fun have changed radically over the years. Today, the only place I want to go backpacking is through the tangled undergrowth of the shag carpet in the lobby of the Hilton hotel. Then I want to lay my weary bones down on a king-sized bed and stare at a color TV which offers me all the standard channels, plus, for a moderate fee, a showing of *Flygirls of Denmark* or *The Naked Rider*. (The latter is an outdoors movie of sorts, since there is hardly room for girls and horses to do unspeakable things to each other in the living room.)

Somehow, I didn't think the Girl Scout Council would spring for a suite at the Hilton, so I wound up instead in a log cabin in the woods at scenic Camp Rowley, Mass., lugging a sleeping bag and a thermos full of orange crush. There were forty girls and nine chaperones, and the first thing on our agenda, after we got our gear stored in the cabin, was a nature hike.

Now, we were all urbanites, living in the most densely populated town in the state, and our idea of the wide-open spaces was a tot-lot littered with beer bottles. This crowd was supposed to instruct the Brownies about nature?

We started off down the nearest trail, the girls excited and chattering, the mother-chaperones looking as if they were starting Mao's long march.

"What the hell am I doing here?" one mother remarked as a formation of darning needles buzzed our column. "I panic when there's a moth in the house."

We tramped on down the wooded path. First we paused to look at a disgusting growth on a tree stump. The girls agreed it looked exactly like the veal parmigiana served by the school lunchroom.

I tried to be helpful. "Perhaps we could find some lichens," I said to another mother.

"I thought they only had those in the South."

"No, no, lichens are things that grow on rocks—like fungus."

"Terrific. Why am I wandering around in the woods looking for something I can find in my toilet bowl?"

We paused to inspect a bush in which, nestled among the branches, were gauzy, podlike sacs in which God-knows-what was growing. The troop leader waxed eloquent about butterflies. I was thinking about *In-*

vasion of the Body Snatchers. Being eaten by a plant is not high on my list of ways to depart from this vale of tears. (We used to have a game in elementary school to while away recess—it was called How You'd Like to Die. The fact that our classroom calendars at St. Michael's School featured the Martyr-of-the-Month in technicolor mid-martyrdom may have had something to do with it. We all agreed that getting tortured by the Godless Atheistic Communists was no fun. Being eaten by lions was no picnic either. Burning at the stake, hanging, and getting drawn and quartered were thought to be disagreeable. Freezing to death was said to be quite nice. I, myself, opted for the firing squad, which was quick and had a touch of panache.)

As we walked, little girls would come up to me and ask a question about pieces of stuff sticking up out of the ground. Prior to the nature hike, the only flora I'd seen recently was in full-color photographs in *House Beautiful*—and then it was usually something like "How to Re-create the Gardens of Versailles in Your Window Box."

"You're not supposed to pick toadstools, right?" one of the girls asked me.

"Right."

"Why?"

"Why? Because the toad will get angry. He will have to go out and buy a Barcelona chair, which looks terrible without a half-decent Kerman rug to go with it, and it will cost him a bundle."

The farther we went into the woods, the thicker the underbrush became and the bigger the bugs got. It was the first time I had ever seen a mosquito with an FAA license number.

One mother gazed at a mosquito with a two-foot wingspread. "If we had saddles, we could just throw them across the bugs and ride home." We were dousing ourselves constantly with bug spray. We were probably breathing more carcinogens here in the forest primeval than we would have inhaled loitering about a smokestack at a steel plant. The underbrush grew so thick we had to walk crouched over. The mud sucked at our feet while the mosquitos made kamikaze runs. I suddenly had a feeling of déjà-vu. Where had this happened before? Then I knew. In an Errol Flynn movie called *Objective, Burma!* Any minute I expected to hear Tokyo Rose from loudspeakers hidden in the trees: "Think about Babe Ruth and mom and apple pie and Betty Grable, *Amelican* soldiers. Throw away your guns and go home before you die in this jungle hell."

A mother behind me pulled her shoe out of ankle-deep mud. "Did we sign our kids up for Brownies or is this the Green Berets?"

"We're working for our counterinsurgency badge. After this, all we have to do is invade Guantánamo and we've got it sewed up."

"You think this is bad," another mother chimed in. "Just wait 'til we get to the creek."

"What creek?"

"The one with the dead tree in it that we have to walk across."

One of the Brownies piped up, "Last year Mrs. Grasso fell in. I hope somebody falls in this year!"

"Oh, boy!" said another Brownie. "I can hardly wait."

"Rotten kids," murmured a mother.

A few more minutes and we came to the creek, a rippling body of water, which, indeed, had a fallen tree across it. The Brownies scampered merrily across, leaving the mothers on the other side.

"I think I'll call a cab," said one.

"Listen to the little darlings now," said another.

On the far side of the bank, the Brownies had started up a chant: "Fall In! Fall In! Fall In! Fall In!" like bloodthirsty spectators watching a would-be suicide tottering on a ledge on 52nd Street. When Mrs. Grasso fell in again, they all cheered.

Once across the creek, we came to a rock marked with red, yellow, and green trail markers, each pointing in a different direction.

"What does that mean?" we asked one of the troop leaders.

"How should I know?"

"Oh, boy, we're going to get lost again!"

The troop had hiked its way into local history at the overnight last year, when it couldn't find the trail back to the cabin. But the troop, with the pioneer self-reliant spirit of scouting, found a way to solve the problem. They stood in a circle and screamed "Help!" until a forest ranger came to get them.

This year, we had all come equipped with compasses. One of the mothers examined her compass as we set off down what we hoped was the right trail. She said she was waiting for the day they'd invent a compass with a magnetic needle that pointed directly to the nearest McDonald's. I said that if you wanted to find which way was north you just had to look at a tree. Moss only grew on the north side, I said.

We stopped to look at a tree. It had moss on both sides. My credibility as a nature expert, none too high after my toadstool explanation, vanished completely.

Alyssa sighed. "She's even worse at math," she said to a friend.

I gave the tree a vicious kick. "Joyce Kilmer is a rat fink and you are a lying swine," I hissed.

We stomped along, pausing, as was our wont, to peer at some little bit of vegetation or animal life. One of the Brownies summed up what the girls had learned as we looked at a particularly smarmy piece of gunk growing under a rock.

"Nature is gross," she said.

"What they have learned on this nature hike," I said, "is that if God had any taste he would have done the whole place in Astroturf."

Just then we entered a lovely, sunny meadow. The only problem was that we had been in this same meadow an hour ago.

"Damn," said the troop leader, "I thought we were heading back to the cabin."

We plunged into the woods again. We hit the meadow two more times before we finally staggered onto the right trail. Then we tried to keep the girls from immolating themselves along with the hot dogs at the cookout. We bedded the Brownies in their sleeping bags on the floor. One little girl, clutching a Pink Panther doll, began to sob, "I want my mommy!" When she finally got quieted down, the other girls went on a gigantic giggling spree. At 1 A.M. the chaperones were prowling the cabin, threatening to disembowel any Brownie who let out so much as a titter.

When things were quiet, one of the mothers brought out a thermos —filled with sombreros. We said to hell with what the Girl Scout Council would think and lapped up the booze. That made it a little easier to sleep on the hard floor of the cabin.

We awoke in the morning feeling as if we had been beaten with truncheons. The day was sunny, warm, and fine. The mosquitos were dive-bombing the screen doors. A whole glorious day in the outdoors awaited us.

"Oh, well," I said to another one of the mothers, "look on the bright side."

"What bright side?"

"It's only another twelve hours before the buses break through to get us out of here."

"That," she snorted, "is what they kept saying at Dien Bien Phu!"

Alan

Dawn's Early Light

LET THEM go in good health to the woods. They're getting exactly what they're paying for. I've been in woods occasionally and I know for a fact you can get sick in them. Woods give you warts. Woods are for tinkers, horse thieves, the Hitler Youth, and bugs. I steadfastly remain in Urban America, where you just reach out and whatever you need is right there. I can walk or take a very short ride to places that feature all the necessities in life—deli, dry goods and garments fresh from an unscheduled truck, pinball machines, even an ocean. We have our own sewage treatment plant. Go eat your heart out. Our own prison. How many communities have one of those? We even have our own international airport a couple of hundred yards from our bedroom. I admit I do not like the airport as much as I like the pizza places and the ocean, because the planes using it make noises that no human should ever have to put up with. But I'd rather be going deaf and know where I am than be lost in the woods and hear perfectly the thousands of little creatures making their little sounds of warfare and illicit mating. The airport also provides a little fringe benefit that I've never mentioned to anyone before.

Sometimes, I like to drive over to the airport just to one of those machines in the lobby and take out an insurance policy. It has nothing to do with flying. I just go back to my car and drive off to whatever I'm supposed to do that day. The policy is just a hedge to provide for those I leave behind when I decide to drive into that land that husbands go to when they decide they've handled as much as they're going to and that it's time to find a motel in Duluth and a job washing dishes in a diner frequented by forest rangers, trappers, and others who will never ask you about your past.

Ideas of deserting come closest to reality in the mornings. In the parlance of sociologists, "Morning is a time for the members of the working family to share." I'm all for that. I love to share. When it comes to sharing tasks in the morning, I'm at least a socialist, probably a commie. I often wonder, when I'm alone in the kitchen doing the kids' lunches, everybody's breakfast, the previous night's trash cleanup, and other little chores, how come the members of my working family aren't taking advantage of the morning to share all this?

I am the first human up in the morning. There are farmers who get up later than I do. I get up before those who are arrested for burglary in the nighttime have even left their homes to begin burgling. I am awakened usually by dreams, all of which share one common element—anxiety. In one dream, I am a freshman in college and haven't finished a composition on *Moby Dick*. In another dream, I'm driving in a strange city and can't find my way back to wherever it is I'm supposed to go. In yet another, I've driven off that city's main road and skidded off a cliff, tumbling into a large body of water, where I'm pursued by Moby Dick.

Once having awakened, I have a variety of options. I can turn to my right and try to figure out whether I'm staring at my wife's head, my wife's arm draped over her head, my wife's pillows on top of her head, somebody else's wife's head, a white whale. Or, I can turn to my left and stare at the airport runway and listen as the winds carry the voices from that facility's public address system: "Paging Mr. Mrfghrmn, Mr. Mrfghrmn. Your koalas are at the ticket counter." Or I can just lie there, staring at the ceiling, and wonder: (a) if either car will start later; (b) which kid will wake up with a stomach bug; (c) how to deal with the two international terrorists who have somehow slipped by the dog downstairs and are at this very moment making their way upstairs; (d) whether the dull sensation in my large right toe is a telltale sign of something terminal.

Mostly, I lie there wondering whether it's worthwhile to go back to sleep, given that the alarm is set to buzz at 6:15 A.M., which is only four hours away. I wonder a lot about that until I drift off around 6:08 A.M. Seven minutes later, as the buzzing begins, an arm, presumably belonging to whoever is holed up under all those blankets next to me, shoots out to the night table. The arm is like Godzilla's tail. It carves a swath of destruction as it seeks out by some system of sonar the origin of the buzzing. It knocks the phone receiver off the cradle. It smacks a box of facial tissues to the floor. It finally grasps the little clock and chokes it to death.

Now I am officially up. The terrorists have apparently left, frightened away by the dawn after having climbed the flight of stairs for four hours. The ache in my toe is gone, replaced by a mild form of bronchitis, the beginning of an anxiety headache, and a twitching of the right eye, where I have a recurring corneal abrasion. (This is treated once a year by non-English-speaking doctors wearing tennis sneakers who hand me the same tubes of salve and say, "You must to put in regularly. You must to put in regularly.")

Jane bounds in and jumps on the inanimate form next to me. "Grlumph," the form says. Ahh, life signs. Jane pokes her wet nose into where the form's head appears to be hidden. "Getouttahere, dumbdog," the form says, rearranging itself under the covers. "Get outta there, Jane," I add, "you don't know what that is or where it's been."

Jane jumps off the form and begins rubbing up and down against the foot of the bed. "Grrrrrlllllll," says Jane, "grrrrrlllllll." See Jane. See Jane pace. See Jane grrrrrlllllll. See Jane do this every morning for as long as she lives, or as long as I live, whichever comes first. See how it stops being cute after the first morning or two. Jane wants to go out. Daddy will take Jane out. Daddy always takes Jane out. Why the hell Jane doesn't know this yet, after seven years, is a big mystery to Daddy.

I wash, brush teeth, shave and stimulate my gums with a piece of wood, because, if I don't, the hygienist said, she will make even more pain and blood for me the next time. It is 6:30 A.M., three-fourths of the way through the twentieth century, and I'm in front of a mirror sticking wood into my gums. Every minute or so, I yell out, "OK, time to get up." Nobody answers, and nobody gets up. Why I yell this, I'll never know. Why do I take the dog out? Why do I stick wood in my mouth? I have certain tasks in life. I shall do them. When I go, they'll find me clean shaven with good breath, lying behind a pile of dog mess in the backyard with a mouthful of splinters. "He did his damnedest," they'll say.

On this particular morning, the dog, having done what she must do, has to be coaxed upstairs into our bedroom, so we can let Kitty Widdums out of the kitchen. Today is a big day for Kitty Widdums. She is going to the vet to be spayed, or as every kid says, "Get spaded."

"Get the kids up!" I yell to Caryl.

"Kids, get up," she mumbles into her pillow.

Nobody gets up.

I go into Alyssa's room. "Alyssa dear, get up. C'mon, honey. Time to get up now." I gently stroke her head. Nothing. Louder now. "Alyssa, get up! Now! Okay, Alyssa, c'mon. Now, up. Up, Alyssa, up! It's late. You're gonna be late." She emerges from under the blanket and stares at me through the hair that's fallen over her eyes. There's a word for the expression on her round little face staring out from under the Snoopy sheets. Ahhh, what is that word? The snarl would indicate the word is fury.

All right, she's got her eyes opened anyway. I run into Steven's room. On the way, I yell, "Hey, Caryl, whaddya say, hah? This is no damn luxury hotel here."

"Right, we gotta get up," she whispers faintly. I often wonder why she says "we."

"Hokay, Steverino babeeee!" I announce with a jolly air. I try to remain jolly, as I trip over his train track and plunge face forward into his double-decker bunk. "Hey, that smarts, hah? C'mon, Steve. Time to get up now. It's late. You're gonna be late." Nothing. The pile of two blankets and two quilts has not moved. Louder now. "Steve, get up! Now! Okay, Steve, c'mon. Now, up. Up, Steve, up. It's late. You're gonna be late."

I do this a lot, and I always do it the same way. Why don't I learn? These are not threats, these foolish things I utter by rote. "You're gonna be late" is not a threat. It's a promise, a sign of hope. They want to be late. Or, if choices are offered, they'd just as soon not go at all.

Steve stirs. I'm reduced to prodding him in the ribs with my forefinger. It's cruel, but effective. He jumps up and stares at me, as I say, "C'mon, you have to get up." He stares as if this were the first time in his life he had ever heard such a thing, as if he had not been getting up at this time in this manner five mornings a week every fall, winter, and spring for eight years.

"Kids, make your bunks. Caryl, make the bed." These are the instructions I leave as I run back downstairs to make breakfast. The kids will not make the bunks, and Caryl will not make the bed, but if I'm ever in a play that requires me to say, "Kids, make your bunks. Caryl, make the bed," I won't stumble over the lines.

Breakfast is not the only meal I make in the morning. Despite the hour, I'm also into lunch. Alyssa has turned her back on school food. How can school food compare to the varied delicacies we pack for her in a brown bag? "You want tuna or peanut butter?" I yell upstairs regularly. What I hear in return is:

"You can't wear a short-sleeve shirt and that light jacket, Steven, because it is five degrees below zero!"

"Maaaaaa, you tell me to act my age, and then you tell me what to wear!"

His door slams. His door opens again immediately, because the doors don't work. Grumble, mumble.

"Alyssa, that's a perfectly good jumper. What's wrong with that jumper?"

Her door slams. Her door opens again immediately. Grumble, whine. "It iiiiitttccchhheeessssss me!"

All this is called: Caryl helping. I rest my forehead against a cool wall downstairs and whisper piteously, "C'mon, make a choice. It's not forever binding. It's not marriage. It's not life or death. It's not for a career. Tuna or peanut butter?"

"Tuna," Alyssa shouts down.

Oh, joy. Oh, bountiful discovery of that knowledge that allows me to move on, to take another step through life.

"With or without lettuce?" I shout back up the stairs.

"With!" she shouts back down.

Ahhh. The morning is looking up now. I pity those fathers who work so hard at their paying jobs that they can't share these quiet moments with their children. It is only 7:30 A.M., and look at the dialogue we've established.

Now, the family gathers around the kitchen table. My son is on the left, my daughter on the right, my wife near the stove, myself poised and ready to send off my kids to school in a good humor feeling good about themselves as human beings, and the cat . . . The cat. The frigging cat is standing in the tuna.

"*Get outta there!* Get outta the tuna!"

"Oh, Kitty Widdums," Caryl says, in a tone of voice that suggests that a cat standing in my daughter's lunch is something cute.

"Hahahahahahahahahahaha." Alyssa is convulsed with laughter and can no longer eat.

"Mrmph," Steven says, as he launches into the eighth of seventy-six comic books he will try to read between now and 7:45 A.M., when he is supposed to leave for school.

The rest of the time is taken up by announcements:

Me to Steven: "Don't read. Eat."

Me to Alyssa: "Decide what you want to eat and then eat and then comb your hair and then make sure you put your money in your pocket and then make sure you take your bookbag and then don't forget your hat and gloves and coat."

Me to Steven: "Don't read. Eat."

Alyssa to the world: "You know, uh, the cake?"

Me: "Not by name."

Alyssa: "The, uh, cake that Mommy made last night, right? The one for the Kids Curtain Call party after school, right?"

Me, wondering why kids that age sound like Edward G. Robinson in *Little Caesar:* "Right, sweetheart, the cake Mommy made, the one I'm looking at now in the cake plate."

Alyssa: "It has to be cut up into slices, because we don't have any knives at Kids Curtain Call."

Me to Alyssa: "Why didn't you tell us earlier? Why do you save these things for the last minute?"

Alyssa to her plate: Sulk, sulk.

Me to Caryl: "Slice the cake, please."

Caryl to me: "What cake?"

Steven to us: "Are there any more comic books?"

Me to Steven: "You're late. Get your head gear."

Steven to me: "I hafta put on my sneakers."

Me to Steven: "Why do you save these things for the last minute? I'll go up and get the damn head gear."

The orthodontic head gear is lying on a shelf in his room. It is holding back a platoon of toy Union Army soldiers. Very good. His teeth will sprout out unrestrained, but the Confederacy will be saved. The next time the orthodontist asks for a payment, tell him to wire General Longstreet.

Steven leaves, and I walk Alyssa down the street to Aimee's. I also walk the cake down the street. I have to give the cake to Aimee's father, to give to Aimee's mother to take to Kids Curtain Call. I try to explain this rapidly to him, as I hand him a pistachio cake. He is too nice to say anything, but he can't conceal the look in his eyes, a look that says, "Why is this screwball handing me a green cake at 7:50 in the morning?"

At the corner, Aimee says suddenly, "Oh, nooooo."

I panic. Is she ill? Did I step on her foot? She's not going to throw up or anything, is she? "I forgot my money for potato chips. I'm supposed to buy potato chips, and I forgot my money. We have to go back to my house."

"No, no way, kid. Here, here's a buck. It's on me. That enough? Hah? You want more? More than a dollar? You got it. Two dollars? You name it. I just want to clear this neighborhood of kids."

They walk away, also regarding me with some suspicion. I make my way back for adult conversation, for adult tasks. First, I stop to pull Caryl's car out of the driveway, so I can pull my car out of the driveway. This makes sense. What fails to make sense is her car's inability to go "Grrrrrmmmmmmpppppphhhhhsssss" when I turn the ignition. It goes, instead, "click." The battery is dead. Of course the battery is dead. And where is it written that a battery lives forever?

Caryl throws a coat around her robe. Her hair is in curlers, which makes the top of her head resemble no-man's land laced with concertina wire. Very fetching. "You get in your car," I explain, "and I'll get in my car. I'll back up my car and push your car out of the driveway, and you steer it up against the curb, right?"

"Uhhh, right," she says, uncertainly, and heads for my car.

"No, Riv. Let me do it so you'll get it right away. Get in your goddamn car!" I open the door on the driver's side and push her in. I rush to my car. It starts. I know when it starts, because the muffler and tailpipe are broken, and when it starts, I'm enveloped in a dense cloud of white exhaust.

I back up. She backs up. I back up some more. She backs up some more. I've done as much as I can do with machinery. Now, for brute strength, I shall go out and push her car the lousy few feet back to a curb. But no. No, because Caryl is shouting (with the window closed) that I must do something else. I am getting irritated, especially when I notice that in shoving her car with my car, I have broken some more of the front of her car. Pieces of plastic are on the street. Plastic, for Chrissakes. Ralph Nader may be on the right track after all. Failing to read her lips, I beg that she open the window, which she consents to do.

"Don't push me. You'll get a heart attack."

"I won't get a heart attack."

"You will get a heart attack."

"I push cars a lot. I won't get a heart attack. Don't you have any confidence in me? Where in hell has the confidence gone?"

"I just don't want you to get a heart attack from pushing the car."

"Obviously you'd rather I get a heart attack from arguing."

"All right," she says with that shrug that's supposed to make me feel guilty. "You want to get a stroke, go ahead."

"When did the diagnosis change? I thought I was having a heart attack."

"But don't push me backwards. Push the car forwards."

"Forwards is uphill, Caryl. Backwards is downhill. Look at the street, Caryl. You see?"

"It all looks the same to me."

"When *you* push the car, it'll look different. It's my stroke. I'll get it my way."

With the car secured against the curb, with Caryl's head free of curlers, with both of us dressed for work, we pick up Kitty Widdums and arrange the drive. I drive, and Caryl sits in the back seat with the cat so the cat will not climb up on my head and sit there as I drive in traffic. This seems to be working. The cat, apparently scared shitless, is burrowing her way into Caryl's coat. Caryl is calming her: "Ooooohhhh, nice Kittums Widdums, nice kitteeeee cat. Ohhhhh, don't worreeeeee. Nice Kiddums. Nice Widdums. Christ!"

"Pardon me? What did nice Kiddums do to Mommy?" I ask with the proper sarcasm. "Did nice Kiddums chew on nice Mommy's little finger?"

Mommy is not amused. "The cat is scared."

"So?"

"So, she's farting."

I reach over with my right hand to open the glove compartment. I start poking around.

"What are you doing?" she asks.

"Looking for a road map."

"To the veterinarian's?"

"To Duluth."

"Duluth?"

"I bet they've got a couple of diners there," I mumble.

"What? I can't hear you back here. The muffler's making noise. What?"

"I said, 'My God, it's not even nine o'clock.' That's what I said."

Caryl

The Big Sleep

MORNINGS SEEM to get to Alan. I don't understand it, the mornings seem fine to me. But then, I don't come out of a dreamlike trance until 10 A.M., so I am only dimly aware, before that time, that I am in fact out of bed and walking about. It is at night that my patience starts to wear thin. I always thought that when I had a family, my evenings would be tranquil as a mountain lake; I imagined sweet little tots sitting at my knee, the way Longfellow wrote about it:

Between the dark and the daylight,
When the night is beginning to lower,
Comes a pause in the day's occupations,
That is known as the Children's Hour.

When night starts to lower at our house, the children are not at my knee. They are in front of the TV set, watching reruns of "The Brady Bunch." They want to eat in front of the television so as not to miss a single minute of the idiotic drivel.

"*Turn off that goddamn TV set!*" I shriek, having had enough noise all day at work. Suddenly, it dawns on me that I am screaming at more children than the ones I gave birth to. Often, they are little-girl persons, and they are planning to eat dinner at my house. They have other plans as well. In such cases it always seems to be my job to break the news to Alan.

"Alyssa wants a slumber party," I said to him recently.

He stiffened, as if he had just been told he was being sent off to the Russian front. His eyes shifted about, his hands shook. It was sad to see such stark terror evoked in an otherwise healthy, normal American male by those dread words: slumber party.

Finally he got hold of himself. "Have you forgotten," he said in icy tones, "the last slumber party—Apocalypse Now?"

"It wasn't that bad."

"What do you mean it wasn't that bad? That's like saying World War II wasn't that bad. The screaming, the kicking, the thudding of hooves, the ceilings that almost collapsed, the bags under my eyes."

"Alyssa's friends have invited her to slumber parties, so she owes them. Besides, they're older now. They won't be so wild."

So we started planning for the slumber party, a small, *intime* group, perhaps three or four.

"Trina says she can't come unless Kim comes too," Alyssa said.

"Well, she's Trina's sister, so that's OK."

"Deanna's coming."

"Sure, Deanna may be a little younger, but her feelings would be hurt if Thi came and she didn't."

"Lulu wants to know if her niece can come." (Lulu is the youngest of eleven and her niece is two inches taller than she is.)

So, one night at seven-thirty, little girls began streaming through the front door, with sleeping bags and pillows thrown over their shoulders. Alan watched the milling horde with awe.

"Is this a slumber party, or have we just volunteered to take 500 boat people? Who are all these children?"

"Just a few of Alyssa's best friends. Aren't you glad she's so popular?"

"Maybe we should run her for president. There are enough votes in this house right now to put her ahead in the Harris poll."

The crowd milled around in the dining room, where it ate its way through three bags of popcorn, four bags of Doritos, a carton of potato chips and a gallon of Coke. We sat in the kitchen as the din grew louder and louder. Steven added to the general air of jocularity by walking around in a sheet saying he was the Ayatollah Khomeini. Girls started to punch Steven. He started to punch girls. Girls started to punch girls. They began giving each other Miss Piggy karate chops— aiiiiiiyyyyyaaaaaahhhh! There was much laughing, shrieking, and moaning. One of the girls came in, irate. "They're laughing at me because my nose shakes. It only shakes because of the germs!" And she let out a cough that made Typhoid Mary seem the picture of health by comparison.

The shrieking grew louder, bodies hurtled in and out of rooms. Steven came flying into the kitchen. He got up and started toward the living room.

"Steven, don't provoke the girls!" I ordered.

"Who, me?" he said, innocent as a lamb. "I'm not provoking anyone." The fact that he had stuffed the cardboard center of a roll of gift wrap—perfect for use as a bludgeon—down the back of his shirt did not exactly signal peaceful intentions. Alan confiscated the weapon.

"I'm not doing anything. *They're* coming after me," Steven protested as he was body-searched. He pointed to a sweetfaced little blonde who was lurking outside the kitchen doorway. "She's kicking me. She's got a lethal foot."

The noise escalated from deafening to impossible. I called Alyssa into the kitchen, and I said to her sweetly, "Alyssa, sweetheart, would you ask your friends to make a wee bit less noise? Could you do that, please?" (I had just read *Mommie Dearest* and I had been sweet as hell for a week. You weren't going to catch *me* shrieking at these nice little girls; one of them might be taping the whole party.)

Alyssa nodded, walked into the other room and screeched, in a voice that would unsettle a banshee, "MY MOTHER SAYS YOU ALL HAVE TO SHUT UP!"

Alan and I moved upstairs to the bedroom to get a semblance of peace and quiet. Then the girls decided they were going to do a musical revue, and the nearest thing they could find for a stage was the stair landing. We had box seats to a musical. Alyssa and Trina did a disco version of "Silent Night." Somebody else sang "Jingle Bell Rock," off-key. But the real show-stopper was the girl with the germs; apparently they made no impact on her vocal chords. She did a star turn with the Muppet song: "I'm the inspirational, so sensational Wendy . . ."

Alan sighed. "Ethel Merman is alive and well halfway up our stairs."

We finally got the girls herded downstairs into the family room, an ideal spot. It had a door that could be closed.

The girls decided to play séance. First there was blessed silence. Then we heard a caterwauling chant, in unison: "Spirits of beyond, if you hear us, knock twice!"

I said to Alan, "Where is Steve?" He had vanished, suddenly.

All at once the air was rent with ear-splitting shrieks and squeals. The door to the bedroom was flung open and in burst seven-year-old Deanna, clearly on the verge of tears. "I'm scared. The Deadly Babies are gonna get me."

"Deanna, this is supposed to be fun. It's just a game. Don't be scared!"

"It's the Deadly Babies."

Steven marched into the room, wearing a sheet and carrying a hockey stick. "I really scared 'em," he announced. Where he had been, it turned out, was on the porch, impersonating a spirit.

Deanna stomped out. "You're a jerk, Steven. The Deadly Babies are gonna get me."

"Steven," I asked, "who and what are the Deadly Babies?"

"Oh, Deanna saw *It's Alive*, about a bunch of dead babies that rise up and strangle people."

"They have big claws," Deanna called back from the hall. "The Deadly Babies eat people."

We heard the chant again—"spirits of beyond—" It took me back to my Girl Scout days, when ghost stories were the rage on overnights.

"Steven," I said, "I've got a trick that will really get 'em. Where's the flashlight?"

I took down one of the gruesome Peruvian folk-art tin masks from the bathroom wall. "I'll sneak around and shine the light on the mask and that will really be scary."

I threw my coat on over my nightgown, tiptoed out the front door, across the lawn, and around to the back of the house. I stubbed my toe on one of the two-by-fours left over from the construction of the family room. It was pitch dark. I had a sudden horrible thought. What if I tripped and broke my neck—one misstep and it would be all over. Did I really want to be found sprawled in the backyard in my nightgown wearing a tin mask? The papers would have a field day.

WEIRD SEX RITES SUSPECTED IN DEATH OF WOMAN

Victim Sprawled in Yard Wearing Fertility Mask and
Black Nightgown

Husband Found Alone in House with Little Girls

"A Likely Story" Says DA of Slumber Party Alibi

I crept up the back-porch stairs, stuck my masked face against the window, flicked the light off and on, and gave a series of low moans. I was a smash. Shrieks and squeals exploded from inside the room. I did this twice, and was preparing for a second encore, when suddenly I was tackled from behind. Down I went, smashing my face—in the mask—

against the side of the house. The sharp edge of the tin ground into my forehead.

"Steven, for God's sake, what do you think you are doing?"

"I figured I'd tackle the ghost for the girls and be a hero."

"In the future, remember this piece of wisdom from your mother. Do not knock people over when they are wearing masks of tin." The blood was trickling down my face. I went in the house to the excited jabber of the girls:

"I was scared but I recognized that thing from the bathroom," Deanna chirped. "I thought it was the Deadly Babies."

I went upstairs and Alan got out the alcohol to swab on my forehead. I peered into the mirror and saw the jagged gash.

"If anybody asks me about this," I said, "I am going to tell them you hit me. You are not going to catch me explaining, 'You see, I was crawling around the back porch in my nightgown with this tin mask on . . .'"

It was getting very late. We decided we would go to bed and try to ignore the noise from downstairs. Alan tossed and turned. I kept waking up and hearing the TV. When the clock said 1 A.M., I marched downstairs and demanded that all the girls get into their sleeping bags.

"We can't," they chirped. "It's too hot in there."

I opened the door to the family room and was hit by a blast of air that felt like it came from the sub-Sahara. Someone (Steven later confessed) had turned the thermostat up to ninety degrees. I went into the room, opened all the windows and flailed my arms to get cool air circulating again. By the time the room was cool, I had a fever that felt like 106. Sweating, I herded the girls into their room while they laid out the sleeping bags. I went upstairs to bed, trying to ignore Jane whining in Alyssa's room. I slept fitfully, waking now and then to the murmur of voices below. Alan had been dozing, but I began to notice a strange sensation. Was I dreaming? It felt like something was nibbling on my toes. Something small, with beady eyes. With claws.

"Aaarrrggghh. It's the Deadly Babies. They've got me. The Deadly Babies are nibbling on my toes!"

Alan leaped up and switched on the light. There was Kitty Widdums, happily perched on my blanket, gnawing on my toes.

I looked at Alan. "I guess it's not the Deadly Babies. Heh-heh. It must be Peruvian jungle rot from the mask—I'm hallucinating."

I took one look at Alan's face and figured I'd do better with the babies with the fangs that ate people.

"Have you ever heard of the Deadly Husbands?" he said, steel in his voice. "They strangle mommies who tell little girls they can have slumber parties."

He couldn't get back to sleep because Jane was whining so pitifully. He put Kitty Widdums in my office, and Jane in our room, where she slept on his feet. Kitty Widdums spent the rest of the night in my office—*without her litter box.*

Alan woke me up the next morning with a benign smile on his face.

"Good morning," he said. "Kitty Widdums left you a gift on your shag rug."

Alan

Intime Dinners

SLUMBER PARTIES were not in my game plan for adult life. I used to daydream about the kind of homelife I would lead when finally I became a family man. No more Army barracks or dingy dormitories. No more raucous fraternity houses or low-rent apartments with somebody else's furniture. I would have a home. I would sit in a comfortable leather chair near a fireplace, complete with appropriate crackling wood, and my children would sit on the floor around me. One would play with toy soldiers, another with dolls; yet another would pat the large but gentle Rover. I would be reading a book selected from my collection of leather-bound volumes (to match the chair), now and then looking up to see the clipper ships coming in on the tide while awaiting wifey's call to dine in the dining room that would adjoin the spotless kitchen.

"Dinner, dear," she would announce.

"Come, children," I would command softly, as I stood up and straightened out my leather smoking jacket. They would all jump up at once and grab for my hands. "Heh, heh," I would say. "Now, Daddy can't hold all of you. Go help your tired mother with the six-course dinner she has prepared."

Much of it came true. We have a home, a rug, and a dog. And when Heartburn Pizza Heaven is closed, Caryl cooks dinner. And, of course, we have the children. We have our children and other people's children. It's not quite what I had in mind. I have, in fact, sent in applications to a number of colleges, asking if they accept persons not for study, but just for dingy dorm residence.

What we have here on any given evening is about as *intime* as an Automat at lunchtime, with fewer choices.

I sit at one end of the table and Caryl at the other. On one side sits Alyssa and one of her friends; on the other side, Steven and one of his friends. We are careful to balance the seating arrangements carefully, just as Amy Vanderbilt or Emily Post would have suggested. "When preparing seating arrangements for dinner at home, it is considered gauche, *très*, to seat the junior high school boy next to the elementary school girl, especially if they are related by blood. If no other arrangements are possible, remove the knives from their table settings. By far the best arrangement is one of diagonal opposites so that if they must fight, they will be forced to duel with the butter knives over the open table in plain view of the stern looks of their parents."

"Gotcha!" Steven addressed Alyssa as he spronged a pea at her face by making a catapult of his fork.

"Missed me! Missed me! Now you gotta kiss me!" she rejoined.

"Cut the shit!" Pater retorted.

Dinner usually begins when Caryl's finely honed sense of dining etiquette signals her that it is time to begin cooking. This happens when Alyssa grimaces, holds her stomach and groans, "I'm hungry, I'm so hungry. When are we gonna eat? Are we gonna eat now? Soon? Please, soon. I'm so hungry. Maaaaaaa, I'm starving!"

Or, sometimes, one of the visiting children will say softly, "Mrs. Lupo, my mommy said I can't come here again for dinner if I don't get dinner when I come for dinner," and begins to eat a sandwich that she has pulled out of her jacket pocket.

As Caryl starts to boil rice (we have rice with meat, fish, fowl, lunch, dinner, and sometimes breakfast), the children proceed to set the table at a prearranged signal from Father.

"Set the goddamn table or you don't eat!" he so signals.

The children have been doing this for years, but every evening they manage to add a delightful little twist so that no one in the family is faced with the drabness of routine.

One plate has a napkin, two forks, and a spoon. The next plate has no napkin, no forks, two knives, and two spoons. The third plate has two napkins, one fork, no knives, and three spoons. At the other end of the table is one napkin, perfectly folded, with one fork, one knife, one spoon, and no plate. Continuing to the right, we have one plate, no napkin, no fork, no knife, no spoon, and finally, a plate with napkin, fork, knife, spoon, and two doggie biscuits. In mid-table is salt but no pepper, or, for a variation, pepper but no salt. On special occasions there is neither. And often, a lucky wanderer invited to dine might find both a saltshaker and a pepper shaker—clogged to prevent pouring.

Everything is in a state of readiness as Caryl brings us one of her famous creamed-chicken-in-gravy dishes. Steven and his friend Kevin are reading war comic books. Alyssa's friend Aimee is at her place, asking softly if we have any peanut butter and jelly, and Alyssa is upstairs hugging the cat.

"Watch out!" Caryl screeches as she lumbers in with a gruel pot that is smoking with the intensity of a three-alarm fire. "This is hot stuff here, hot stuff here."

"Steve," I ask, "where are the cups and glasses?"

"Huh?"

"Cups, glasses, the things we use to drink from."

"They're in the kitchen."

"But we're in the dining room."

"Hey, Alyssa," Steven yells, "on your way in, get six cups, thanks." Back to American GIs as they whack out more Panzer brigades.

"Oooooooooooo, she's so cute," Alyssa announces as she appears with the cat. The cat is cute. The cat is also no longer in Alyssa's arms. She is, instead, standing on my plate.

Aimee is saying that she doesn't even need the jelly, or for that matter the peanut butter. She is now talking bread and water, which we can't give her, because there are no cups.

"Aren't you through with that one yet?" Kevin asks Steven. Kevin has finished *GI Blood, War, Death, and Guts.*

"No comic book reading at dinner," I remind them. No expression of any sort is apparent on their faces. They have learned to deal with this command by closing their comic books on their right forefingers and, moments later, when I allegedly have forgotten about my command, once again opening said comic books and picking up where they left off—a fairly easy task, given the plots.

"No comic book reading" is one of the many flashes of bright and witty conversation that dominates our dining room. The repartee sparkles with subtle humor and deep thoughts in the New England tradition of Emerson, Thoreau, Whittier, Hale, and Channing:

"There are two ways you're gonna eat those stringbeans—by yourself or with your jaw forced open while I pour them down your throat."

"Alyssa, you have to learn to eat without dipping your sleeves in the gravy."

"Aimee, you haven't touched anything. Is anything wrong?" A pale, wan look, followed by a shake of the head and no eating.

"Cheez, Kevin, I really am sorry I can't give you any more chicken." Usually said after Kevin's ninth helping, which includes what was going to be my third and Caryl's second, and the dog's main course.

"For Chrissakes, somebody get the goddamn phone and tell whoever it is that we're eating."

"Maaaaaaaaa, it's for you!"

"For Chrissakes, somebody get the goddamn doorbell and tell whoever it is that we're eating."

"Hi, there, sorry to interrupt your dinner, but I'd like to give you some Salvation Army booklets and just wonder out loud here whether you, as you're eating so sumptuously, realize that less happy souls are begging in the streets of Boston for a bit of soup."

"Who let this guy in here?"

"Arf. Arf. Bowowowowowowowow. Grrrrrrrrhhhhhhhhhgggggg."

"Oh, Migod!"

"It's the dog! The damn dog got loose. Somebody catch the damn dog!"

Caryl reenters the room and surveys the scene. "Steven, do as Daddy says and get the dog before she kills the Salvation Army man. May I see one of those booklets, Loop? Maybe they pay for articles."

"That dog should be put away!"

"Shaddup, mister."

"Steven's kicking me," Alyssa whines.

"I'm not kicking."

"Yes you are," I snap, "because Kevin is too far away to kick her, and Aimee doesn't kick, and Ma is busy reading the Salvation Army booklet, so if you kick her again, you won't have to eat the stringbeans, because you'll be eating dogfood."

"Hahahahahahahahahahahahaha," interjects Alyssa, who falls flat onto the rug to do her special dinner-time laugh.

"Get up and eat your dinner!"

"I'm full," Alyssa says.

"Me too," Steven decides. "If I eat any more I'm gonna puke."

"Caryl, hey Riv. Caryl? I'm *leaving* you, Caryl. Tonight. I'm leaving. I'm also leaving all the kids and animals. Caryl?"

"You know, I bet I could rewrite my piece on gene splicing for this Salvation Army magazine. If I just change the lead a little, they'll never know. Yes, Alyssa, what is it?"

"Why is Daddy dribbling food off his lip and staring funny at the table?"

Caryl

Making It

THERE ARE certain illusions some people cling to even in the face of incontrovertible evidence to the contrary. Alan still thinks one day we will have a dinner scene right out of a Victorian novel. I picture myself whipping up a coffee table or a highboy that would make Duncan Phyfe turn green with envy. I think of myself as "handy." I believe I have a gift for putting things together, which leads me to ignore the printed instructions that come with things to be assembled and plunge ahead on blind instinct.

I once tried to put together a store-bought sandbox and it came out looking like those modern sculptures you see on college campuses that are called either "Birds in Flight" or "The Muse Celebrating the Transcendental Spirit of Poetry in a World Devoured by Technology." I built a wall for what was supposed to be a basement playroom by nailing slabs of Sheetrock to four-by-fours. The only problem was that I never bothered to learn how to score the Sheetrock before cutting it to make it even, so the top of my wall looks like the rim of the Grand Canyon. (On rainy days the basement leaks like a sieve anyhow, and the Grand Canyon effect is heightened. My children are the only kids in the neighborhood who can shoot the rapids under their own Ping-Pong table.)

But I plunge onward, doggedly. One day Alyssa and I were looking through a magazine and we came upon a picture of a dollhouse, one of those Victorian numbers with a mansard roof, cunning little window panes, sweet little shingles, and an exquisite little price tag of seven hundred dollars. Alyssa gave a little moan of delight. My "handywoman" instincts came racing to the fore. "The kid wants a dollhouse, I will build a dollhouse!" I thought. "Nothing is too good for my little girl!"

A Victorian mansion was a bit beyond my ken—even I knew that. I decided on something more like a Cape Cod saltbox, and I sat down to sketch out a design. The dollhouse in the book had been made with quarter-inch plywood and the magazine gave the dimensions. I decided to make my dollhouse bigger, so I wouldn't have to mess with tiny nails with my less-than-tiny fingers. I just multiplied by three. The lumberyard was out of quarter-inch plywood. They offered me three-quarter-inch plywood.

"What the hell, I'll take it, how much difference could it make?"

My first job was to lug the plywood up to the second floor where construction was to begin. After about my seventh trip up the stairs with a board on my back, I realized that the slaves who built the pyramids would have called a work stoppage if they were asked to do this. But finally I got it all up and began to build. I hammered and smashed and hammered some more, and soon noticed it was getting dark. Had I labored well into the night on the dollhouse? No. It was only three o'clock in the afternoon. The Darkness at Noon effect was due to the dollhouse. It was blocking out the sun.

But I carried on. Finally, it was done. I called out to my daughter, "Alyssa, sweetheart, Mommy has a surprise for you. Come up and see!"

Alyssa came scampering up the stairs. She got three-quarters of the way and then stopped dead in her tracks. She stared, with the awed expression of one who has just seen an overpowering work of man or nature: Grand Canyon, or the World Trade Center. There before her was a stark, four-foot high structure of gray wood that looked about as much like a Victorian mansion as did Sing Sing prison.

While Alyssa gaped, speechless, I stepped back to admire my handiwork. The building looked familiar. Very familiar. What was it? Suddenly, I knew. I had just built a perfect replica of Pruitt-Igoe, the housing project in St. Louis that the city finally had to dynamite because even poor people refused to live there.

"Is that my dollhouse?" Alyssa asked, shaken.

"Yes, sweetie, that is your new dollhouse."

"Oh," she said.

"Look," I said to her, "everybody and her sister has a Victorian mansion. They are a dime a dozen. You have something different. You have a high-rise, maximum density, low-income housing project. You can play Urban Living. Your Barbies can take turns mugging each other. Your Farrah Fawcett doll can be a social worker checking up on Malibu Barbie to see if she's shacked up with Ken and ought to have her welfare check cut off. Tuesday Taylor can run numbers. You're the only kid in the neighborhood who can call up her friends and ask them to come over and play in her slum."

And then came the Pinewood Derby fiasco.

The Pinewood Derby is a project dreamed up by the powers-that-be in the Cub Scout organization, people who are adept at devising new and clever ways to humiliate parents. My most vivid memory of my brother's days as a Cub Scout is of the time he announced at 9 P.M. one night that he had to have a leaf collection for the pack meeting the next day. My father led him out into the backyard with a flashlight, and a few minutes later I heard my father's voice drifting in from the darkness: "I don't care what the hell it is, pick it up, glue it on, and call it a goddamned maple."

Steven came home one day all excited about something he said was to be the Pinewood Derby. Alan shrugged, pulled out a five and told Steven to bet it on win, place, or show. "It's a helluva way to raise money for Cub Scouts," he said. "Didn't they used to sell cookies?"

The Pinewood Derby, it turned out, was not about horses, but cars; little cars that the Cub Scouts and their daddies were to build. Steven produced a box which contained a block of wood and four wheels. It said on the box, "Instructions inside."

"Where are the instructions?" Alan asked Steven, there being none in the box.

"I lost them." But he told his father that all they had to do was to put wheels on the block of wood and decorate it so it looked like a car.

"Oh, boy," I said, my "handy" instincts about to run amok again, "we can chop her and channel her, put a pair of duals on her—"

Alan leaped up and clutched the piece of wood to his bosom. I could tell by the glint in his eye that I was not going to lay a paw on that block of wood. Alan has always felt a deep psychic pain about the fact that he messed up a match scratcher in junior high. Here was a chance to redeem his honor, in the eyes of his son, yet. He and Steven would make the derby car.

Alan plunged in with zest. Steven said the leader told them the rule was that the finished car couldn't weigh more than five pounds. No sweat, Alan figured, since the block of wood couldn't have weighed more than ten ounces.

Alan and Steven worked at a feverish pace. Steven scrounged old parts from his models. Alan designed a handsome cab from old pieces of plastic. They glued on glittering gimcracks: jazzy fenders, silver horns, a little gilt mirror—and they painted it in bright colors until it looked like a vehicle any high-class pimp would be proud to own.

The night of the derby we arrived *en famille*, at the local auditorium where a wooden track had been assembled for the derby. No one, we were certain, had a vehicle as classy as ours. Haughtily, we deigned to peer at some of the cars the other kids had brought.

They didn't look like ours. Not at all. They were *carved*. The blocks of wood had been planed, carved, and sanded into the shape of sleek little Indy racers. We looked at Steven.

"I goofed," he said.

And then we discovered he had made another slight error. The racers couldn't weigh more than five *ounces*, not five pounds. A scale was set up in the corner for the weigh-in. Steven took his beautiful little pimp-mobile over and set it on the scale. Zonnnggg! The needle fluttered wildly.

"We'll just have to get it down," the cubmaster said. They started to strip it. *Rip!* Off came the beautiful chrome windshield. *Tear!* Off came the silver horn. *Crack!* The gilt fenders broke off.

It was like that scene in *"J'Accuse!"* when they rip the epaulets from the arms of Dreyfus while the drums roll. I could see Alan flinch as each doodad came off. He groaned with the little windshield. He grunted as if hit in the stomach as the silver horn dropped on the floor. When the mirror went, Alan muttered through clenched lips, "I'm going to kill myself!"

In a minute, all Steven had left of his beautiful little car was the block of wood and the wheels. Alan's face was drained of color.

"Can you commit hari-kari with an exacto knife?" he said. "Tell Steven my last words were, 'I'm sorry.'"

"It's not your fault," I said, trying to be soothing.

"First the match scratcher, now *this!* If I drink the turpentine, maybe it'll be quick."

Steven was sad for about twelve seconds. Then he ran off to get into a shoving match with his friends and had a wonderful time.

We figured maybe Steven had a chance to win the race with his stripped-down block of wood. We didn't know that auto racing is a cutthroat sport, even in Cub Scouts. Especially in Cub Scouts. The kid who won the grand prize had a father who was a chemist and injected the car with mercury to give it a better center of gravity. After the final run it leaked and the mercury slid all over the track. The second-place winner had a father who made seven trips to the butcher shop to use the scale to see that the car wasn't overweight because of all the coins he had taped between the wheels to make it faster.

"I never won these things when I was a kid," he said with a beatific smile. "When I was a kid, I was honest." He kept a firm grip on the package of cheese from the local grocery that was second prize.

"Winning isn't the most important thing," he said. "It's the only thing."

Wait 'til next year. I know a guy at MIT who does NASA contracts. For a small fee, he ought to be able to whip up something tricky: Magnets, an electromagnetic force field. Maybe he could give us some little heat-seeking rockets so we could nuke the other cars as they approach the finish line. We won't be suckered again!

Part Three

Leisure World

Caryl

On the Beach

It is a lovely, sunny summer day, and the temperature is hovering in the mid-eighties. I come into the family room and announce, in my best sugar-wouldn't-melt-in-your-mouth, Mary Poppins voice, "Let's all go to the beach!"

Do my children leap up, childish joy sparkling in their eyes, and cry, "Oh goody, goody, our wonderful mommy is taking us to the beach?"

They do not. Steven does not lift his eyes from the "Sgt. Fury Firebombs the Dirty Japs" comic book he is reading. "I hate the beach. The water's too damn cold."

Alyssa is coloring, intently. She says, "The beach is yukky. It's all covered with sand. Why can't we have a pool like Lulu does?"

Alan scrunches himself behind his newspaper and tries to make himself invisible.

At times like this, my entire childhood flashes before my eyes. Or, to be exact, the part of my childhood I spent sitting on the cement steps of my front porch on unbearably hot days, sweating, and dreaming—with the passion of an alcoholic imagining a pinch bottle of Four Roses—of any body of water large enough to immerse my entire person in.

There was a creek a block away—Slimy Sligo, we called it, but Sligo's waters were not sufficient to cover your ears if you lay face down in it. Besides, my friends and I were bombarded with warnings from our parents to the point where we believed we could actually see the polio microbes floating with the green crud on Sligo's brackish bosom. I was convinced that if I stuck as much as a sweaty toe into the water I would immediately fall down in a paralytic seizure.

Sometimes on weekends there were trips to the shores of the Chesapeake Bay, a body of water noted for the production, in great quantity, of two particular life forms—jellyfish and beetles. I would splash along doing my Esther Williams impersonation—a dazzling smile and a dog paddle—while floating corpses of Japanese beetles knocked against my teeth. But these delights were only occasional pleasures. Some days, when the mercury and the humidity both went off the scale, my friend Beano and I would interrupt our endless game of Washington Senators trivia ("What Senator pitcher speaks only Spanish and is legally blind?") and get on our bikes in pursuit of the Holy Grail: a swimming pool.

We would ride for miles until we found one, and we would park our bikes up against the fence watching the owners frolic. We were poor, damned souls permitted to gaze on paradise; nobody ever invited us in. So we would sadly get back on our bikes, ride home, and go back to trivia. ("What Senator outfielder lives in a walk-up in Alexandria and gets total disability from the Veterans Administration?")

Mine, you see, is a story of aquatic deprivation, a childhood in which I dreamt of sparkling blue waters and had to settle for the sprinkler. To this day, my idea of heaven is the MGM set for an Esther Williams movie. The first thing I plan to ask St. Peter is "Which way's the pool?" I am like the little match girl, grown up to unexpected affluence, whose kids turn their noses up at roast goose.

Here the Atlantic Ocean beckons, a mere half-mile away, and my family does not hear the siren song. Something inside me snaps. I undergo an instant metamorphosis: From Mary Poppins to the Madwoman of Chaillot.

"YOU CHILDREN ARE SPOILED ROTTEN! I WOULD HAVE GIVEN MY RIGHT ARM WHEN I WAS A KID TO HAVE AN OCEAN RIGHT NEARBY AND IF I SO MUCH AS HEAR ANYBODY EVEN BREATHE THE WORD POOL IN THIS HOUSE NO MOVIES FOR A MONTH AND BREAD AND WATER FOR DINNER! WE ARE GOING TO THE BEACH AND WE ARE GOING TO HAVE FUN!"

They take one look at my glittering eye and acquiesce. I drag them out to the car to go to the beach. I am mollified, and happily expectant. They all wear the expressions of Russian dissidents about to board the train for the Gulag.

We arrive at the beach and spread out the blankets. Alan turns his back to the water and continues to read the op-ed page. Steven still has on his sweatshirt and long pants and is muttering about the cold. Alyssa huddles in the middle of the blanket so that the grains of sand will not touch her delicate epidermis. I decide to ignore them, to bake in the sun and meditate on the sheer joys of beach-going.

The first summer we came to this beach, Steven was only a year old. That was the year we discovered it takes only slightly more equipment to get a one-year-old child to the beach than it does to get a thirty-year-old astronaut to the moon. There was, for instance, the fifty-pound playpen to ensure that a child who could crawl the four-minute mile would not try to retrace the route of the Mayflower in reverse. And of course, to protect the tender skin of said infant, a forty-pound beach umbrella—not to mention various changes of clothing, bottles of orange juice, diapers, lotions, and ointments. It took us a half hour just to get this stuff from the car to the beach. I put Steven in his playpen. He took one look at the whole setup and began to shriek. He was too hot.

I picked him up and marched him down for his first encounter with the Atlantic. It was hate at first sight. He screamed. He was too cold. I took him back to his playpen and gave him a bottle of orange juice. He smiled. I smiled back at him and prepared to bask in the sun.

Steven went glug-glug for three minutes and twelve seconds. Then he started to shriek. He had a load in his diapers and did not like it. I plopped him down on the blanket to perform a series of ablutions. He smiled. He was clean. I, however, was holding a paper diaper full of one of the largest mounds of infant excrement I have ever seen. How could a child that small have produced such a massive creation?

Alan gagged and ran for the ocean. I marched about looking for a trash can. There was none in sight. I started walking up the beach, noticing that people were giving me a wide berth. I walked half a mile up the beach. No cans. To make matters worse, the diaper was beginning to sag and tear. I decided to bury it. I came back to the blanket and quickly shoved the diaper under a corner of it. I did not want my fellow beachgoers to see what I was doing, so I kept up an ersatz conversation with Steven the whole time I was digging: "See, Mommy is digging you a nice tunnel. See the pretty tunnel. Isn't this fun!"

Then I jammed the diaper in the hole and threw sand in on top of it, breathing a sigh of relief.

A strange look came over Steven's face. At first I thought he was smiling. But then he gritted his teeth, as if he were attempting to bench-press 300 pounds.

I looked at him with horror. "You wouldn't do that to me. Have a heart, kid, it's my vacation too!"

His face got red, the veins stood out on his neck. Then an expression of blessed relief came across his face. Another masterpiece. Like Michelangelo, he smiled in triumph. Then, of course, he screamed. Michelangelo did not have to sit on the ceiling of the Sistine Chapel.

But things got better as he got older. He went through a phase, when he was three years old, when he actually liked the beach. In fact, he liked it so much that he refused to leave it. The words, "Time for Mommy and Steven to go home" produced in him the same reaction that police dogs and fire hoses elicited from marchers in Selma. At age three he had civil disobedience down cold. Like a rock standing in the water, he could not be moved.

So I had to try to wrestle with the blanket and the beach toys with one hand and carry a limp child in the other. But one day I decided the time had come for a showdown.

"Time to go home," I announced.

Steven sat there like Mahatma Gandhi.

"If you do not come now, Mommy is leaving."

Not a whimper. Not the flicker of an eye. He was stonewalling. But two could play that game.

I picked up the pail. "See, Mommy is taking the pail. The pail is going home."

He didn't blink, he just sat there with his toes in the water, defiant.

"The shovel is going too. And the towels." I stuffed the towels and shovel in the beach bag.

He gave me a look that said clearly, "Who gives a damn about the towels and the shovel?" It was time for my trump card.

"Mommy is taking the roly-poly beach toy." I jiggled it so the little bells rang and the little boats moved.

He blinked. "Ah-ha," I thought, "he is on the ropes." I began to pour it on, relentlessly.

"See, roly-poly beach toy goes in the beach bag. All gone. Roly-poly beach toy is going home. Now Steven is going home with Mommy, right?"

He sat still, looking at the bag with the pail, shovel, and roly-poly inside. Then he said, "No."

"No? What do you mean, no? You are three years old and I am your mother and it is against law, tradition, and precedent for you to say no to me. Do you understand that?"

I hunkered down to his level. We were eyeball to eyeball. He didn't blink. He said, "No."

"All right," I said to myself, "now he's asking for it."

To him I said, "Well, then, Mommy is going home. Good-bye."

The ultimate weapon, infantile fear of abandonment. I had read Jean Piaget, the psychologist. I took several steps up the beach saying to myself, "Sorry to do this to you, kid, but with my superior knowledge of psychology you're no match for me."

I turned around. He sat there. I took five more steps. He didn't budge. "Soon," I thought, "he will crack. He will come running to me crying, 'Mommy, Mommy, don't go!'"

In a minute I was on the sidewalk, twenty-five yards away. He sat unmoving by the shore. I shook my fist at him, "You'll crack! It's just a matter of time! They all do!" I hollered. Three teenagers looked at me strangely.

I got into the car and ducked down out of sight. It was the final blow, the naked use of power—a rotten thing to do, but it was him or me.

Silence. No whimpers, no pitter-patter of little feet on the sand. I raised my head and peered out of the window. Steven was making a sand castle by the edge of the water, happy as a pig in swill. I pounded my fist against the car door. "Curse you, Jean Piaget, your infantile fear of abandonment isn't worth a damn!"

I marched down and scooped up Steven. He went limp. "No," he said.

"Kid," I said, "if only we'd had you at Panmunjom, North Korea would have had a franchise in the NFL by now."

But I never got discouraged. The beach remains, for me, a promise of sensual delight—the sun on my back, the warm sand between my toes, the cool water against my skin. Ignoring the rest of my family—now huddled in the middle of the blanket as though they are in steerage—I leap up and run with my arms outstretched to embrace the sea. I plunge in, executing a perfect shallow dive.

My blood-curdling scream unsettles oysters nestled in their beds. At first I think I am having a coronary. Then I remember that this is the North Atlantic, and the amateur town athletic teams aren't called the Vikings for nothing. I grit my teeth and begin to swim. In five minutes, I have lost all feeling in my extremities and my lips are turning blue. I splash around, telling myself what a good time I am having. I give an energetic kick, and begin the breast stroke. Suddenly, I stop. There, floating just under my nose is one of the exotic bits of flora and fauna that these waters are noted for.

And isn't it nice that I don't have to be a marine biologist to recognize it—Trojanus Discardus—courtesy of the sewage treatment plant in Boston Harbor.

Alan

Sportin' Life

THE BEACH intimidated me. You couldn't eat plums there. As soon as you pulled a plum out of your brown lunch bag, it automatically covered itself with sand. The water sometimes produced squishy jellyfish, which, according to neighborhood legend, sought out kids to poison them with their tentacles, right through the soles of one's sneakers. When I was a teenager, a lot of the guys took up weight lifting. It looked boring. I never took the time to develop "definition" in my arms. They do not exactly ripple with muscles. Going to the beach meant sucking in my stomach and not breathing a lot. It meant that most of us had to watch the rest of us sit around and flex deltoids or tripods or whatever the little bumps under the skin are.

The rest of us could take solace in swimming. When most of you is under water, nobody cares if you are fat, skinny, or well muscled. Mostly, the boys swam. In those days, girls didn't swim much, because it would "roon" their hair. That's how they said it, when we asked how come, when it was ninety-two degrees and they were twenty feet from the shoreline of the Atlantic, they never went into the water.

"You wan' me to roon my hair?" one would respond. Instead, they rooned their bodies by constantly exposing their skin to heavy solar rays, sweating profusely and greasing their sweat hourly with glop from a tube. Sometimes, when we tried to throw a girl in the water (hey, I bet nobody else ever thought of that, hah?), she would slip out of our arms into the sand, which would immediately cake on the sweat and glop.

At summer's end, we launched football season. Pro football then was just a sparsely attended game played in a few cities by guys who didn't look that different from most adults, in that they weren't seven feet high and did not weigh in at 250 pounds minimum. It was also an easier game to understand, because specialists and complex plays hadn't been invented yet; a lot of guys played both offense and defense; there was more kicking, and quarterbacks, ends, and fullbacks were known to engage in said kicking.

Football was at its most complicated down at the street level. We played tag rush, usually on the street or in a driveway. If there were three guys to a side, the field was crowded. The captain and his team of two would "huddle" on the pavement, while he took a stone and drew the play. Even if we could have seen what the hell he was drawing, it wouldn't have made any difference, because it was so complex. To do those plays we made up you'd need not only an eleven-man squad, but the whole bench and maybe the band. While we huddled, the other side would try to shake us up by yelling, "Hey, c'mon, it's gettin' late," which it was, or, "My muddah wants me home fah lunch," which she did. We would scream back, "Tough luck, we got our lasties," which was not quite how Sid Luckman or Sammy Baugh would have put it. Sometimes, one of the other team's players would accidentally step over the line of scrimmage—that is, the ball lying in the middle of the street —and would be accused of "tryin' to steal our play." We never questioned how he could possibly do this, if we could not even see the damn thing from three inches above the pavement.

Winter was basketball season, which meant two guys in a vacant lot shooting baskets, except in heavy sleet storms. In spring, we officially reopened the baseball season. All it took to do this was one other guy, one bat and a rubber ball. We "opened" with one of us throwing the ball to the other. The other would drop the ball, and we'd both applaud. Unless somebody was around to sing the national anthem, we then broke for lunch.

On Sundays, when most of us were off, we walked a mile to the one alleged baseball field and played two seven-inning pickup games, a doubleheader, no extra charge to the fans (the latter consisting mainly of small kids who sporadically chanted, "Canweplayyyyy? Canweplayyyyy?" prompting the larger people playing to respond, with sportsmanlike character, "Screw, kid, getattahere!"). Between innings, we showed off for the girls by performing such athletic feats as heaving the baseball at their faces or chasing them around the infield while try-

ing to trip them with bats. As one grew older, some of the more individ-
ualized athletic endeavors were introduced, such as pool, bowling, and
chasing one girl around her living room.

The University of Massachusetts opened my eyes to other sports that
I never had imagined existed. Like javelin throwing, which consisted
mainly of predominantly white sophomores running around the football field with spears and shouting, "Haya, haya, haya, kill the white
hunters!" In this sport, the wind usually was against me. I felt like a
World War I German cranking out poison gas only to feel the wind
turn it back on him. I'd throw the javelin, the wind would turn it
around, and it would pursue me down the field.

There were hurdles, which dramatically increased the number of hernia cases at the infirmary. There was volleyball, in case anyone wanted
to join a nudist colony someday. There was wrestling, which I almost
got away with, because I worked out a deal with my cousin Lenny. One
day, he'd beat me. The next day, I'd beat him. On the last day, the
coach smiled at me and said, "Today, you go against *him*." Him was a
very quiet western Massachusetts farm boy, very polite kid. He could
afford to be polite. God had carved him from one muscle. He pinned
me in 3.2 seconds. It still stands as a university record for inglorious de-
feat.

The best athletic offering was archery. All the city kids liked archery,
because most of them had had to leave their weapons at home. Bows
and arrows were the closest they could get to zip guns. Just touching
the quivers brought tears to their eyes, usually because they grabbed the
wrong end of the arrows. The trouble was that city kids did not take
naturally to the bow and arrow. A lot of arrows didn't hit the straw tar-
gets. A lot of arrows, one might say, fell short. They fell off the bows.
They pierced the ground in front of the archers. They came close to
piercing the archery instructor, who concluded that the safest place to
stand was near the target. The injury rate was higher than at Little Big
Horn.

I retreated often at UMass to the pool room, where I felt more
secure in the smoky haze of a hundred unfiltered cigarettes, where I felt
some kinship with the pale young men who scurried around the tables
like rats and whose idea of a declarative sentence was, "Shit!"

Caryl introduced a whole new world of sports events to me. She described it all as a step up to the sort of high society of sports. Her lesson
plan, or as I came to know it, her *Mein Kampf*, included four basic activities—tennis, skiing, boating, and horseback riding. Under duress, I
tried all four very early in our career, when we lived in a somewhat rural
area of New York State. In New York City, I had impressed Caryl by

beating her in footraces on the sidewalks, pothole jumping, and catching subway doors just at their moment of impact. Now, in the country, her respect for me would undergo awesome challenges.

Boating was the first debacle. She insisted we go to a local lake. That sounded good. It sounded better than it looked. The local lake was covered with a green slime. It looked like a vat of penicillin in its early stages. "I'm not diving into that crap," I said.

"It's just flora and fauna."

"Who?"

"Natural growth," she explained, diving in and reemerging in slime, looking like the creature that ate Tokyo.

"Are you flora or fauna," I asked, before pulling my pants back on over my trunks.

"Okay," she acknowledged, "swimming here isn't great."

"So let's go home and get you disinfected."

"So let's go boating."

I turned as white as she was green. She noticed.

"But you grew up near the ocean. Why don't you like boats?"

"I stayed awake nights, listening to their mournful foghorns, their dirges of death and destruction. I saw them go out to sea, never knowing if or when or whether they would return. Call me Ahab. Also, once when I went out in a dinghy, I got nauseous."

"That's 'cause the ocean swells. This is just a very quiet lake."

For once, her propaganda had the ring of truth to it. Indeed, the lake was quiet. It was more than quiet; it seemed to be dead. But at least I wasn't nauseous. It wasn't bad. Boring, but not bad. We sat in a little wooden boat and rowed in the slime, and the horseflies and mosquitoes bit our cheeks and ears. Even Caryl got bored, so we rowed the four feet back to the dock and tied up our trusty craft. I hadn't screwed up, so I was saying things like "trusty craft" in my mood of euphoria. The mood would prove to be fleeting.

Another couple was trying to shove off, with some difficulty. "I'll help," I announced with newfound confidence. I walked to the edge of the dock, leaned over, and pushed their boat away. Their boat left the dock, and so did I. My departure, unplanned, lacked some grace. My reemergence was worse. I thrashed about in the water and began to panic. The dock was slippery, and I couldn't get a grip on it. I was starting to tire and began fearing the end.

"Caryl, I can't get up. Throw me a rope, a tube, something." She looked worried, because I was worried. When I looked at her looking worried, I got more worried. The process was escalating, and I was nearing an untimely and ungainly drowning in a little-known, stagnant pool of gunk—so much for helping others.

"Loop," she yelled, "how deep is it?"

"How the hell do I know? I'm treading water"—gasp—"trying to"—gasp—"keep my head up"—gasp.

"Have you tried standing up?"

I'm fighting for my life and she's conducting an interview. Maybe before I sink forever she can get in a couple more questions—What do you think of the Cold War? Your hobbies? Something that will flesh out the obituaries. "Are you stupid? Stand up? You want me to drown?"

"Just try."

I would humor her. I stood up. The water came to just below my waist. I spent a lot of time telling Caryl she could stop laughing now.

Of tennis, only the briefest mention is necessary. From playing Ping-Pong over the years, I had developed a great backhand, which served me well in my first tennis excursion with Caryl. "You have a natural backhand, Loop." I puffed out with pride. I even mastered the serve. But Caryl, the expert, said man cannot rally by backhand alone. She tried teaching me how to grasp the racket so I could hit a forehand, like normal people. I never quite grasped the grip; I never learned to hit forehand. In the process of trying to learn, however, I did manage to lose my natural backhand. I also managed to lose every match.

Caryl's attitude is that we must never rest. "We live in such a beautiful area," she said often back then, "it's a shame not to take advantage of it."

"But it's winter," I whined one snowy day.

"Winter sports!" she announced suddenly, pulling out of a closet a uniform of boots, ski jacket, gloves, scarf, and hat.

"You gonna build a snowman?" I asked, jumping up excitedly. "Can I put the raisins in for his eyeballs?"

"Skiing, Loop, skiing."

"Oh my God!" She could have said, "Pogrom, Loop, pogrom," and it would have brought less of a panicked reaction from me.

"Skiing? Who goes skiing? Scandinavians ski, because there's nothing else to do up there. The Finns attacked the Russians on skis during the war. That's it."

"Loop, people pay hundreds of dollars to book trips up here to ski, and it's practically in our backyard."

"There's a big, mean mother of a dog in our backyard too, but you don't see me out there playing with him."

I tried every gambit, including a promise to learn tennis and go boating, come the spring. In desperation, I pointed out that I had no uniform for skiing. All I could do was pull slacks over my pajamas, an old high school leather jacket over my shirt and pajamas and an undershirt, and an old Army fatigue cap.

"Perfect," she said.

As it turned out, I didn't mind falling down thirty or forty times each time I took downhill on the beginners' slope. I got used to the stares of ski instructors, one of whom later said he was laughing at my clothes, not my skiing ability. I didn't even mind when the same guy passed me for the fourth time and yelled, "You're still on your first run?" Nor was I fazed when perfectly suited ski bunnies looked at me as if I were one of those Fresh Air Fund boys up from Queens for a day on the slopes. What tired my body and patience was trudging back up the slope on my skis, a torturous process made necessary by my failure to master the return lift. I would catch the rope just like the person in front of me, but there the similarity ended. The tow would continue up the hill without Lupo. I would be lying there, sprawled in the snow. "Hey, mister, would you hurry up?" a little kid screamed. He would scoot right up there. I took to trudging uphill. After a couple of such trips, skiing lost its glamour. I spent the rest of the afternoon getting drunk in the lodge and discussing the relative merits of Aspen and Vail. I lost a little credibility when I told the other drunks that Arthur Aspen was a damn sight better skier than Vernon Vail would ever be.

I avoided skiing the rest of the winter, a task not easy in a place where winters begin early in September and last through April. Having exhausted my list of excuses, I spent January through April hiding from Caryl. I'd go off early to bars or stay in the closet or just drive around town until dusk. Sometimes, I'd use shopping as an out by purposely forgetting stuff.

"Oh, Jeez, Riv, would you look at what I did. I went all the way to the store and only got one tomato." I'd slap my forehead. "Gee, I don't know where my mind has gone. I'll be right back." Out the door, slam.

I looked forward to May. Winter was ending. Having gone skiing, I figured I didn't owe her boating or tennis. What else was there she could find to torture me with, I wondered, as she burst in one day to tell me she had found a stable.

"Big deal. We got cars. If you can find a good garage in town, I'll get excited."

"For horseback riding, Loop. It's fun. We used to ride in Maryland."

By then, my picture of Maryland was of a vast country club in which healthy looking Nordic people never worked, but spent their lives thwocking tennis balls, schussing down ski slopes, rowing in slime, and also, apparently, galloping about on horses.

"You want horseback riding? Go call your alumnae association from that fancy college. Get in touch with Buffy and Muffy and Puffin and Bobo and Dodo and go prancing around. No way. This is where Tonto leaves the Lone Ranger." I absolutely refused. There was no way I was going to play cowboy. Ever.

We went horseback riding three times.

I never knew horses were so big. I remembered the pony boy, the kid who sold ice cream from a cart pulled by a cute little pony. I remembered the milkman, who delivered from a wagon drawn by an elderly gentleman horse. I had seen cops on horses, but the cops were big, so the horses seemed to fit them.

So how come, when I went to order a horse, it was bigger than any horse I had ever seen?

"You got anything smaller?" I asked the guy.

"Yeah, you want my dog?"

Funny. The whole place turned me off anyway. It stank from manure. All I can remember from the first time is the stink and the bouncing. I would rather not mention which part of the male anatomy gets the worst of the bouncing.

From time number two, I remember again the stink. I also remember the flies and Jerome Aumente's bouncing. Jerry is a swarthy man from New Jersey who married one of Caryl's college friends, Mary Healy, another white woman, this one from the Virginia outback. Aumente is a decent sort who used to play tackle football on the street. In other words, he understood sports—real sports. Mary is an equally decent sort, but like Caryl, had been misled in her middle-class environment to believe that activities like boating and horseback riding were healthful.

"If Alan can go, Jerry," Mary and Caryl scolded, "you certainly can go riding."

"If Jerry's willing to go, Alan," they said, chortling, "you certainly should go."

When this tack didn't work, they tried something more subtle. "The big, tough city kids are yellow-bellies. The big, tough city kids are *yellowwwwwwwwww!*"

At the stable, I quietly spoke to the greaser in charge. "I want the oldest, slowest, smallest horse you got, and I'll make it worth your while."

He brought out a typical horse, big, snorting, with fire coming out of his nostrils.

"This is old? This is slow? This is small?"

"The only older one I got," he said, "is dead."

"I'll take *him*."

"He's gone. It's this or nothing."

I climbed up on the thing, and then I smiled. It shuffled. It actually shuffled. Jerry, fear etched on his face, and Mary and Caryl, smiling, the wind whipping through their Aryan hair, took off at a trot. My horse walked over to a large pile of manure and stopped. The stench was unbearable. The flies were as thick as flies. They rose from the manure and buzzed around my head.

"Hi, ho, *schmuck*, move it!" I kicked her in the flanks, in the bow, the stern, the flanken. I kicked her in the head. I wanted slow, but this was ridiculous. The horse grunted and stood there, in the middle of the manure. I couldn't dismount or I'd sink in manure. The dead horse would have moved faster. I tried to throw my leg over one of the flies. "C'mon, Old Paint!" I urged. The horse remained still. I recited the mourners' Kaddish.

Occasionally, I heard a yelp of pain and looked to the hedges, where I'd seen bobbing up and down the top half of Aumente, a death-mask grin of fear and pain engraved on his face. I didn't know which was worse—bouncing parts of my anatomy or being eaten to death by manure-covered flies. In which circle, I wondered, would Dante have placed this?

When the hour was up, Mary and Caryl, their faces flushed, rode up, reined in their horses, and said something about what a glorious day it was. Jerry bounced in, grinning and mumbling. Yeah, gee, he had a wonderful time, we should do it again someday, preferably after he got out of intensive care. The stable man led my horse out of the manure pile. He smirked and asked, "Was she slow enough?"

The third time was the last time. A Jewish guy from the Bronx had started a combination nightclub and horse riding stable out in the wilderness. He was a heavyset guy who liked to wear a cowboy hat. He got on his horse. Caryl got on her horse. I got on my monster. We trotted. It wasn't bad. I wore a jock and there were no manure piles. Caryl's horse started to gallop. The Bronx cowboy's horse saw her horse and also started to gallop. My horse saw her horse and his horse and, having no mind of its own, started to gallop.

"Whoa!" I yelled.

"Stop!" I yelled.

"Stop, you sonofabitch!" I yelled.

"Oh Christ!" I yelled.

"How do you stop this frigging horse?" I screamed to the birds, the trees, the dirt.

The more I yelled, the faster it went. I watched the earth speed by at warp seven. Astronauts go more slowly than I was going.

"I don't know about you, baby, but I'm getting off at this stop." I lifted myself out of the saddle. The horse panicked. No normal rider gets off a horse while it is galloping. I do. I lifted off. The horse reared. I fell on my ass and bounced on my head. The horse panicked more and took off alone. Caryl's horse reared and, naturally, she brought it under control. What a marriage this was. Dale Evans had ended up with one of the Three Stooges. "Are you all right?" she had the effrontery to ask me as I lay there.

The Bronx cowboy galloped off after my riderless horse. His horse headed for a tree limb. His horse kept going. He did not. A basic rule of the sport is that when a moving rider meets an immovable tree limb, said rider will suddenly stop. To avoid the tree limb; Ringo Bronx fell off his horse and spent the next month with one arm in a cast. Caryl and the three horses arrived safely at the stable.

After that, my reputation got around. Even if I wanted to go riding again, no stable would have me. Parents began telling their children of the urban horseman, and that if they kept still at night they could hear in the distance the cloppety-clop of horses' hooves and a voice singing out mournfully, "How do you stop this frigging horse?"

Caryl

Travels with Alyssa

I HAVE written off horses as a mode of travel for the family. Despite the fact that his grandfather was in the Czar's cavalry, Alan does not seem at all interested in horsemanship. But that's all right. There are other ways to get places. Jumbo jets, for example. They can take you much farther than horses, and to more exotic places as well. I usually try to broach the subject gently to Alan, who believes that the only civilized mechanism for getting from one place to another is the trolley car.

I start with a few subtle hints. A few years ago, after I had wandered around the house for two weeks whistling "Rule, Brittania," Alan got the idea.

"No," he said.

Though I've belted you and flayed you
By the living God who made you
You're a better man than I am, Gunga Din.

He said, "Put it out of your mind."

This royal throne of kings, this sceptered isle,
This precious stone set in the silver sea.

He walked out of the room, saying, "We can't afford it."

"Yes, we can. I'm getting a check for a story that will get all of us on a 747. Roger and Carolyn have been asking us to come for ages."

"We can't go to England," he said. "The V-2 rockets."

"They stopped dropping those in 1945."

"You can't be too careful when it comes to the children."

In the end, he promised he'd go if I promised never again to recite a line written by any person holding a British passport. I think it was in the fifteenth stanza of "They're Hanging Danny Deever in the Morning" that he cracked. Then we came to the Alyssa question.

Alyssa was two at the time, the possessor of a notoriously queasy stomach where travel was concerned. My parents offered to babysit for Alyssa while Alan, Steven, and I took the trip. Alan would not hear of it. I argued, to no avail.

"Look, I'm not suggesting we hand her over to a band of gypsies. My parents will take good care of her."

"Of course they will. She loves them. It's *us* she'll hate for abandoning her."

"We are not abandoning her."

"Tell that to her psychiatrist."

And that was how it came to pass that I was standing in the lobby of the Pan Am terminal at Logan Airport one hot summer night holding the hand of a two-year-old person who looked like a little doll in her Prince Valiant haircut and her lacy pink-and-white pantsuit. Beneath the lace, however, lay a determined spirit that would have done justice to the Iron Duke or an aging mule. Alyssa Rose Lupo had definite ideas about the world and her place in it, and woe to those who would trifle with them.

Alan and Steven came walking toward us across the lobby.

"The bags are checked. My folks are parking the car. We'd better go over by the gate."

As if in response to some cue that only her ears could hear, Alyssa sat down on the floor.

"Come on, Alyssa," I said, "we have to go."

She did not move. The line of her jaw tightened.

"Not *now*, Alyssa. Don't get stubborn with me now!"

Her gaze met mine. The limpid blue eyes had taken on a steely cast seen only in the orbs of Mafia hit men and IRS auditors.

"*Alyssa, get up. Get up or we will leave you here!*" The last was a throwaway line. I had long since given up on infantile fear of abandonment. The steely gaze did not flinch.

This was not exactly a new situation. Alyssa pulled her sit-down strike, on the average, three times a week. I knew what to do—what I always did—reach down, grab her, and pull her to her feet.

So I did.

Alyssa let out a shriek that could be heard at the end of the runway. My heart dropped to my toes. That was not the usual wail of protest. That was pain, pure and simple.

"Omigod!" I gasped, and picked her up in my arms. Her little arm hung limply at her side. Her eyes were filled with tears. Alan's parents came running across the lobby. They looked at me. I read the message in their eyes. It said M-U-R-D-E-R-E-R.

"The aid station," I hollered. "Loop, get the bags, I'm going to the aid station."

I set off at a dead run. The aid station seemed miles away. In fact, it *was* miles away, in another terminal. I ran through corridors, with Alan's parents chugging behind. Alyssa was whimpering and I was chanting, "Oh, baby, Mommy didn't mean to hurt you, *mea culpa, mea culpa, mea maxima culpa,* Mommy will never hurt poor little Alyssa again, Mommy is a rotten mommy, she should be trampled on by elephants wearing cleats. Poor baby, we'll get a doctor right away!"

We finally made it to the aid station. It had a sign on the door: CLOSED.

We double-timed back to the lobby where Alan had reclaimed the bags, rushed out to the car, and drove frantically to the community hospital nearby. The doctor wasn't there. A nurse said, "You'll have to go to the Mass. General."

I was muttering, "Rotten Mommy should be hung up by her thumbs with buzzards plucking out every bleached hair on her head. *Mea culpa.*"

Back we climbed into the car, rode through the tunnel in the traffic and crawled along the crowded expressway. Every time Alyssa whimpered I felt a dagger plunge into my heart. I ran into the emergency room with Alyssa in my arms and gasped, "My daughter, her arm, we need help!"

The clerk at the desk handed me a form. "Fill this out and take a seat," she said, not looking up.

I struggled with the form, trying to balance Alyssa in my arms. Alan was trying to park the car someplace within a ten-mile radius of the hospital.

By this time, it was nearly midnight, and the emergency room was entertaining the usual long-hot-summer crowd. Alyssa and I sat down between the guy with the gunshot wound in his thigh and the guy who had his face slashed with a beer bottle.

Now and then people in white would come by, peer at us, and ask what happened.

"Well, she was sitting down and I pulled her arm, just by accident—"

"Sure," they would say. Then they would examine her arm, point to the spots where the sunburn had peeled, and ask, "How did she get these cigarette burns?"

People started to move away from me in the waiting room, sneering with contempt. Even the guy who got shot trying to knock over a liquor store dragged his bad leg five seats away. Nobody wanted to have anything to do with a child abuser. I stopped explaining. The next resident who asked me what happened, I snapped, "She was trying to roll a drunk and he got hostile."

We sat and sat and sat as the doctors took slugs and knife blades out of people. Alyssa whimpered now and then. It was 1 A.M. when we finally got to a doctor.

"Dislocated elbow," he said. He put his hand on her elbow, pushed, and something went *snap.*

Alyssa smiled. She sat up. "Ooooooooooh," she said. She hopped down from the examining table and started to play with the tongue depressors, happy as a clam. She chattered cheerfully away in the car on the way home. Steven was asleep in the back seat. Alan and I were basket cases.

"We go bye-bye airplane?" Alyssa chirped.

We rescheduled the flight for the next night, despite Alan's mumblings that this was an omen, that we were not meant to set foot on British soil. This time we made it onto the aircraft without mishap. The big jet rolled down the runway, about to lift off. Suddenly, the pilot slammed on the brakes, throwing all of us forward against our seat belts. The pilot's voice was cheery when he came on the intercom.

"Sorry, folks, the tower forgot to tell us there was an Air France plane landing where we were supposed to take off."

"I knew it!" Alan said. "A crazed man has taken over the tower. It is the guy on the zoning board of appeals I said was involved in conflict of interest because he converted his pasta factory into a condo. He is waving a pistol and shouting, 'Lupo will never get to the white cliffs of Dover alive!' "

But finally we were airborne, cruising at 35,000 feet. My game plan was for Alyssa to doze happily in my arms for a few hours, then I would give her a bottle. Alyssa did not like my game plan. She decided it was time to be fussy.

I was prepared. I pulled out her bottle. She slugged it down like a wino with a pint of Muscatel. When there was no more milk she got angry. So she threw her milk bottle. As a two-year-old, she already had an arm like Lefty Gomez.

"*Aaaahhhhhhhhhh!*" came a cry of pain from three aisles back. She had beaned a banker on his way to London for high finance. He glared at me as *I* went back, apologized and retrieved the bottle. I refilled the bottle and gave it to Alyssa. She slurped happily for a time. Then it was empty again.

"*Owwwwwwwwww!*" This time she got a middle-aged lady from Brockton on her way to visit her sister. The bottle hit her on the head, bounced into the air and rolled under a row of seats. Just at that moment, the cabin went dark for the movie. Alyssa began to cry from frustration. Alan and I had to get down on our hands and knees to hunt for the bottle. Each time we grabbed someone's toe because it seemed to have roughly the same shape as an Evenflo bottle, we evoked cries, grunts, or curses. At one point Alan and I met nose-to-nose in the middle of the aisle.

"Remind me," he said, in the measured tones of a man pushed way, way beyond murderous rage, "to talk to you about this trip."

Alyssa did not sleep for one minute of the six-hour trip. Steven kept whining, "Alyssa's making so much noise I can't sleep." By the time we arrived at our friends' house we looked like the cast of *Night of the Living Dead*. Alyssa was thoroughly jet lagged. Her little internal clock was thoroughly snafued. Because of this, she awoke each day at 2 A.M. and began to screech. When she started, the idea spread like the plague. Our friends' children chimed in. Oliver, one-and-a-half, began to shriek; his baby sister, Lucy, opted for rhythmic chanting. The dog bayed. There was more wailing in that house than the entire Greek chorus for *Oedipus Rex* could have produced.

One night our friend Roger, driven to the brink by the incessant crying, stomped into Alyssa's room and hollered at her in her crib, "Shut up, you little twit."

And Alyssa, invoking the spirit of the Boston Tea Party in the face of British authority, promptly threw up over the rail.

Alyssa was probably crying because she was constipated. She had constipation attacks at strategic times—usually at the top of a turret in a castle after we had spent twenty minutes climbing the stairs. One day we planned to meet my best friend from high school and her husband, who were dragging their two children across the map of England just as we were. As we all sat down in a restaurant for dinner, Alyssa started to cry. She turned slightly purple in the face, and the shrieks increased.

"I have an idea," said my friend Clare. She dragged me off to the ladies' room with Alyssa.

"I have been pouring tons of Ex-Lax into her," I said, putting Alyssa down. "No use. She's plugged up tighter than the Holland Tunnel at 5 P.M."

Clare held up a knife she had brought from the table.

"Don't you think murder is sort of a drastic remedy for constipation?" I said.

"We are going to make a soap suppository," Clare said. "That poor kid needs help." Alyssa was now turning deep purple. Clare handed me the soap. "I'll hold and you carve."

"Remember," I said to her, "how in high school when you were the editor of the paper and I was your assistant we said we were going to be big-time journalists?"

"I remember," she said.

"Now we are big-time journalists. You are a producer for a network and I am a writer for the slicks. Remember how we said that we weren't going to be like other women, tied down with kids and laundry and diapers? Remember how we said we were going to get the glamour, the fizz on the champagne, nothing but the fast lane all the way?"

"The Pulitzer Prize by the time we were twenty-five, right?"

"Right? So how come here we are, hotshot journalists, 3,000 miles away from the good old Academy of the Holy Names, and what are we doing? We are trying to carve a depth charge for a two-year-old out of a bar of soap. Did Richard Harding Davis ever have to do this? Did Ed Murrow ever have to worry about the impacted residue of a two-year-old's digestive tract? Would David Halberstam spare an instant's thought in the middle of an erudite analysis on The Making of a Quagmire to the problem of plugged-up plumbing?"

"Oh, shut up," Clare said, "and whittle."

Alan

Now, Voyager

CARYL THINKS I shrink from vacation plans because I am anti-fun, or because I don't like hanging around with my family. Nothing could be further from the truth. I love my family. I love fun. I love watching my family have fun. I don't see why my family and I can't have a grand old time around the house. Why do we have to travel to have fun? Where is it written?

I am sorely afflicted with travel anxiety, which takes all the alleged fun out of traveling. Even when we arrive wherever it is that we are going, I am prevented from fully enjoying it, because I know we'll have to travel to get back to wherever it was that we started. I dearly wish that they would start mass-producing that science fiction invention which rearranges your chromosomes in Daytona and immediately transports you fully assembled to Weehauken.

If we are to drive somewhere, I am anxious about sudden ice storms, oil leaks, brake failures, and flat tires, all of which have happened. If we are to fly, I am anxious about turbulence and air sickness, both of which have happened. If we are shipping out somewhere, I am terrified by gale-force winds, seasickness, and errant U-boats whose commanders have not been told the war is over and they're overdue in Bremerhaven. Two of those three fears have come true.

When I was a kid, traveling meant walking, or, if someone was chasing you, running. Sometimes, it meant subways, trolleys, and the elevated. Once you get over the initial fear of toppling over the elevated or falling on the third rail, such travel was usually more fun than what lay at the end of the ride. The arrival of a 1946 two-door Ford in my family began to signal an end to my carefree and somewhat blasé attitude toward traveling.

Kids in my neighborhood learned quickly that, more than feet and subways, *cars* were a mode of travel to be admired, but to be admired from far away, to be washed and shined and worshiped. Adults who never uttered a harsh word to a kid began screaming from their porches and stoops and corners, "Heyoo, get offa da car!" or "Gedahell away from my car!" or "Get your ass off the car!" The end of the war hadn't brought my neighborhood a lot of prosperity, but what little it did bring was clearly not to be shared by those under driving age.

The actual traveling in cars was not much fun after the novelty of the first ride wore off. The upholstery was scratchy, and it gave off a pungent odor after a rainstorm. The insides of cars always smelled weird to me. And driving meant constant arguing. "Close the window, you'll get a cold; open the window, I can't breathe; close the window, you'll get pneumonia."

In addition to the standard window argument, we had the direction argument. The nondriving adult would question the direction taken by the driving adult. The driving adult would say, "Jesus Christ!" The nondriving adult would tell the driving adult he could swear all he wanted, but he didn't know where he was going. The driving adult would seem to tear the steering wheel from the socket while asking the nondriving adult if she wanted to drive instead. The kid in the back would try to sink deep down into his seat to escape this battle, but this didn't work, because one adult would say, "Sit up, you'll have bad posture"; the other adult, "Let him lie down, maybe he's tired," and a whole new round would begin.

On the way home one evening, after I had spent the afternoon filling my fat little face with every variety of food imaginable, I informed my parents in the front seat that I was about to heave in the back seat. I told them this as we were about to enter the Sumner Tunnel. In those days, there was only one tunnel leading from downtown Boston across the harbor. One tunnel, one lane each way. On the downtown side was the market, clogged with trucks and horses and wagons. On the other side were the beaches and dog tracks. The traffic jams were very colorful. It's a shame there were no helicopter traffic reporters around to record them for posterity, as I'm convinced the reports would have consisted mainly of "Oh, my God!"

My father stopped short in mid-jam. My mother took me out, where

I proceeded to barf to the honking of hundreds of horns. When you're ten and sick and you barf, and you realize your barfing is causing a tense situation, you get apprehensive about your role in life, so you are prompted to barf further. Years later, when, as an adult driver, I experienced a blowout at the entrance to the tunnel, on a very hot day with one wife and some kids in the car, amid much traffic and honking of horns, I announced quietly to myself, "Barf, barf."

Sadly for me, travel and barf have become interchangeable nouns. My first air trip was not only my first air trip, but I was heading off to the Army. A double whammy—two reasons to be nauseated. But when I survived it, and later flights as well, I got a little cocky. That attitude was promptly taken care of during a shuttle flight from Washington to Boston, a flight I had taken so often I felt like a commuter.

Why, then, was I suddenly overcome with nausea? Why was I dizzy? Why was I suddenly sweating profusely, even though I had ripped off my coat and suit jacket, rolled up my sleeves, and loosened my tie? Why were my hands and fingers suddenly frozen in place? Why did the stewardess, prepared for some run-of-the-mill airsickness, stop dead in her tracks, turn white, and groan audibly when she came face-to-face with me?

"Oh, my!" she said, in tribute to her training, for, staring back at her, was a sweating, terribly pale, frightened man, his shirt and tie disheveled, his mouth wide open and his hands clawing the air with paralyzed fingers. Oh, my, indeed. She told Caryl this was certainly very interesting, and she had never seen anything quite like this before. Caryl asked if that were so. Yes, indeed, she allowed, this was so. I am turning into Mr. Hyde, and the two of them are discussing this transfiguration with the detachment of two West Pointers discussing the Crimean War.

She handed me a barf bag and told me to breathe deeply, to chew, to lie back and close my eyes, to relax, to do anything but drop dead on her shift. When none of this advice seemed to help much, she or Caryl got the bright idea that ice would help. Ice would cool me off. Ice would shock me out of my paralysis. Ice it would be, because what else was there? So this lovely woman with long, slender fingers seemed ready to pat me on the back. Hey, nice. Then she dropped two cubes down the back of my neck. Talk about rejection. It cooled me off, and soon, I could move my fingers. I was still shaky, and I had a chill down my spine where the ice was melting. Caryl smiled and said, gee, maybe sitting in the tail when flying through a northeaster was different than sitting in the middle. I had told her that, dammit, I had told her that! I

146   LEISURE WORLD

figured out quickly which one of my fingers had the most life in it and promptly stuck it up in the air to answer her observation.

"I'm glad you're feeling better," she said, smiling. That was 1964.

In 1965, she suggested an all-new adventure theme: ships. I reminded her of our unsuccessful boating trip (see page 131). She said, "Ships are not boats." I retorted, "Geese are not skunks. Your turn." She responded, "Ships are big, especially the ones we're going to take. They have stabilizers in them that stabilize them." I said that was wonderful for the ship, which would not throw up, but what about me, which might? She said I would get my sea legs. I began sweating. "Loop, they're great big ships that cross the Atlantic. They don't pitch and roll." Neither, I reminded her, had the Lusitania.

But Caryl appeared to be right. The Atlantic crossing was smooth. It was even fun at moments, such as eating. Our cabin was not exactly what the movies had prepared me for, however, unless we are talking about movies relating to old submarines. It was the size of a very small closet and seemed, at first glance, to have no beds, windows, or portholes. It contained, imbedded in a wall, a very small vent which, when activated, sent a gush of cool, smelly, forced air into our quarters. I reached the vent by pulling out the bunk bed, approximately the size of a stretcher, and crawling up the wall. If I kept my mouth to the outlet, I could get enough fresh air before Caryl yelled, "Dive! Dive! Dive!" Perhaps others on the ship were lulled to sleep by the sound of water splashing against the ship, but in Black Hole No. 144, we grabbed what shut-eye we could to the steady throb and whine of the engine room.

"Isn't this exciting?" Caryl yelled one night over the whirr and clank of the ship's innards.

"What?" I screamed back from one foot away.

"Isn't this exciting? Isn't this romantic?"

"No," I screamed. "This is what my immigrant grandmother called steerage. And it was cheaper then."

Outside the cabin, however, was a great dining room and some bars, all kinds of decks, swimming, shuffleboard, and whatnot. All that, despite the fatalistic dialogue between two elderly Irish-American female tourists who, as the ship departed New York harbor, said wasn't it a grand day and a grand sight, and well might it be, for it just might be everybody's last trip. I needed that like I needed the engine room symphony every night.

But on balance it was a successful trip, and I was ready to take a ship again, anytime, anyplace. I didn't have long to wait. Early in November that year, we alighted from the train that had brought us to Calais and prepared to board one of the sturdy ferries that ply the English channel.

After we boarded and immediately made friends, I sensed, standing at the bar, a strange movement to the ship. Two visions swept across my mind—one of a man hyperventilating in the back of an aircraft, and the other of a little kid throwing up in front of a jammed tunnel entrance. They passed quickly, but a little voice nagged inside my head, "Barf, barf."

"Is there a dog on board?" I asked.

Two of our new friends looked at each other and excused themselves from the table.

"I think it is going to be a very rough trip here and my stomach is beginning to feel lousy," I said.

"Soft American," some foreigner muttered with a grin.

"Up yours, and I'm taking a stroll outside on the deck." I got up and out. On the deck, something very strange was happening. A storm was happening. A very big storm, as it turned out. In a while, people like me were told to get off the deck. Damn! If the crew was worried, what was I supposed to be, Captain Courageous?

In another half hour, most of the civilian population of the ship was collectively heaving. In another quarter of an hour, the crew members, apparently feeling left out of the fun, joined them. One who didn't was the captain, who seemed totally plastered. "Dinner!" he yelled gleefully at one point, as the crockery crashed to the floor. Another who did not was I. I lay on a couch, my head buried in my jacket, listening to the crash of dishes on the floor and the tinkle of glass as the waves smashed through the front deck and the screams and moans of those who only one hour earlier had questioned my seagoing virility and my Americanism. Caryl was wandering back and forth, trying to find a stabilized area. I told her *home* was a stabilized area. I told her we were not going to travel anywhere again, except by foot to a movie or a grocery store.

It took more than seven hours to make what was normally a three-hour trip. We would later learn that this was a brutal storm, the first of the winter season. When we docked at Dover, an English customs official looked at the wan, sickly people standing in line with their mouths open and tongues lolling about. "Bit of a blow, eh, what?" he said. I wondered how many years in the Tower you could get for killing a customs official.

The English train, as usual, was warm and cozy. We sat back in our seats and sighed together. Everything would be all right now. Returning to England was like returning home. In four months overseas, I had developed a sore on my eye, stayed awake forty-eight straight hours on the Orient Express, and developed the first stages of colitis in a quaint Spanish town called Colera, which I insisted should be spelled Cholera.

Soon, we would be back at our bed-and-breakfast place in London; we'd throw a shilling into the gas heater, crawl under the thick quilts, and sleep peacefully. We were OK now.

"It's nice and warm in here," Caryl murmured.

"Actually, it's a little too warm," I said, looking around.

"Do you smell something?" she asked.

"The frigging train is on fire!" I yelled.

To my right and rear, flames were shooting up from the tracks outside the train window. Two Englishmen were sitting next to the windows. They viewed the fire and looked at their watches. To me, the fire meant an ugly end to an ugly trip, an anonymous and somewhat inglorious death. To them, the fire meant at least a seven-minute delay in departure time. I turned to Caryl and told her that I had put up with an awful lot, and if she wished for some reason to continue this marriage, she would promise me, then and there, no strings attached, that there would be no more channel crossings. *Nada más. Nein. Nyet.* Over.

She agreed.

Why, then, on an August day in 1979 was I breathing strenuously in what should have been a comfortable seat on one of those sturdy little ferries that ply the English channel? We were all staying in Sussex. It was so nice. The house was big and airy and filled with happy kids and adults. The backyard was enormous and neatly trimmed. The temperature in the swimming pool was perfect. The booze was free. We were really leeching off friends in the finest manner. Why was it necessary to go to Paris? Because after I argued Caryl out of side trips to Bulgaria, the Hindu Kush, and the Mongolian border, the only place left on her list was Paris. It seemed the safest.

The day before our departure, it rained heavily. Even the British weathermen, who do not get visible coronaries every night over air masses in the style of their American counterparts, seemed a bit put off by the storm. "Keep raining, you mother!" I prayed silently, knowing our hosts would join me in convincing Caryl that crossing that channel in such a storm was what put an end to Spain as a power—imagine what it would do to us.

But by morning the rain had dwindled to a drizzle. The skies were still gray, but there seemed to be no wind, at least not until we arrived in Newhaven, where the wind suddenly appeared and was happily smashing waves against the dock.

"Well, the ferry is big and it isn't moving much at the dock," I said, with a trace of a whimper.

"Oh, that's a big ship and it's got stabilizers," she said.

"Don't, after fourteen years of relative marital peace, resume that stabilizer routine with me," I warned her.

Within ten minutes after departure, and for the next three or four hours, the only discernible sounds on the ship were the "Breaaaaaaggggghhhhhllllcchh" of barfing and the "Ohhhhhhhhhhhhhhhh" of groaning. The hypertension hit me early. Alyssa was pale and about to use a little baggie. Steven went to the bar to get a crewman. The guy, a wine steward or something, came bouncing down the aisle expecting to find a spoiled American tourist unable to handle a little *mal de mer*. He looked at me and turned the same shade of pale that had afflicted the stewardess in 1964. Yep, partly paralyzed again, the old sweat routine, etc. By now, I knew what I was doing, as I had been told by doctors. I was hyperventilating. When one is apprehensive, one might hyperventilate. If you're worried about getting apprehensive, because you don't want to hyperventilate, you probably start hyperventilating from worrying about it. When you're doing this on a ship that thinks it's an amusement park ride, you tend to scare French wine stewards.

"I don't feel so good," Steven said.

"Breaaaggghhhllch," said Alyssa.

"Breaaaggghhhllch," said Caryl, who now had her own bag.

"CouldImaybeliedown?" I begged.

The steward led me to a small room with double bunks. I smiled wanly, as a soap-opera character about to depart unwillingly but bravely. I rolled with the rolls; I pitched with the pitches, but I was lying down. From outside the room, I could hear the moans, groans, and an occasional scream or cry. If I was going to go, I thought, I might as well be lying down ahead of time.

A burly deckhand showed up in the doorway to tell me in French (the goddamn boat goes to England every day, but nobody speaks English) that I am not supposed to be in the room. I point to my heart, indicating that this is more serious than a bit of barfing. "*Non mal de mer. Non.*" The guy ran away.

Moments later he reappeared, this time with a female bureaucrat. We went through the same routine. I was magnificent. She shrugged. After a babble of exchanges with the wine steward and the burly guy, they left me in my misery. My fingers were coming back. I could feel a little life in them. I was beginning to relax, when a young couple stumbled in. With barely a look in my direction, he propped his back against the bunk and held her tightly around the waist, while she barfed into the sink—or tried to, beset as she was with the dry heaves.

"Oh, O-li-ver!" she screamed repeatedly. "I'm going to die! I'm going to die!"

This was not good for my mood. Too much of this and I could start getting nervous again. It would be hyperventilation time again. I pushed myself up on my elbow and asked weakly, "Would you like to lie down?" (Please say no!)

"No," Oliver answered. "It would be better if she could throw up. I have to hold her like this because I think she threw out her back, and it hurts her to bend over."

"Oh, Oliver," she rudely interrupted, "I'm dying!"

Once or twice in a man's life, the man and the moment are joined. Some call it grit. At such moments, the quiet guy in the platoon charges the enemy tanks—which, having been on the tank end of that, I think is pretty piss poor strategy—but, be that as it may, there are such moments of heroics for all of us. It was here, in mid-hyperventilation, in mid-storm, in amid-ships, or wherever the hell I was lying, that I reached such a moment. I pushed myself up again and said, for some reason in a Bogart accent, "You're not gonna die, *shweetheart*. You're gonna be OK. Now, I got a bad heart [OK, I lied—but "I got bad hyperventilation" doesn't quite make it] and I'm gonna make it, kid. If I can make it, you can make it!"

I fell back down on the bunk from the sheer exhaustion of my small act of courage. Oliver seemed ready to applaud. He smiled in appreciation. The woman turned around for the first time and looked at me as if to say, "What kind of screwball is this and where did he come from?" She would have said it but nature called. "Arrgghh, Oliver . . ." Etc.

Once on shore, in France, I touched Caryl's hand, gave it a gentle squeeze and suggested, "I think what we need is either a marriage counselor or a travel agent."

Caryl

The Magic Kingdom

ALAN TAKES more vows, where travel is concerned, than a cloistered nun. His list of Things I Will Never Ever Do Again is by now quite lengthy. But I am resourceful. My tactic is to start with something that really makes his skin crawl—like the four-color brochure on the four-teen-day walk in the foothills of the Himalayas with four gurus and fifteen Sherpa guides sponsored by a travel agency that is a front for Reverend Moon. After that, selling him Disney World was a snap.

He knew we'd have to go to Disney World eventually. It's middle-class America's version of a pilgrimage to Mecca. Every family that can scrape up the cash must make the long and arduous journey to a shrine peopled with more minor deities than the slopes of Mount Olympus: Mickey, Donald, Huey, Louie, and Dewey. With frayed nerves and tat-tered wallets the faithful stream through the turnstiles of the Magic Kingdom, intent on giving every child his or her birthright: the oppor-tunity to gawk at a six-foot duck in a blue jacket—the only place you can see that outside of the delirium tremens—throw up on Space Mountain, and run through more coin of the realm than a high-class Bar Mitzvah could account for.

The first thing we realized, as we drove up to the borders of the Magic Kingdom in our rented, super-economy-rate sedan, was that we had left American capitalism and rugged individualism behind. For the next six hours, every move we made would be ordered, planned, and directed, first by perky female voices on the Disney radio network—all we could pick up on the car radio—and then by a series of squeaky clean adolescents who seemed to belong to a family of clones. Disney World may be the world's first *working* socialist state. Everything is timed, planned, orchestrated. The trains do run on time. "This is what it must have been like in the early days of Mussolini," Alan observed as a clone waved us into our assigned parking spot, Goofy 54. If only Eastern Europe had taken its cue from Walt Disney instead of Karl Marx, the West wouldn't have had a chance. The dummies built the Berlin Wall, when they could have put up Cinderella's castle and had the people battling to get *in*.

Once inside the park we wandered, mouths agape, down Main Street. If Walt Disney ever read Sinclair Lewis, he never let it show; no dusty, provincial little hicksville here. Main Street was so perfect it took my breath away. The paint fairly shone on the buildings, the window glass sparkled, the gutters were unmarred by as much as a gum wrapper. I began to wonder, could this be what heaven is like? The perfection set my teeth on edge. I began to long for just one shifty-eyed mugger; a lone panhandler with stubbled chin and rancid breath, bumming a dollar for a cup of coffee; one piece of racist graffiti spray-painted on a wall: "Minnie Mouse is a honky." There was none to be found.

Alyssa let out a squeal of delight and began tugging me in the direction of a ride called "Flying Dumbo." I soon found myself standing in a long line, looking up apprehensively as, directly above me, very large Flying Dumbos wearing idiot grins dived out of the sky and then climbed again. As a Dumbo zoomed overhead, my palms began to sweat. I became convinced that this was how I was going to die, on a sticky afternoon in Orlando, Florida. I was going to be fallen upon by a 300-pound Flying Dumbo.

There I would lie, only my sneakered feet protruding from beneath the still grinning, fallen behemoth—just like the scene in *The Wizard of Oz* when Dorothy's house falls on the Wicked Witch. People would snigger reading my obit: "Mother of Two Mashed by Falling Dumbo." I suddenly felt waves of nausea. My daughter smiled up at me. "Isn't this fun!" she piped.

On and on we went, standing in lines, perspiring in the heat, being whirled nearly to unconsciousness in a spinning teacup. But it was for the children, no sacrifice too great to bring them joy! At one point Alyssa stood absolutely still, amazement and rapture on her face. "Oh, my God!" she said, her small voice full of absolute wonder. This made it all worthwhile, the plane tickets, getting lost trying to find the motel, getting lost trying to find the car rental place.

"What is it, Alyssa, sweetheart? What do you see?"

She pointed down at her shoes. "Look! Look! My shoelaces make a perfect figure eight!"

Three hundred dollars for the plane tickets alone. Not to mention the motel, the rental car . . .

Steven looked up at the sun. "You could sweat your ass off in this place," he said.

I saw the news stories in my mind's eye: "A mother of two was arrested in front of Mr. Toad's Wild Ride today when she apparently went berserk and tried to garrote her children with strings of licorice purchased at the Main Street candy store. Police said she was babbling something incoherent about shoelaces as she was carried off in a strait-jacket."

Still, we pushed on. After all, this was once in a lifetime. We still hadn't been through Pirates of the Caribbean. As we approached the entrance, we gave a sigh of relief. No lines in front. We bought our tickets and entered, to find ourselves in a winding, narrow corridor built to resemble an ancient dungeon—and the corridor was packed with people. Each time we turned a corner there was another corridor—and wall-to-wall humanity. A half hour passed. Forty-five minutes. Alan is prone to claustrophobia. The crowd began to murmur, the mood turning ugly. Alan's palms began to sweat, he found it hard to breathe.

"A thirty-nine-year-old father of two suffered a coronary today in Pirates of the Caribbean," he muttered. "When he fell, he tumbled into the underground stream and his bloated body floating through the pirate displays immediately became one of the most popular tourist attractions."

A man directly in front of us in line put his ear to the wall. "There's a man on the other side of the wall tapping out a message in Morse code," he announced. "He says he's been in line for four years now." Finally we reached another turn. There before us was—another corridor, another sea of people. Alan peered at a skeleton propped up in a cell off the corridor. "That's Irving Shapiro, a real estate salesman from Perth Amboy. He bought his ticket in 1969." The grumblings from the crowd grew louder. "How thick could these walls be, anyhow?" someone asked. People can be oppressed for only so long. The spirit of rebellion was brewing. I could see how it could be:

"A group of middle-class American tourists rioted today in the Pirates of the Caribbean attraction. They began a frenzied charge through the corridors screaming revolutionary slogans, 'Death to Mickey Mouse!' and 'To the guillotine with the lousy dwarfs!' Staff workers in the Disney World attraction had to beat the crowds back with maces and axes from the displays."

Rebellion was averted only by the fact that around the next turn was —the ride. We sailed through pirate battles and emerged, weary, on the other side.

"My shoe hurts," Alyssa whined.

"I'm hungry," Steven whined.

"I'm thirsty," I whined.

Alan hummed his own version of "Cocktails for Two." "In some secluded rendezvous, that's where I'll leave the lot of you."

Alyssa wheedled me into another ride on the Flying Dumbo. Alan looked up at the two of us flying through the air, a beatific smile on his face. "I'm leaving now. You can have the kids and the house and the dog and the cat and the five books of tickets to the rides."

I shook my fist at him. "I'll track you down to the ends of the earth!" I knew how it would go:

"A mother of two went on trial today for hunting down her estranged husband—who had deserted her five years earlier on the Flying Dumbo—and beating him senseless with a Mickey Mouse cap with the ears filled with lead. The judge, who had just returned from Disney World for two weeks with his four kids, ruled it justifiable homicide."

After ten hours, we broke for dinner. Our motel was outside the park. It is easier to get an audience with the Pope than a room inside the Kingdom. We got on the monorail, then on the steamboat, then on the tram that took us back to Goofy 54. After dinner we decided we had to see the fireworks, so we drove back to the Kingdom, parked in Mickey 73, climbed on the tram that took us to the steamboat which took us across the lake where we stood in line and bought our tickets. Once inside, Alyssa stood still and looked at her shoes.

"What's the matter, sweetheart? Don't you want to see the fireworks?"

"No."

"Don't you like fireworks?"

"Yes."

"Well, Alyssa, what is it that you want?"

"I think I want to throw up."

Alan

The Last Time I Saw Paris

"I READ," Caryl says one morning, "that you can get a wonderful lunch in Paris just by picking up stuff at the stalls. It's like a picnic."

Caryl has a habit of believing what she reads. She told me that she read that Disney World was cool and not crowded in March. But then, Caryl believes things she reads in pamphlets handed out by Moonies. Why do I listen to her?

A picnic, though, sounds like a good idea, given that after throwing up across the whole English channel (see page 147) and sitting for hours on a train while my kids whine "Everybody on this train has something to eat. We're hungry. If we stare at those people with bread, will they give us some?"—after all of this, we blow eighty bucks for dinner slightly larger than the Parisians had during the Prussian siege of 1870.

I do not ask where Caryl got this information about stalls and cheap eats, perhaps because I am hungry and we are fast going broke. So Caryl takes us on a forced march, which she calls tour, of Paris. We are duly fascinated. There is water in the fountains, people feed the pigeons, the grass is green. Nobody pees in the Palais Royale garden. No one gets mugged under the Arc de Triomphe. The people are pleasant, for now that the U.S. dollar is worthless, Parisians feel no need to be rude to Americans anymore. Algerian beggars give us money. "Very nice, Caryl. Oh yeah, look at the flowers, kids. Mmm, very large boulevard they got here." But by 2 P.M. it is six hours since *le petit déjeuner*, and that was pretty *petit*. Alyssa's hair is over her face—at least, I think the kid behind the hair is Alyssa. She is the same height, and I hear kvetching from behind the hair. Steven is lying on the hood of a parked car, not ours, and breathing dramatically. He may be trying to tell us something. I am sitting on the sidewalk. My clothes droop more than usual. Caryl is hunched over from the camera around her neck and the pocketbook on her shoulder. She looks like a female Quasimodo. Very lovely. I must look at our wedding pictures when we get home.

For an hour we have been looking for stalls: the famous food stalls she read about in the book whose title I never learned. "So far," I say, gasping in the midday heat, "this is not a picnic. This is the Bataan death march."

We are getting desperate and begin looking for cheap restaurants, a search that proves as successful as the trip to the stalls. Most of the restaurants have in their windows signs which, when freely translated, say: "We're on vacation until the return of Charlemagne and the greater glory of France. You wanna stand out in the heat, stupid tourist, that's your business. We're swimming in post-Franco Spain. Go eat your heart out."

"Steven," I command. "Steven, look for a restaurant! Steve, look, boy, look! Look for one with a Master Charge picture on the door."

Steven hones in on a building across the street and points. We follow. It is a restaurant. It is open. It takes Master Charge. That we can tell from the outside. Inside are other details we hadn't counted on.

The place is dark, not poverty dark, as if they can't pay the light bill, but expensive dark. The place is carpeted. On the floor. On the walls. When I think back, I think I remember carpeted urinals, but trauma does that to you. It takes awhile for our eyes to focus. I remember an Army lecture on night vision and how they told us we shouldn't be scared when we were alone in the dark in the woods because our eyes would get used to it. (My eyes got used to it. They communicated to me that I was alone in some dark woods.)

Now, in the restaurant, my eyes focus on what appear to be some gleaming white specks in the distance. I stare hard. They seem to be moving. After a few minutes, they take shape. They are the teeth of the headwaiter, who is dressed in dark, formal clothes, and the movement is that of his mouth as he asks in French if he or any other human can help us. The look on his face suggests that we are beyond help. The French is polite in tone, but I am convinced that he is saying to the other life forms near him, "*Alors*, a light-skinned gypsy family has come for a handout. How quaint. Take them to the kitchen."

Caryl and I are not to be deterred by our sloppiness, our less-than-Continental appearance. We jabber back in English, high school French, Spanish, mainly sign language punctuated by Indian grunts.

"Uh, this restaurant, no? You serve food here, *oui?* Uh, *deux* big persons, *deux* small. Small persons hungry. Uh. Master Charge. Not too late to eat, *s'il vous plaît?* Tired, *mucho. Merci.*"

Ahh, they are laughing. Clearly we have captivated them. They show us to a table. It is in a corner, a good distance from the door. It takes awhile to get there. The table is in Belgium. We have to step over the body of a waiter who was sent to this table as punishment some years earlier. It is hard to see him because of the underbrush and wild flowers. There seems to be some arguing to our rear among the assorted waiters, waitresses, host, bartender and others. Again, I can only infer from the tone that the subject of the debate is us. Could it be that our dirty, sweaty bodies, clothed in basic American urban relaxing weekend garb diminishes their enthusiasm as restaurateurs?

Given the lateness of the hour, few others are in the restaurant. Across the room are three middle-aged men around a small table. They wear magnificent suits, which fit them. They drink coffee from small cups. They smoke cigarettes, holding them the way an artist might hold a brush. I am convinced that when they light up, no one says, "Butt me, Billy Baby, will ya?" They stare at us. They all grin at once. They leave quickly. We sit there, staring at the menu, stupidly written in French. I don't understand French menus. I always misread them. *Roast boot with verdes? Fresh poison garnished with chicory?* Also, there is another element nagging at me. Something is out of place here. Besides us. It has something to do with the Oriental carpets on the walls and the scimitars. It is related to the music being played on the stereo. It is Arab music. Oh my God, it's an Arab restaurant! We not only don't find her stupid stalls with the pickup food, but in the middle of Paris we don't even find a French restaurant.

"Jeez!" I announce. "I don't want to get caught in the middle of a cross fire."

"Now what are you talking about?" Caryl asks.

"This is an Arab restaurant."

"No kidding, Dad," Steven says sarcastically.

"A Doiiiiiiii!" Alyssa responds in a Mortimer Snerd voice. It's her cute way of saying, "Stupid!"

"I've been reading about guerrilla warfare in Europe between the Israelis and the PLO. If anyone comes through that door, they're gonna shoot first and ask questions later. Hit the floor, and I'll cover you all with my body."

"*Pardon, monsieur?*" The maitre d' has appeared. I wonder how long he has been listening. Can he tell I am Jewish? Who are those three other guys and why did they leave so fast? What the hell is on the menu anyway? I grin back at him.

In broken English and Spanish, in French and with much movement of the hands, he explains that this is a Lebanese restaurant. I am relieved. With broken French, Spanish, and English, I explain that back where I come from there are many Lebanese, that I have eaten at the restaurants of the Lebanese, that I have drunk the wine of the Lebanese. "Some of my best friends are . . ."

What would we like to eat? Oh, well, heh, heh. Yes, the menu is up-side down, we can fix that. Heh. Heh. Hmm. Would I mind if he suggests something? Why, no, given that my family has aged visibly since we first entered. He smiles. "An assortment of hors d'oeuvres and mixed grille?"

Hey, not bad. It makes sense. I had a mixed grille at Barney's in East Boston a few weeks ago—a little lamb, a little kielbasa, a little Italian sausage—about six or seven bucks at the most. It was a good meal.

Having ordered, we sit back to hum along with an Arabic version of the Mormon Tabernacle Choir, complete with massed violins wailing in a minor key. We are immediately attacked by five waiters, four in the front line, with a linebacker in reserve in case one up front falls in the line of duty. They attach a small table onto our regular table. They rearrange our plates, our glasses, our wine, our silverware, our clothes, our chairs, the pocketbook, the camera. One is about to begin ortho-dontia on Steven's teeth when the food arrives. It arrives in a truck. The five waiters begin piling saucers of appetizers everywhere they find a space. One waiter thinks he is re-creating the Eiffel tower. He keeps building the plates higher and higher. When Alyssa moves her right hand from the table to scratch her forehead, bang! they slam a platter down where her hand had been. They are putting plates everywhere, on the table, on chairs, on the floor . . .

They are suddenly gone, all five of the waiters. They have come and gone like raiders in the desert. They leave behind them four persons whose lives will never be the same, four persons stranded in a foreign land with thirty saucers full of Middle Eastern hors d'oeuvres.

Steven and Alyssa decide they like the chicken wings. Steven and Alyssa decide that's *all* they like. That leaves twenty-nine other appe-tizers and only two persons to share them. That leaves, for example, three dishes of cut-up cucumbers in some kind of sauce. It leaves ground meat, some in loaves, some in balls, some just floating around waiting for a rescue team. Twice during the appetizers, Alyssa goes to the bathroom. Steven hits the rest room once. I go twice. Caryl can't get up out of her chair. Since she travels with a great fear that she will lose her camera, she always wears it. It weighs her head down, and her head seems stuck in some sort of vegetable dish.

"Mpphh," she says.

"Ma's eatin' vegetables," Steven exclaims.

"Alyssa, pull your mother's head out of the plate and ask her to pass the stuff that looks like polluted shrimp."

For an hour or more, we eat. First, we say things like, "Oooohh," and "Umm, interesting." Then we say, "Oh my" and "I wonder what that is?" Then we say things like, "Gee, I think I'm full" and "I wonder if we can get a doggie bag—*un* bag for *chiens?*" And then we say things like, "Urgghh" and "I gotta go again" and "Oh, my God, will this never end?"

The smiling platoon of waiters returns. They begin taking plates away. God bless them. They actually are cleaning the table. Caryl and I rub our stomachs and grin and say, "Mmmmmmmm." The waiters smile. Good. They know we liked the thirty appetizers. I kick the kids under the table. Alyssa has her pre-throw-up face on, but manages to groan, "Hmmm." Steven looks up and says, "I gotta go!"

Now the pressure is off. We can have a small coffee and relax. We have met the appetizers, and they are ours. They have thrown everything they have at us, and we haven't caved in. We ate it up and forced it down. We did it our way. We joked about how they were force-feeding us, about how we'd grab the daggers and spears off the walls and fight our way out of the restaurant, how they would pursue us down the Champs Elysées throwing kibee balls at us, while we dueled our way to freedom. And now, now . . . now they are putting clean plates in front of us and clean silverware. There are two reasons to do such a thing. One is to get rid of customers fast to make room for new ones, but we are the only ones in the place. The other is—oh, no—the other is to serve more food.

"*Non!*" I scream.

"*Non?*" a waiter echoes with a look of disbelief.

"*Merci, non!*" I plead.

He gets the maitre d'.

"*Non?*" says the maitre d'.

"Was very good. The food. *La comida.* Grub. Nice. Ummm. *Nada más.* Eat more, children get sick. *Comprendez?*"

He looks like a dog who has been told that he cannot go out. He looks, in a word, hurt.

"He's hurt," I tell my family.

Alyssa is groaning quietly, rubbing her stomach. Steven is slouched down in his chair, eyeing a gilded knife on the wall. Caryl is pleading with her eyes.

"We can't do it, guys," I say. "We're not gonna be the Ugly Americans. We're gonna eat."

"We just ate," Caryl whimpers.

"We just ate the hors d'oeuvres, Caryl. We have not eaten the mixed grille."

"You're kidding me," she says.

"*Un peu*," I plead with the man. "*Solo un peu*." I hold my thumb and forefinger up, parallel, with only a tiny space between them.

"*Un peu*," he says, reassuringly.

He returns, bent over from the burden of lugging in four massive trays of meats—lamb, veal, kidney, steak, beef, brontosaurus, wild boar, canned boar, dog, cat, pigeon. Whatever fleshy animal ever existed, there is a piece of it on each tray. Each of us gets a tray. Steven looks at me with eyes that beg for relief. Alyssa is no longer in sight, as she has sunk past the level of the table. Caryl is laughing, some might say hysterically. She still has veggies on her nose.

"Everybody make believe you're eating," I command. "Move your forks around, kids. Caryl, you do what I do."

I eat from my plate and Caryl eats from her plate. I eat from Steven's plate and then from Alyssa's plate. Caryl eats from Steven's plate and then from Alyssa's plate. I eat from my plate, Steven's plate and Alyssa's plate. Caryl eats from Steven's plate, Alyssa's plate and her plate. Caryl is now sinking down in her chair, perhaps to check out Alyssa under the table. I eat from my plate, Steven's plate, Alyssa's plate and Caryl's plate. Then from Alyssa's plate, Steven's plate, my plate and Caryl's plate again.

A half hour later, they find us. Caryl is choking on her camera strap. Alyssa is lying under the table. Steven is sitting transfixed, his eyes resting on the glittering blade handles. I have three forks and two teaspoons in my right hand and one fork, two knives and a napkin in my left hand. Pieces of meat are splattered over my face and stuck in my hair and I am muttering to myself, "Clean your plate like a good little Alan. Clean your plate like a good little Alan."

They tell me a few days later that the bill was 699 francs, which came to $175 that day on the international exchange. They tell me I laughed and threw down the equivalent of another twenty-five dollars for a tip. They tell me I didn't stop laughing for the rest of the afternoon. I heard the three of them say often that they were so full they would never eat again. A few hours later, Steven and Alyssa asked if there was anyplace in Paris where you could get pizza. They say I had to be physically restrained from attacking my children.

Part Four

Muddling Through

Caryl

Good-bye, My Fantasy

I WISH to propose a moratorium on sexual fantasies; not on having them, mind you, but on writing about them. I do not want to hear one more word about anybody's erotic imaginings. I suggest we stomp through My Secret Garden and trample all the blossoms and we assign the psychologist who writes "Sexual Fantasies, case # 573" for a hip women's magazine to the nutrition beat where he can wax eloquent over the sensual delights of cauliflower. I have had it with SF—and I don't mean science fiction.

The reason is not that I am a bluenose. I have no objection to whatever consenting adults do—as long as they don't do it on the freeway and frighten the automobiles. But I now find myself in the same position in the sexual fantasy department as I was when I was fifteen years old—too mortified to talk about it. The reasons, however, are different.

When I was fifteen, a sweet and innocent product of a convent school, I was not supposed to know anything at all about sex, much less to have fantasies about the delights of the flesh. Said flesh was to be kept buttoned up inside the blue serge uniform with the sailor collar and cuffs.

And, in fact, my body was as pure as the driven snow—it was just inside my head that one could find a veritable Sodom and Gomorrah. Or so I thought, at any rate. My actual knowledge of the field of erotica was not huge. I thought that sodomy was the act of living in the place that got destroyed by lightning and that oral sex was something dirty done by a dentist. The literature I had read on the subject included *Kiss Me Deadly* by Mickey Spillane, a bootlegged copy of the University of Maryland freshman hygiene text—it had a paragraph on VD and masturbation—and my grandmother's library of books by Frank Yerby.

I sat and thumbed through my grandmother's gothic romances, knowing full well I was skating on the thin edge of eternity. Sister Angela had described eternity in a valiant effort to keep the sophomore class away from the mortal danger of the soul kiss. "Think of a high mountain, and a sparrow flies by once every thousand years and brushes the tip of the mountain with its wing. The time it takes that sparrow to wear down that mountain is only an instant in eternity."

I risked damnation for Yerby's purple prose, in particular *The Saracen Blade* and *Goodbye My Fancy*. The former featured a great deal of pseudo-medieval grammar, and much rending of garments accompanied by erotic moans. " 'Ohhhhhhhhhh,' she said as his virile hands probed beneath her tunic." That sort of thing. *Fancy* had a southern motif, and rending of garments was also very popular, except that taffeta bodices replaced Byzantine silk. In these epics, men were whipped into fevers of lust by female bodies, but mine did not seem to have that effect on people. I kept half hoping that as I walked home from school one day, some errant male—who looked just like James Dean—would be so blinded by feverish lust that he would lure me to some exotic and secluded spot, rend the blue serge, rip off the little red tie, untie the brown oxfords, and teach me about Being a Woman.

I was, I thought, a hopeless lecher, doomed to that special circle of hell reserved for the degraded ones. There we would be, hanging by our thumbs and roasting nicely to a turn, Bluebeard, Jack the Ripper, the Pope who had all the illegitimate kids, and me—still in my sailor suit and oxfords. Every now and then a devil would come by and give me an extra poke, reminding me that I had brought eternal shame to the Academy of the Holy Names, the National Honor Society, and the Catholic Students Mission Crusade.

Now, the problem with all this is that early developmental experiences tend to stay with you—some people, after all, have traced Watergate to Richard Nixon's potty training. It is very easy to get stuck in the stage of one's early fantasies, and I am forced to admit that Adolescent Convent School Imagery leaves something to be desired. I get this sinking feeling inside when I read the tide of literature that has come upon us about other people's erotic imaginings. I pride myself, after all, on my creative imagination—do I not make my living as a writer? It seems that it is required of me to have more inventive fantasies than,

say, a plumber or a dental hygienist. But I am awed by the sheer poetry
of the things *they* come up with.

One woman, for example, said she imagined herself in a lovely garden filled with huge, exotic flowers. They all turned, at her whim, into
sexual organs with which she could experience ecstasy. Now there is a
class fantasy. I could never have dreamed it up. Never, in my wildest
imaginings, have I considered transport with a tulip. Or for that matter,
a black-eyed Susan or a hibiscus. I totally overlooked the erotic potential of flora and fauna.

Then, I discovered that animals are very sensual to other people. I
still think of animals as cute and cuddly, as in "The Wonderful World
of Disney." Dumbo was not, as far as I was concerned, a sex object. But
other people's fantasies have a starring role for animals—German shep-
herds being the quadrupeds most often doing a star turn in "Sexual
Fantasy, case # 4172." Little did I know that when I thought I was
being avant garde by leering at the hairy chest of Robert Redford, somebody in the row behind me was casting lascivious looks at the furry
front of Rin Tin Tin. Where did I go wrong?

When I was fifteen, I couldn't talk about my fantasies because they
were so terrible, so lurid. Now I can't talk about them because they're
boring. *Déclassé.* If the roving psychologist with the tape recorder came
along to hear *my* wild imaginings, how could I tell him about this guy
in a leather jerkin wearing a jeweled Saracen blade at his waist, declaim-
ing, "Maiden, I wouldn't unlace thy smock!" Or the tall fellow with
the top hat and ruffled shirt who is saying, "Mah name is Courtney
Beauregard and Ah must have you-all, mah fancy, or Ah shall diah!"

I would have to make something up, and everything I can think of
sounds so dated: red velvet whips or Oriental potentates or motel room
orgies. You can see all that at your local neighborhood theater. (My
mother-in-law once took the kids to a kiddie matinee of *Tom Thumb*
and freaked out when the previews were for *The Marquis de Sade.*) I
have to face it, I am a failure in the fantasy department. I have no wish
to be reminded of it. So if you have this terrific fantasy about making
love to Quasimodo while swinging on the rope of the bell tower, or
performing perversions with the Archbishop of Canterbury during high
tea, just shut up about it, thank you. I don't want to hear.

Alan

Mid-life Crisis

You KNOW you're past your prime, when instead of fantasizing about that old Jane Russell poster in *The Outlaw* or Raquel Welch in that cave-girl outfit, you begin daydreaming too much about pension benefits, a lack of political or commercial clout, and job descriptions.

"And what else can you do, Mr. Lupo?"

The lady in my daydream sits behind a desk and diddles around with a yellow pencil. This is daydream No. 46 of the currently popular series, "What Will Alan Do for a Living If and When He Grows Up, His Parents Should Only Live to See the Day."

Alan is trying to get out of journalism, which he's been in for almost two decades. Two decades have made him decadent. After years of newspapers, magazines, books, and television, Alan has a funny idea that all his new stories are reruns. The Wandering Jew of Journalism has reached the end of the road. He wants lucrative new career opportunities. Somebody make him an offer, even one he can refuse just for the joy of it. Why isn't anybody calling? Why is it so quiet in the house? Why is the only knocking coming from the radiator and not from the door? It's time to answer the mid-life-crisis interviewer.

"I was a stock boy and a soda jerk and short-order cook and waiter. I can do all of those. If you're talking seasonal, I shovel snow. I got four shovels—two for regular snow, one for hard snow and narrow passageways, and an ice breaker. I can make school lunches for kids. I do that very good, so the tuna doesn't fall out from between the bread when you cut the sandwich diagonally."

The lady smiles. I notice she has stopped diddling around with the pencil. She looks at me with what appears to be ill-disguised contempt. "You are forty-two."

"Don't remind me. The last place I worked, I was the only one who remembered Pearl Harbor. I don't mean remembering reading about it. I mean remembering *it*. Everybody else thought Tojo was the way I said HoJo's. They thought 'Tora! Tora! Tora!' was an Irish lullaby. I even remembered the song, 'Remembaaaaaa Pearlllll Harbaaaaaa. . . .'"

The lady cuts me off with a jab of the pencil. "Forty-two is not very old. Forty-two is very young. You're as old as you feel, as they say."

Who says these things, anyway? Who are *they*? My whole life, people in authority tell me things like, "Whadda you wearing white bucks for? *They* aren't wearing those anymore." Who isn't? Who, for God's sakes? If enough of us resume wearing white bucks, do *we* become *they*, or do *we* remain *us*? And who's responsible for saying, "You're only as old as you feel." I got a picture in my head of a group of people dressed like monks, with hoods on their heads, wandering around the streets very quietly, and suddenly, like a Greek chorus, in the middle of a crowd of shoppers, they yell in unison, "Better to have loved and lost than never to have loved at all," or "You can lead a horse to water, but you can't make him drink." And everybody stops and shakes his or her head up and down and mumbles, "Yeah . . . right . . . that sure makes sense . . ." and resumes his or her business, while *they* move on to the next town.

"But forty-two is a bit old for soda jerking, is it not?" the lady is asking.

"It's a living."

"You have two college degrees, Mr. Lupo," she says strongly, accenting the words *two* and *degrees*. She adds that I have a lifetime of wondrous journalistic adventures that would come in handy to the lucky employer who should pick up my option.

I'm sure she's right and that it's just a momentary lapse of memory that has totally wiped out all those wondrous experiences. Maybe if I strain hard, some of them might come back.

Like the time I was about twenty-two or twenty-three, late at night, alone in a newspaper bureau, teletyping my story back to the main office from my cold Catskills outpost. Suddenly, a man appears beside me. I am startled. Before I can yell, he shoves a jar under my nose. There is no cover on the jar. Inside the jar is a pile of chicken dung, drying out. The guy is big on the properties and potential of chicken dung. "This," he yells, "is the key to the future!"

Three years later, Omónia Square in Athens. Citizens are demonstrating against the government, which is pretty hard inasmuch as there does not happen to be any government in power at that particular time. Just like foreigners, they are demonstrating in their native tongue. I turn to Ms. Rivers, whose language facility was demonstrated to me in Paris, where she asked for two railroad tickets and was directed to a place where they sell pineapples. "I wonder what they're shouting," I say. No sooner do I say it than a man separates himself from the crowd and offers help. He speaks English, he says. His name is Sam, he says.

"Sam?"

"Sam."

"We're with a newspaper, Sam, called the *Baltimore Sun*."

"Yes, in Maryland," he answers.

"Hey, not bad, Sam."

"Where you live in Maryland?" Sam asks.

We lived in Laurel, halfway between Washington and Baltimore. An international spot of repute, it wasn't. The big restaurant was the Little Pigs of America Barbecue, or something like that, at the corner of our street and Route 1.

"A small town, halfway between Washington and Baltimore."

"What town?" Sam asks, getting impatient.

"You never heard of it. Don't worry about it. I'll spell your name right. What are they shouting?"

"Is it near Bowie?"

"What the hell kind of thing is that to be shouting in the middle of Athens?"

"Where you live, is it near Bowie?"

"How do you know about Bowie?"

"The racetrack. I go to the horses there, when I go to America."

"We live in Laurel."

"They have a track there, too!" Sam is getting excited.

"Sam, what the hell are they shouting, already?"

"Pimlico. You ever go to Pimlico?"

This is called Being a Foreign Correspondent.

The lady in my daydream is unimpressed with what turned out to be my memorable experiences in journalism.

"Have you thought about a related career, such as public relations?"

Then it happens. This is where the daydream gets good. No matter how it starts, it always ends up this way. Sometimes the lady in the day-dream asks me about becoming a scientist and I tell her how it was with me in Chemistry 101, freshman year, University of Massachusetts, when I was the only person who couldn't make right-angle bends in my glass tubing and how I cost the Commonwealth of Massachusetts hundreds of dollars in broken glass tubes. Sometimes they ask me about craftsmanship and mechanical ability and I tell them how it took me three months in junior high school to make a match scratcher, which is a piece of wood planed smooth with some sandpaper glued to it.

"Public what?" I say, getting up slowly but deliberately. I'm wearing a trench coat, slightly soiled from my last urban riot coverage. My El Producto wooden-tipped cigar (eight cents) is dead, but it protrudes menacingly from my abundant lower lip. "I don't flak for nobody, shweethaaart. Not Big Al. Not anybody worth the name reporter. Not when you've stood out in the rain with your guts hangin' out, and ya know ya got a dime left and one chance to crawl to that phone booth, baby, and get rewrite and you dictate, lady, you dictate right off those notes without so much as a pause, you dictate the kind of copy that makes 'em cry at their breakfast tables the next morning: 'A three-alarm fire tore through a two-story wooden frame house at 1314 Crumpet Street, Southwest, last night, forcing residents to flee with only the clothes on their backs. Fire Department spokesman Paunchy Halliday said it was the worst blaze to hit that block since he can remember. The flames were visible from across the street. Thick black smoke spewed from the second-floor windows. The cause of the conflagration is undetermined. No estimate of damage was available. Fireman John Borkowski, of Engine Company 14, suffered abrasions, contusions, and lacerations of the right back when an unidentified male near The Shamrock Hearth Tavern threw a bottle of Budweiser at the firefighter. Police gave chase but failed to apprehend the suspected subject.'"

The lady is somewhat taken aback, as *they* say. She removes the glasses from her eyeballs and suddenly shakes out her hair, which has been in a bun. She smiles coyly and begins to toy with the top button of her blouse.

"Fahget it, shweeeethaaaart. I guess maybe after all I got a couple of good stories left in me yet." I turn and walk out, flicking my cigar stub in her direction.

Enough cigars and dreams and I'll make it to forty-three.

Caryl

Rational Chic

THE LADY in the daydream obviously wasn't me. My hair is short and curly, and that's the way it will stay. I don't have enough hair for a bun. I never really did, except for a period when I went through my fake hair phase. I wore a chignon with so much dynel in it that I was a fire hazard within six feet of an open flame. A cigarette lighter could have turned me into the Human Torch. I tried shoulder-length falls when they were chic. All that hair was supposed to be erotic, but it kept tangling. I usually looked like an extra in *The Snake Pit*.

These days, I no longer pursue the grail of fashion. When I walk into a store I march up to a rack and pick out a jacket, blouse, and skirt all coordinated by the manufacturer. "That, that and that. Wrap them up," I say. I would like to tell you the reason I do this is that I have more valuable things to do with my time than to spend hours shopping for clothes to put on my back, that I object to fashion as an image of idleness and frivolity foisted upon women, and that it is beneath my dignity to trifle with it.

Now, all of those things are true to some degree, but none of them really explains my buying habits. I have finally admitted to myself that I have no "fashion personality," as the magazines put it. Or, to be accurate, I have one, but it is not the sort of thing that would bring Richard Avedon on the run. I discovered my true fashion personality leafing through an old scrapbook, when I came upon a snapshot of me at age eleven, posing at Camp Mayflather. (That was its real name; Miss May Flather was a lady of some repute in the Girl Scouts, despite—or perhaps because of—her unfortunate name.) There I am, standing beside a wooden bridge, my socks drooping limply about my ankles, a wrinkled camp shirt hanging out over stained shorts, my hair curling in random directions in the area of my forehead, and a toothy grin in the midst of it all. I experienced the shock of recognition. It was the quintessential me.

I was relaxed, happy, and obviously not giving a damn that I looked like a movable trash heap. It would not be until some years later that I would begin to follow the dictates of fashion. My most treasured piece of wearing apparel in my childhood was a white holster with a fringe and huge fake gems brought back from Texas by my father which I wore as an accessory to everything. When I went to a convent school I had to wear uniforms, which did not exactly sharpen my fashion sense. My high school uniform was a heavy blue serge dress with a white sailor collar and cuffs and a red tie. We amused ourselves in the cafeteria by dipping our ties in the mustard jar, and since the showers in the gym didn't work, we had to change directly back into our uniforms after sweating through forty-five minutes of girls' basketball. The uniforms soon developed little red rings of perspiration under the armpits, accompanied by a ripe aroma. The finishing touches to this enchanting little ensemble were the triple-roll bobby sox and thick brown oxfords. The look might be called Early Catholic Military.

When I chose my own outfits, therefore, I let my creative imagination run wild. My very favorite little nothing for an evening at the St. Michael's teen canteen was a wide red corduroy skirt worn with a black elastic cinch belt pulled so tight my face turned the same shade as my skirt, a fuzzy white angora sweater, and, at the neckline, an inventive touch: a little piece of red velvet ribbon fastened with a medal emblazoned with a picture of the Madonna and the words, "Excellence in Spelling." It would have put Halston into a catatonic trance.

The next fashion period I lived through was Movie Star Baroque. In my neighborhood, nobody read Vogue. We all wanted to look like the people we saw up there on the silver screen. When Marilyn Monroe was big, the look was peasant blouses worn off the shoulder, hoop earrings, and a sleepy-eyed stare. My friends and I all looked like the children of itinerant fruit pickers hopped up on cocaine, not sex goddesses. I was particularly keen on Kim Novak for a while. The movie flacks let it be known that Kim Novak wore nothing but lavender, so lavender it was for me. I wore lavender skirts, lavender shorts and, on top of those, my CYO all-star basketball jacket which was sort of purple. I would practice my jump shots in this outfit, which Kim Novak was not noted for doing. In my Grace Kelly period I wore long white gloves and long formals when the style was for cutesy-poo little ballerina-length tulle numbers. At five-eight, with a reputation as a jock, I didn't have a prayer of making it as cutesy-poo. I went for regal. At least I was tall, and if I kept my mouth shut the braces wouldn't show.

Movie stars went out with a bang senior year in high school. "Collegiate" was the "in" look, which meant pink shirts, charcoal gray Bermuda shorts, and pink knee socks. I looked pretty ridiculous in those, but not as bad as the kids who were five feet one and shaped like a pear. I bought a camel-colored polo coat for my freshman year in college, but it didn't fit right and always looked like I got it by rolling some tall English gentleman. I got a rash from Shetland sweaters, and nearly went lame hobbling around on three-inch spike heels that would have brought ecstasy to the face of a sado-masochistic foot fetishist.

The search continued as I went out into the real world to seek fame and fortune. I tried all the looks, but they never came out right. In a cape I felt like Batman; I was too healthy for the Victorian pallor of the *My Fair Lady* look, and would have felt ridiculous trying to cover a meeting of the FCC dressed like a Cossack. The Jackie Kennedy look was very big when I was working in Washington, but once I wore an El Cheapo imitation Jackie—Chanel jacket and little skirt—to a party and the genuine item was there. She glanced at me and turned away with what I am certain was a sneer of cold contempt.

When the women's movement came along I tried the jeans-and-boots number, but I kept streaking my hair and wearing eyeliner. It was not precisely a political statement. The miniskirt was fine for petite little things, but when I wore it I looked like second-from-the-right in the chorus line of the Roxy and received obscene suggestions for afternoons of sweaty passion from dirty old men on street corners.

So now I have decided I am going to make things easy for myself. I am never again going to try to mix and match any articles of clothing, for I now have a closetful of stuff which would be worn together only by a person high on sacred mushrooms or totally blind. I will never again try to look like a rajah, a hooker, an astronaut, or Mao Tse-tung. No more fashion-personality nonsense for me. From now on, nothing but the real thing.

Anybody know where I can get a good buy on wrinkled camp shorts?

Alan

Rhapsody in Blue

JEANS, SLACKS, tennis outfits, pantsuits, that's all she wears. Whatever happened to those strapless gowns with the corsages? I liked those. I keep telling her to get one. She says they're dated and adds that we do not go anywhere that one would wear such a thing. She forgets. We may yet.

Years ago, when cops walked the beat, and there wasn't so much crime in the streets because it was confined to the back alleys and the upstairs hallways, a friendly policeman would arrive at the door and ask if we would like to buy a ticket for one buck or less to the policemen's ball. Given the price, most people bought one ticket, which pretty much implied that not many were going, unless all the male heads of households intended to quietly slip away and dance with one another—not a likely event.

People bought the ticket with relief that the cop wasn't there to arrest somebody's brother for kicking out all the support beams of the public library. Numbers players also bought tickets, because it was like gambling: you put a little down now, you never knew what you might win later. Maybe the next time little Nathan hotwired a hook and ladder truck, the policeman who would collar him would be the one you bought the ticket from and maybe would look kindly on the misunderstood kid.

Some people didn't go to the dance because the law was looking for them, and there would be great embarrassment if they were arrested doing the box step. Others didn't go because watching a bunch of cops dancing did not turn them on. Still others were immigrants and couldn't dance in English anyway. The only dances they went to were at the weddings of relatives, or, occasionally, to the funeral of an old enemy. ("When you die, gonif, I'm gonna dance on your grave.")

Now, the cops don't walk the beat anymore. They ride around, two men to a cruiser; and given the size of today's teenagers, two men to a tank ought to be the next clause in police union negotiations. What that means, however, is that instead of a friendly knock on the door, you get a phone call from a policeman asking if you'd like a pair of tickets to the annual ball. Not only is the personal element gone, but the sales pitch has changed from one ticket to two.

This call comes one day when I am not around and Caryl is answering the phone. She will go anywhere. If the morticians were having a grand ball, highlighted by a lecture on "Embalming Since the Harding Administration," she would sign us up.

"Sure," she says happily to the cop on the phone. A few days later, I look at the mail, and there are two fancy engraved tickets to the policemen's ball, each with a tab of something like $2.50.

I was feeling pretty tough. After all, there was no cop at the door waiting for my answer. The mails are impersonal. I knew nothing of the earlier phone call. All the teenage bravado regarding cops came out. "They gotta be kidding," I said, sneering, as I stuck the invitation back into a pile of mail that had been gathering since we bought the house a decade earlier.

Then came the second phone call. I answered it. An officer identified himself and asked if we had received the tickets. If we hadn't, he said, two more could be sent out. I stammered. I felt a rush of guilt.

"Yes, sir," I answered. "Tickets. I think I remember the tickets. Gee, haven't we sent in our check yet? Gosh, time has a way of rushing by." I went on like that for a while. The bravado of pockmarked adolescence was gone with the 195cs.

The problem, it being an inflationary age, was a lack of operating funds to pay for utility bills, much less cop dances. I put the whole issue out of my head. Police are not like fund raisers who come out of New York or Washington who collect for liberal causes and follow up with letters. They're not like the credit departments of stores that send polite notes ("Perhaps you have forgotten the $80,000 you owe us, and that is certainly understandable, and if you've mailed it in, please spit on this note and tear it to shreds and accept our apologies") and then follow through with tougher letters ("Our records indicate an outstanding charge on your part. Failure to pay will result in appropriate measures: arrest, trial, conviction, hard time, and a record for life").

No, I figured, the cops are busy out there deterring crime, saving lives and, for the more courageous, directing traffic. They're not going to notice if one couple fails to send in five bucks, right?

Wrong. There was another phone call. Caryl took this one. "Yes, officer. Gee, I think we did get some. Hey, Loop, did we ever send in that money for the policemen's ball?"

I was too stunned at first to answer. Clearly, the cops were not going to let go of this one. The heat was on, and I knew my days were numbered. Somebody up high must be putting on the pressure and the men in the ranks were up against it.

"Tell them the check is on the way," I whispered. She happily told the officer the check was on its way, as I rushed up to the third floor to write it out, stuff it in an envelope and place it on the top of the dresser, so I wouldn't forget to mail it in the morning.

I did not have a good night.

"Why can't you sleep?" Caryl asked.

"These guys mean business," I said.

"Why are you doing your Jimmy Cagney imitation?"

"Maybe I shouldn't cave in to those coppers. Maybe I should just keep that envelope here and let 'em come and get it, if they got the guts."

"Maybe you should go to sleep."

She was about to nod off herself.

"You know what they're gonna do, don't you?"

"Who?" she murmured, sleepily.

"The fuzz. They don't get that check soon, they're gonna come down here in cruisers, on bikes, maybe an armored car with a SWAT team. They're going to surround the house and play big searchlights all over it.

"'All right, Mr. and Mrs. Lupo. We know you're in there. Come out with your hands up and the check clearly visible, and no one will be harmed.'"

All the neighbors would be standing outside in their nightclothes. They would be straining to see and talking excitedly to one another. "He never was any good, you know. She smiled a lot, but I never really trusted her. The poor children, what they've gone through. You know, they've trained that dog to kill. This was a nice neighborhood before their kind moved in."

"Here's your answer, coppers," I'd yell back, smashing a window. Rat-tat-tat-tat-tat-tat. Screams from the neighbors. Bam! Slam! Kerplow! Fragmentation grenades from the SWAT team. Hssssssss! Tear gas. They rush the door, but I'm going to take as many of them with me as I can. Despite my family's screams of terror, I rush downstairs to meet them with my Thompson submachine gun. The bullets from their service revolvers slam into my chest and I lunge forward and crumple into a bloodied heap at the bottom of the dusty stairs. (For dust, see page 11.)

"Hold your fire, boys," says the sergeant in a thick brogue, which belies his Italian background.

"Jeez, would you look at those dusty stairs," says a young patrolman.

"What's that in his hands?" a plainclothesman asks.

The sergeant bends over me and pulls the bloodstained check from my hands.

"My God," he says, "he had made the check out, too. All this was so unnecessary, so unnecessary."

I hear a familiar voice and look up. My blurred vision clears momentarily, and I see a familiar face. Why, why, the sergeant is the cop who used to come to the apartment when I was a kid and knock on the door and ask if we'd like to buy a ticket for half a buck or so! Had I only known! He recognizes me also.

I try to raise a hand. "I didn't know . . . I . . . I . . . would have mailed the check, had I known it was you . . . I . . . I . . ."

"Don't try to talk, my boyo. The meat wagon is comin'." He turns to the other officers, one of whom says, "You know this bum?"

The sergeant bristles. "Don't you be talking like that about this boyo. He was a good lad, and he came from a good family. They gave every year to the ball, not missin' a one. And he grew up the same way, he did. But something happens to the best of us. Maybe him marrying out of the neighborhood and all, Jaysus, will you look at the dust on those stairs."

"Loop? Loop?" She calls to me in my sleep. "You're restless, honey. Are you OK?"

I wake up in a sweat and stare at her. "You got a nice dress?"

"What?"

"Get one. We're going to a dance."

Caryl

Heel Thyself

So we're going to the policemen's ball. I can't figure it out, Alan was never that big on law enforcement. But when I ask him, "Why are we going fox-trotting with the fuzz?" he gives me this glittery-eyed stare and mutters something about Jimmy Cagney and Thompson sub-machine guns. I decide to humor him. Mid-life crisis makes some men a bit quirky at times.

This means I am going to have to go out and buy some shoes to go dancing in; my blue and white Pro Keds will look pretty silly with a black chiffon skirt. I go to the shoe store and discover with a shock that all the shoes have heels that resemble a letter opener owned by Lucrezia Borgia. Spike heels are back. Terrific! Next it's going to be the rack and thumbscrews. I know from experience that spike heels are strictly for masochists. You'll love three-inch stilettos if you're the kind of person who thinks a fun afternoon is sitting around having somebody rub ground glass into your cheekbone.

I saw my first pair of spike heels when I was a sophomore in high school, at one of those "Back to School" fashion shows sponsored by a department store. A model tottered along the runway wearing a pair of black patent leather spikes that narrowed at the bottom to the width of a ball-point pen. I was hooked. I had to have a pair.

The reasons for my fascination had more to do with my particular pair of feet than with fashion in general. I am one of those people who grew like a German shepherd puppy. My feet grew first. I caught up to them, eventually, but the growth lag left me with a permanent sense that my feet wore name tags—the Monitor and the Merrimack. One of my favorite children's tales was one called (honest to God) "Fairy Foot," which was about a prince with normal-sized feet who lived in a land called Stumpingham, where everybody else had feet the size of rowboats. Fairy Foot suffered much discrimination, and not being smart enough to dream up Affirmative Action, he just sulked a lot. I identified with Fairy Foot, a projection of wish fulfillment, no doubt. Like the black folks who used to use hair straightener and skin bleach, I could not afford the psychic cost of identifying with my own kind—the big-footed Stumpinghamians.

The wonderful thing about the spike heel was that it changed the entire structure of the foot. No longer did the foot just lie there, stretched out, its entire length exposed to public gaze. It would tilt into the air like a high-rise building, and while the foot would not actually shrink in size, it certainly would appear to do so. Suddenly, the flat, "ballerina" shoes in my closet looked obscene, ugly barges designed more for the conveyance of sludge than for the enhancement of feet. Whenever I ventured into a shoe store, after admiring a cute little size-five flat shoe in the window, I was always aghast at the sheer magnitude of the size ten that the salesman brought out. How could a mere five sizes make so much difference in the esthetics of a shoe?

My greed to own a pair of spike heels was unhampered by practical considerations, like whether or not I could learn to walk in them. I had barely managed the style that used to be called "Cuban" heels. (Why they had this particular nickname I don't know, except that they were so squat and comfortable that Fidel could have worn them on a dead run carrying a submachine gun in the Sierra Maestra.) I saved up my shekels for a pair of white linen spikes, and after a half hour of practice, I was almost permanently crippled. If I had been a horse, they would have shot me. But I worked at it, and after considerable time I could move around with the same ease as one of those Chinese women with hobbled feet. So what if I looked arthritic? My feet seemed, if not exactly small, different. More like the Washington Monument than the Pentagon.

The problem was that three-inch heels put me over the six-foot mark. I had been tall before. Now I was the Wilt Chamberlain of high school girls. I gazed desperately about for anybody tall. If a tall ax murderer had asked me to the prom, I would have said yes like a shot.

As it was, I had a lot of thrilling conversations on dates about free throws and the zone defense. I had a wardrobe of spikes for tall fellows and a neat row of ballerinas for short fellows. A cold chill would run down my spine at the question, "What if I fall in love with somebody short?" Would I wear my ballerinas and look him in the eye or clamber aboard my spikes and stare out over the top of his head?

In college, I hung around with a group of girls who averaged five ten in height. In our spike heels we were a formidable group, outlined like the Four Horsemen of Notre Dame against a gray-blue October sky. We ruined more vinyl floors than I care to remember.

I got to the point where I could move pretty well in my spikes by putting most of the weight on my toes and moving at a half trot. I was working as a reporter in Washington then, and there were times when my feet just gave out. I was not an uncommon sight in the halls of Congress, walking from a hearing room barefooted, my shoes in my hand. My worst moment came in the Rose Garden of the White House where I was covering President Johnson, who was receiving a delegation of farmers who were presenting him with a bagful of soybean seeds. (As a glamour beat, the White House is highly overrated, but that's another story.) It had rained the night before, and to my dismay, my heels sank to a depth of three inches in the damp loam. When I tried to move, nothing happened. It took a UPI reporter and a Secret Service man to haul me out. But for them, I might have withered and died on the spot, and White House tour guides could have pointed me out as the first person to die of terminal spike heels.

Spike heels went out of fashion, finally, and my toes uncurled. I now rely on sneakers, boots, wedgies, and—when the occasion demands— shoes with heels that one can stand upon without being in constant danger of falling sideways. I no longer look like a foot-fetishist's mad fantasy of a character in the "Stomp 'em, Tromp 'em" variety of porno flick. I have come to terms with my feet, and I no longer worry about their size. After all, Jackie O sports a pair of size tens, and the *paparazzi* do not turn away in disgust. So what if my lower extremities are large and flat? They run fast, and when I treat them properly they never cause me any pain. Theirs is an inner beauty, and I have a new respect for them. I have made them a vow: I will never, never again torture them by cramming them into a pair of spike heels. They are, and they shall remain, free feet.

Alan

Primitive Passions

LIKE FAIRY tale heroes can hear giants, I can hear her approaching in the distance, coming on homeward in her size-ten shoes. She struggles toward the door. Both arms are full of shopping bags, the kind with rope on the tops, so you can blow a lot of cash in the stores and still carry around the stuff as you go up and down the aisles to spend even more. The guy who invented that big bag did for retailing what Ford did for the assembly line.

She holds one bag in the left hand and one in the right. She carries one bag under her right arm and another under her left. The rope from another bag is draped around her neck. There's yet another held in her teeth. It's the Quasimodo effect. The dog, fearing some alien being and not being smart enough to recognize her anyway, is attacking the door. I let her in, so the dog can jump on her and the bags and slobber her face.

"There's more in the car," is how she greets me. No hello, no how-areya, just, "There's more in the car." She goes out to get it. I don't touch the bags. I'm afraid. In fact, I don't even hang around. I disappear. When I was a kid, I got the impression that it's a sin to spend money. For anything. You're supposed to save money so the next generation can get educated for the kind of work that will enable them to save money for the next generation. I'm not sure which generation is allowed to begin spending some, but I know it's not ours. The trouble is, she doesn't know that.

"Hey, c'mon downstairs and see what I got."

"Do I have to?" I whine.

"C'mon."

I go downstairs.

"Did you get the kids some pants? You said their pants are all short, you know, the ones that last year were too long? You said they have no pants."

She slaps her forehead. "Oh, gee, I forgot to get them pants. I *knew* there was something I forgot."

"You've been gone since 9 A.M. It's now 5 P.M. All day you're in stores and you come home with enough bags for a hernia, and you forget the pants? How about the underwear? You said I needed underwear, because my shorts are torn and shredded. Did you get some underwear?"

"You know, they didn't have any in your size. I looked, but they didn't have your size."

That smarts.

"Ah, what the hell, who's gonna see my underwear. Let's start dinner. Did you do the food shopping on the way home? You told me not to do it. You said you were going to do it. What'd you get?"

She puts on her confessional guilt look.

"You didn't buy food? You got nine, ten bags there, and you didn't buy food? No pants—the kids are gonna walk around with trousers up to their knees. No underwear—I'm gonna be the only forty-two-year-old man downtown with diaper rash. No food either? What the hell did you buy? Nine hours shopping!"

"Eight hours, if you count commuting."

I begin chewing the rope on one of the bags. I read somewhere that if you're starving, you can get nutrition out of almost anything.

"Do you want to see what I got?"

"No."

She doesn't listen. She begins to take something out of the bag. I know already what she got. When I see the white wrapping paper, my fears are confirmed. What she got is what we don't need, because we already got it. We got them, to be precise. We have got them on bookshelves, on the floor, on the tops of tables. We have got them hanging on walls. They stare into our eyes, down onto our heads, up to our navels. They are a collection of statues, face masks, retablos and pots. They are called folk art. Not by me and the kids. The kids call them dumb, and I call them expensive and a few other names. But those who sell them, and those who buy them and those who tromp through the house to admire them call them folk art.

So, in the dining room is a statue of a well-endowed African native pointing his parts in the general direction of where I eat. She got her first inkling of my attitude toward this folksy art when I muttered one evening at dinner, "That guy thinks I'm a white colonialist, and he's gonna piss in my salad."

The kids were laughing. They thought it was funny. Sometimes, it takes awhile for Caryl to get a joke. I said that two, three years ago, and she hasn't laughed yet. She also didn't laugh when Steven and Alyssa paraded their friends into the rooms to make appropriate anal remarks about the other natives.

"He looks like he's makin' a doo-doo," one volunteered. They all broke up, they being at the time kids age eleven and under and me, not her.

She lectured the kids on the meaning of art and how people in far off Zaire and Mexico worked for weeks, making these things out of wood and stone, by hand, et cetera.

"They're made in Rahway, New Jersey," I tried telling her. "They're made in a factory by machines. And the last machine on the line is the stamping machine. You want Taiwan, the machine stamps Taiwan. You want Upper Volta, the machine stamps Upper Volta."

She looked at me the way a patrician Roman would have looked at a Visigoth. "You can tell they are handmade, because they are roughly hewn."

"That's another machine," I explained. "It's called the bruiser. It comes before the stamper. They feed the stuff into this machine and it knocks the thing around for a while, so people like you can tell people like me it's handmade."

She didn't buy the factory explanation. She doesn't have my street smarts. Worse, she had a classical education. It tends to muddle the mind.

"Okay, let's take your scenario and look at it," I told her one day, after she came home with a statue of a lady who was not wearing a bra, a piece of work clearly calculated to prompt great derision from the neighborhood kids. "Some poor sonofabitch in a village somewhere is working for a month on this one statue, nothing else. Just him and his little whittling knife. Then, the big white wholesaler comes up from Nairobi and gives this guy two dollars, a week's supply of unfiltered smokes, and some orders for more statues. By the time it gets to the store where you bought it, the price is up to $85, and you're convinced it's a bargain, because if you bought it in New York, where we don't live, as opposed to Boston, where we happen to live, it would have cost $115, not counting parking."

"This is art!" she screamed. "You want the children growing up without an appreciation of art?"

"Why the frig not!" I parried intellectually. "I didn't grow up with no appreciation, and it didn't do me no harm!"

Apparently, my rapierlike responses in countering her theories on her own intellectual level overwhelmed her, for she just laughed and went back to reading some book on Mexican rug weaving and how you yourself can do it at home with only a few simple pieces of machinery. "One begins by remortgaging the home. . . ."

So, here she is again, pulling this stuff out of the bags. The only things I'm looking at are the Master Charge slips falling onto the floor. "See? A spear carrier. Look at the detail. Look at the face. Look at the design on the shield."

See the nice design. See the nice bills. See Alan get a night job. See Alan on his hands and knees trying to pick up loose change after parish hall bingo games. See Alan fail to pay his bills. See Alan skip town. See Alan doing time. See the folk art that keeps Alan company in his cell, while all the other guys have tape decks and TV.

There's no reasoning with the woman. I can't walk into a room where I'm not being stared at by the death mask of an Aztec. In the middle of summer, I look at Nativity scenes, one of which seems to be taking place in a three-story tenement house with cows and sheep wandering about.

All of this implies good news and bad news.

The good news is that she alone is going to upgrade the economy of the Third World, so that it is on a per capita income level with Sweden and the Arab Emirates.

The bad news is that in order not to go broke we are going to have to sell folk art, and given that she will not part with what she has bought, I'm going to have to learn to whittle. The trouble is, aside from my total lack of any proven ability in this field, there isn't much of anything folksy or quaint left in America to reproduce and sell elsewhere. My only hope is that somewhere in Paraguay an emerging middle class family will want a hand-carved bas-relief of a typical native American boy vandalizing his elementary school or boosting his grandmother's purse.

Caryl

Das Kapital

THAT LITTLE business enterprise Alan dreamed up is a good example of the business acumen of both our families. Between us, we have the genes of industrious Germans, clever Jews, colonizing Britishers; why has nobody in either of our families ever made a dime? (I did not even mention the Irish and the Romanians, because nobody expects a lot from those genes except poetry and the ability to carry a tune.)

It seems that both Alan and I are much better at observing people who make money than by joining them at it. He has criss-cross references on who is on how many boards of directors, his reporter's tools. I fancy myself a critic of business trends, which means the fact that I can't balance my checkbook is beside the point.

It is in this role that I have taken notice of the newest movement of American capitalism—straight for your local college campus. "Free Enterprise Goes to College" is the name of the game. *Newsweek* ran an item not long ago about the fact that American corporations are subsidizing the study of Truth, Justice and the American Way of Making Money. The University of Texas has set up an Institute for Creative Capitalism, with generous donations from such folks as Mobil Oil. Petrodollars ease the way for the Texas A&M Center for Education and Research in Free Enterprise. Goodyear is the sponsor of a chair in free enterprise at Kent State, and similar programs and centers seem to be proliferating at least as fast as nuclear weapons.

The prophet of this movement is former Treasury Secretary William Simon, who suggests that big companies ought to spend their dollars on campuses which are simpatico. He says that the free enterprise system should not "finance its own destruction" by giving money to universities which display a weakness for radical thought.

As an academic myself, I am intrigued by the movement of big business into academe and spent some time looking into the progress that has been made. There is so much valuable research to be undertaken in the name of free enterprise! After I took a survey of the programs now being financed by the corporate sector, I came away much impressed. A few examples:

The Emery Chemical Company Institute on the Civilian Uses of Napalm: The precipitous end of the Vietnam War brought about a crisis for our napalm reserves. It had been believed that we would be in Southeast Asia for at least twenty years, pacifying the countryside with napalm and ensuring healthy profits for those who make it. The institute's researchers have been investigating alternative uses for the sticky stuff. One promising approach is to use it in the war against organized crime. Strategic hits on bookie joints in Bayonne, the baronial mansions of Mafia chiefs in Phoenix and on small groups of undergraduate marijuana peddlers on the campus at Berkeley would keep the need for napalm constant.

Researchers are also looking into the feasibility of using napalm for pest control. Persons having trouble with pesky mosquitos at lawn parties could merely dial a toll-free number, give the digits of their Master Charge card, and order a strafing run by two Phantom jets that would bomb the little buggers back to the Stone Age.

The United Petroleum Famous Capitalist Composers Symposium: Capitalism has chronically suffered because the unions and the Socialists have all the good songs. "God Bless Free Enterprise" is derivative and trite, and nobody remembers the lyrics anyway. Capitalism needs a rouser like "Joe Hill" but it may be hard to come by. "I dreamed I saw J. Pierpont Morgan last night, alive as you and me" doesn't quite make it. Free enterprise needs an epic, a Beowulf for the boardrooms. One promising work is the saga of a petroleum executive who was caught by the SEC trying to bribe a Korean minister of commerce, hauled before a Congressional committee, and for his valiant efforts in behalf of free enterprise is now pining away in the same prison where they sent the Watergate felons. It is set to the tune of "John Brown's Body."

Leonard Evans' body lies
  A-tanning in the sun
At Allenwood Federal Penitentiary
  Where he's 75401
But his spirit marches on.

Leonard went to prison saying,
  "I am not a crook."
Why should he be punished
  Just because he bribed a gook?
But his spirit marches on.

The Wilbur Eaton Chair for Research of Apartheid (named for the president of that venerable university who said nix on divestiture): A team of eminent biologists and political scientists, funded by a consortium of American companies doing business in South Africa, has discovered that apartheid is in fact beneficial to South Africa's black majority. The blacks are growing hardy and strong from all that physical work, digging diamonds out of the mines and raking up hardscrabble earth to plant subsistence crops. The whites are growing soft and lazy, what with their servants and leisure time, so much of it spent on the tennis court. In fact, one biologist has observed that the hands of South African whites are beginning to evolve in a peculiar way. The digits are disappearing and the palm is expanding, so it resembles the sweet spot of a Dunlop Jack Kramer. When all the whites in South Africa evolve to the point where their hands are shaped like tennis rackets, they will be unable to use their automatic weapons and the blacks will simply take over under the law of survival of the fittest. So it's clear that American universities should not divest themselves of holdings in corporations doing business in South Africa, but rather should increase such holdings—in the interests of the black race.

Not only are corporations funding special programs at universities, but they are also creating propaganda for free enterprise. The Center for the Study of Private Enterprise at the University of California turns out red-and-white bumper stickers that read: "The American Economic System: It Works When We Do." I discovered that this is only the first in a salvo of free-enterprise bumpers. Soon to be available from other sources are:

"Support Your Local Strikebreaker: Take a Goon to Lunch."
"Capitalists Do It Profitably."
"Honk if You Love Tax Loopholes."
One center is even working to enlist corporate executives in political

activism. Justin Dart, president of Dart Industries, says that many universities are "plotting the destruction of the free enterprise system."

Executive Action 101, which I was allowed to sit in on, ought to go a long way toward remedying this problem. The class that I observed included two vice presidents of corporations, a network censor, a production manager of an auto company and the national manager of a chain of hamburger stands. The men were carrying M-1 rifles and wearing three-piece suits, ski masks from L. L. Bean and bandoliers of ammunition bearing the Halston monogram. They were about to begin target practice on a life-sized cardboard cutout of Ralph Nader.

Later in the course they would undertake one search-and-destroy mission to cut down redwoods in a national park, another to Newfoundland where they would club baby harp seals. They would learn the proper technique for burning crosses on the lawns of members of the Sierra Club, and the final exam would be a midnight mission in which the students would assemble a fully operational nuclear-power plant on the lawn of the Kennedy compound in Hyannisport.

Not everybody who is a philosophical champion of free enterprise is overjoyed about the movement of business money onto the campuses. Economist Milton Friedman, for one, thinks it goes against the very idea of a university to appoint academics to shill for one point of view. But money is getting tight in higher education these days, and one wonders what's next: The Meyer Lansky School of Criminal Justice? The Burger King Chair of Theology? The Consolidated Edison Center for the Study of the Benefits of Radiation? The Larry Flynt School of Family Studies?

The mind boggles. Who knows? Academic freedom may finally fall from the fast buck from within, rather than the Philistines outside the walls.

Alan

Bureaucracy in Bloom

CARYL, HAVING grown up in a very law-abiding community, is prone to making light of endeavors just on the other side of the law. Indeed, there are those who could sing their way off to the slammer, but I am not one of them. I am in awe of the law, and not just the criminal law. Let some bureaucrat pen a regulation, and I'll abide promptly. And I'm not that passive about it either. I lust after the latest regulations, statutes, guidelines and findings of investigative bodies. Let others more romantic than I drink after hours or double park, just give me a deskful of General Accounting Office reports. Like this one, for example:

"Management and control of personal property is poor and procurement controls should be strengthened at U.S. embassies in Latin America."—Feb. 11, 1980.

To some people that might just be a jumble of bureaucratic verbiage, an unimportant memorandum that shall be little noted and not long remembered. Most people would read it and yawn. Not me. It sets my imagination aflame. I can See It Now:

The chanting and the cursing of the crowd pounds with the rhythm of waves against the walls in the embassy in downtown Hijo de Puta, the capital city of the Republic of Burrito. "Abajo Conglomerates! Abajo Imperialistic malfeasance! Burrito for los Burritanos!"

The cadence is broken only by the sporadic smashing of glass, as an occasional frozen burrito finds its mark. The siege at the U.S. embassy has been going on for what seems like an eternity, so long that the news media personnel who had crowded into the quaint alleys around the compound are long gone on other assignments.

Only the Burritanians of the Front for the Liberation of Burrito, led by El Chaucero, their English-major dropout from B.U. (Burrito University), remain, and their mood is growing angrier each day. Their original 376 non-negotiable demands have been scaled down to 142 unshakable demands, dealing mainly with working conditions on Burrito's lush grape farms.

"We will make no wine before its time," they insisted in the beginning, and now, it is their basic chant, their trademark, already picked up and emblazoned on undershirts by half a dozen Maoists on New York's East Side. "We will make no *wine* before its time! We will make no *wine* before its time!"

Franklin Ferret, the embassy security officer (Saint Mary's Star of the Sea High, Fordham, Georgetown, OSS, CIA) looks hard at his boss, the ambassador, Payola Pruitt (St. Paul's, St. Mark's, Beaver Country Day, Princeton, Fletcher School of Diplomacy, State Street Bank and Trust, Mobil).

"Pruitt's a pro," Ferret had been briefed at Foggy Bottom. Pruitt, indeed, is a career man, Ferret thinks. Who else, in the midst of such obvious danger, would be worried about a report from the General Accounting Office?

"Will you look at this, Franklin?" Pruitt asks in his thick north-of-Boston accent. "Dahn it ahl."

"With all due respect, sir," Ferret interjects quietly, "I should like to direct your attention to the left wing of the embassy, which is on fire."

Pruitt shakes his head and continues, as if he hasn't heard a word. He waves in the air a document labeled "Acc. No. 111526 (ID-80-23)." Ferret's trained eye sees all that he needs to. The GAO had been asking a lot of questions all over Latin America, tough questions that no embassy staff likes to hear or answer:

"Is the guacamole in your commissary purchased by open bid or from selected dealers?

"Is the linen laundered in-house or farmed out to the State Department's approved list of native sweatshop laundries?"

The casual air of the GAO investigators had kidded no one. GAO is on a witch hunt, and the paper Pruitt waves about documents problems "in personal-property management at U.S. embassies in Latin America."

"No nuclear testing on Burrito's plains!" the crowd outside chants.

"Listen to this, will you, Franklin?" the ambassador asks in that tone of voice he uses when his perception of fairness has been assaulted. He reads from the report, "Periodic inventories were not performed, property records were incomplete and inaccurate, and property-requirement standards were not established."

"No more drafting of Burrito's free agents!" the crowd outside is chanting. Their mood is turning ugly.

"For gosh sakes," Pruitt exclaims, "how does one inventory property, when militants keep burning our flags and mattresses? How do we keep property records intact, when indigenous labor, posing as housekeepers, keep stealing our accounts receivable and displaying them as evidence of spying?"

"Environmental-impact statements or death!" the crowd outside is chanting. Now, even Pruitt's ears perk up.

"Where the heck are our Marine guards, Franklin?"

"As you may recall, sir, we were assigned a full Marine platoon, which, given the strength of today's all-volunteer armed forces, numbers three persons, to wit: one infantry person, one radio operator/clerk-typist/motor-pool person and one maitre d'. We have instituted emergency procedures and have armed the radio operator/clerk-typist/motor-pool person and placed him with the infantry person." Ferret pauses uncomfortably.

"And?" Pruitt demands.

"Well, the combat infantry person is a female person, and the radio operator-etc. person is a male person, and one hour after they were posted guard at the windows, we found them in a linen closet doing what they insisted was close-order drill. They've been put on report."

"What about the other Marine?"

"He's been acting strangely, sir. He's been walking around dressed only in a jockstrap asking embassy personnel to take his picture. He says that if female personnel can now make a few bucks on the side posing out of uniform, a man who stormed Lebanon's beaches for Ike should have some equal opportunities. He's been put on report."

"So, we have no Marines?"

"That's right, sir, but it makes no difference. The Gatling gun is rusted, and even if it weren't, Marines are under orders from the State Department never to shoot in self-defense."

"The crowd is getting harsh," Pruitt observes.

"Kill Babe Ruth!" the crowd is chanting.

"Kill Babe Ruth?" Ferret asks.

"You forget, Ferret, that this has been a hell of a long siege here."

The jangling of the phone on Pruitt's desk startles them. Pruitt grabs for it and hears the nervous voice of the embassy information officer, Sheldon Stonewall. "I've been fielding calls from the networks and wire services all morning, sir. We're gonna have to come up with some kind of cover story."

"Cover story for what?" Pruitt asks with the impatient and patronizing tone he reserves for ethnic American employees. "The embassy's under siege by communist elements directed from Moscow and infiltrated by Castro's agents and fake priests. It's the story we've been using for years."

"They're not asking about the siege, sir," Stonewall says. "They've got the GAO report on procurement controls. Apparently it's broken everywhere."

Pruitt holds the receiver away from his ear. He seems to age suddenly before Ferret's eyes. The militants must have broken into the compound, Ferret concludes.

"The GAO report on procurement controls," Pruitt says, his words barely audible. "The press has it!" He buries his head in his left palm.

Ferret can hear Stonewall's chatter on the line. "NBC wants to know why procurement regulations and prudent management practices were not followed to ensure against fraud and abuse. ABC is asking why competition in bidding was inadequate. CBS is harping on why purchases exceeded authority. Public Television has a seventeen-year-old unpaid intern from Radcliffe who calls every five minutes asking why files were not documented. What do we tell them?"

Pruitt has ceased functioning. Ferret takes charge. He firmly but gently takes the receiver from the ambassador's hand, places it to his own mouth, and says in clipped tones, "Stonewall, this is Ferret. You want to know what to tell 'em. This is what you tell those leeches. You tell them the GAO report isn't worth a kettle of warm spit. You tell them that a great American went to pieces today. You tell them that the GAO did to him what a bunch of rotten commies couldn't do. You tell them he was stabbed in the back by his own snoopy countrymen, while he defended their interests in a far-off distant corner of America's manifest destiny."

Ferret replaces the receiver quietly. Pruitt is slumped in his chair staring off into space. And then Ferret hears what he feared he would hear. Stonewall is right. The procurement report is out. The crowd outside has taken up a new chant, and Ferret knows the embassy's days are numbered:

"No more failure to follow procurement regulations and prudent management practices to ensure against fraud and abuse!"

"No more failure to follow procurement regulations and prudent management practices to ensure against fraud and abuse!"

"No more failure to follow procurement regulations . . ."

Caryl

Reader's Digest

ALAN LIKES reading the serious stuff like government agency reports. Not me. I am into trash. Give me a schlocky best seller I can read in the john and I am happy. But you won't find me wading through a gothic, or one of those orgasm-every-page epics. I like nonfiction junk, the stuff that purports to be serious but is, at the center, marshmallow fluff. Because of this avocation, I regard myself as something of a critic where the literary marketplace is concerned. For those of you with an interest in where the market is heading, let me fill you in on a couple of the latest trends.

A real "surefire" category of best sellers is the genre best represented by *Winning Through Intimidation*, by Robert Ringer. This book, and others like it, gleefully instruct the reader to jettison some 2,000 years of Judeo-Christian tradition in the interest of upward mobility. They point out that turning the other cheek is strictly for losers, and that anybody who thinks the meek shall inherit the earth hasn't been to the Harvard Business School lately, where one course instructs students in a ploy called strategic misrepresentation—i.e., lying.

Getting ahead, it seems, is chiefly a matter of Doing Unto Others, using people like so many paper towels. The rewards for this are money, fame, and power. Guilt is never mentioned, since it has no place in the annals of making it.

Several new books elaborating on this theme will soon be in the bookstores, and I would like to mention a few of the ones that will undoubtedly make the "list."

Getting Ahead by Being Thoroughly Despicable, by Dr. Ronald McIver, a psychoanalyst and Toyota dealer from Duluth, maps out a clear path to success in the boardrooms of American business. Among the subjects he treats at length are: Computer Fraud for Beginners; the Etiquette of Blackmail; Discreet Embezzling; Kissing Ass with Class; and Sammy Glick Was a Right-on Guy.

If McIver takes a contemporary approach to success in America, another author, A. J. Breathwaite, a corporate executive who also teaches psycho-history at Herkimer Technical School, looks to the past with *Career Tips from Great Men of History.* Breathwaite suggests that people who want to get ahead in business study the management strategies of some of history's famous can-do men. The chapter titles offer a capsule look at the book's extremely practical approach:

Getting Your Rivals out of the Home Office—Joseph Stalin
Picking Junior Executives—Julius Caesar
Getting Reliable Information from Your Employees—Torquemada
Managing People Effectively—Gregory Rasputin
Assertiveness Training—Attila the Hun (when he talks about severance, he doesn't mean a paycheck)
Finding a Mentor—Iago
Breaking with a Mentor—Judas Iscariot.

Success seems to be the number-one theme of popular literature these days, taking the top spot from that old standby, sex. It's not only how you behave that will affect your climb up the ladder, but you must also learn to dress for success as well. For too many people, however, the concern with appearance, which starts with Grecian Formula to wash away gray temples, stops short of the ankles, and can be the Achilles heel of the upwardly mobile individual. Realizing this, Thomas Brady, general manager of Brady's Brogans, has some valuable advice to offer in *Your Feet Are Your Fortune.* He advises would-be executives that a pair of Gucci loafers may be more important than an MBA—even if they do cost more. He adds that if you jog in your old black high-top basketball sneakers from high school, no one is going to give you the big account. The "hooker look" in spike-heeled slingbacks, he warns, doesn't make it in the corporate boardroom—especially if you're a guy.

Success, of course, isn't the only popular theme on the best-seller lists these days. There is another kind of book that is selling like hotcakes, and it falls—vaguely—under the heading of psychology. These are the books that suggest that as long as you like yourself, everything will be hunky-dory. Why bother with expensive analysis when you can get all the answers for $11.95? These books insist that every experience, whatever its nature, can enrich your life if you've got the right attitude. A few of the promising titles due out soon:

The Joy of Dying, by Damon (Digger) O'Dell, a mortician and junior high school guidance counselor. Dr. (mortuary science) O'Dell offers well-thought-out ways to make dying an opportunity for personal growth. He believes that death suffers from a poor image and that an aggressive advertising campaign could increase its popularity. "Going with gusto" sounds like a lot more fun than shuffling off this mortal coil. A catchy jingle could do wonders for death's poor PR track record. Among the subjects O'Dell deals with in this sensitive and understated book:

> Is Dying Really Bad for Your Health?
> Planning the Bon Voyage Party
> Living with Brain Death
> Who Says a Shroud Has to Be Dowdy?
> The Fun Funeral
> The Designer Look in Burial Urns

But perhaps the most impressive aspect of Dr. O'Dell's pioneering work is his carefully researched "Two Hundred and Thirty-seven Positions for Passing On," taken from ancient drawings on temple walls at Ankor Wat.

Fun Divorce, by Marvin and Miriam Weisskopf. (He is a dentist and she is a computer programmer. They have been happily divorced for three years now.) The Weisskopfs report that the main problem with divorce in the past was the lack of ritual. After all, we have rituals associated with all the important events in our lives—marriage, birth, death—but divorce has been allowed to creep up like a thief in the night. There is no social stigma to divorce, say the authors. In fact, these days, anyone who hasn't had at least one divorce is out of the mainstream. The Weisskopfs suggest that each couple which is parting throw a gala party and invite all their friends. The authors have come up with a number of games which will have symbolic meaning for the divorcing couple:

Charades: The guests must guess the identity of the husband's mistress or the wife's lover through the familiar parlor game. ("Small word . . . four letters . . . rhymes with . . . hammer? No, nail . . . rhymes

with nail. . . . Pail? Jail? . . . Snail? . . . Mail? . . . Mail! *I got it!*
Mail! It's the mailman!")

Monopoly: The couple put the stocks and bonds, the car, and the
stereo on Park Place and battle it out. It is therapeutic for all concerned.

Scrabble: The guests see who can be first to spell out the major
reason for the divorce: S-E-X-U-A-L-D-Y-S-F-U-N-C-T-I-O-N or
M-E-N-T-A-L-C-R-U-E-L-T-Y.

Las Vegas: In this game, the couple shoot craps for the custody of
the children. The winner gets them for weekends and Christmas vacation. The loser gets them for the rest of the time and pays the orthodontist.

How to Be Your Own Best Buddy by Sam and Selma Snodgrass, who
operate a car wash and primal-scream clinic in Mobile. The authors advocate that you sing into your mirror every morning the words of Mister
Rogers, "I like you just the way you are." Then you should make a list
of your good qualities and take out ads proclaiming them in *The Progressive* and *Car and Driver*. When your mother hollers at you, "You
bum, why don't you get a job?," you smile and say serenely, "Every day
in every way I am getting better and better." When your boss fires you
for incompetence and stealing from petty cash, you simply grin and say:

Fe fi fo fum,
I am my own best chum.

And when the Internal Revenue Service comes to take you away for
claiming your disco lessons as a business expense, be lighthearted as
they snap on the cuffs. Sing out:

I am as good as I can be
Despite five to ten for felony.

Alan

Brevelnick at the Bat

I'M NOT as good as I wanted to be.

I didn't want to be Ted Williams. I wanted to be Sid Gordon. There were differences. Ted Williams was a super-hero, Sid Gordon was a damn fine ballplayer. Ted Williams came from a strange sunny land called California. Sid Gordon was born in Brooklyn.

Ted Williams gave the finger to the press, an act that struck me as showing some dignity. Sid Gordon just played ball. First, he played with the New York Giants, and then he came to Boston to play across town from Ted Williams, to play at Braves Field, where he stood at home plate and hit balls out of the field and into the railroad classification yard. Somebody told me once he hit one into the Charles River. Could be. He was some hitter, that Sid Gordon.

There was another difference. Sid Gordon was Jewish. And when you're a kid, and times are not good for you because you feel that you have to defend yourself every day for being what you are, then sports heroes are very big—sports heroes, cops, and gangsters of your own ethnic group.

Boston gave up Ed Stanky and Al Dark to get Sid Gordon and Buddy Kerr and Willard Marshall. Stanky became a manager later on. Dark became an all-star, a manager who said strange racial things to members of the San Francisco Giants, and then a reborn Christian. Marshall and Kerr played admirably and retired. Gordon kept going, even as the Braves moved from my city and my heart to a place called Milwaukee, an alleged community in a state where they grow cheese. At this writing, they are in Atlanta, and I don't even know who plays for them, and I don't care. The Boston Braves are dead, and so, sadly, is Sid Gordon.

And so, by the way, was my big dream. I knew I wasn't good enough to be a professional ballplayer, a minor leaguer, a college ballplayer, or even a high school ballplayer. I was a steady Sunday doubleheader sandlot ballplayer—lots of singles and doubles, a nice secure job in right field where hardly anybody ever hit anything and where you could get a nice tan and think about Sunday's upcoming pot roast.

So my dream, realistically, was not to be a baseball player. My dream was to be a baseball card. In other words, I didn't want to work at the game. I just wanted its glories, my picture staring out from a two-and-one-eighth-by-two-and-one-half-inch Bowman bubblegum card with my whole life story written in one small paragraph on the back. The guys who wrote that stuff really had to write tight copy, boy. One inch of copy because you had to leave room for white space, vital statistics, and advertising. Yet they did it with a style and grace rarely found in writing today.

Take Bill McCahan. He pitched for the Philadelphia Athletics. Who knows what crime he had committed to warrant that fate, but such was his lot. He was No. 31 in the 1948 series of cards. They posed him with his hairy arms over his head as if he were going to pitch. Great photojournalism it wasn't. But on the back, on the back was the poetry. In one concise paragraph, nudged between McCahan's vital statistics and an ad ("Ask for Blony Bubble Gum, the Bubble Gum with three different flavors") and the copyright, was this:

> Pitched a no-hit, no-run game against the Washington Senators. Last year was his first full year on the A's. He had only been in the minors for two years. He pitched for Wilmington in 1942, spent three years in the service and came out to pitch for Toronto in 1946 to win 11 and lose 7. He's a pitcher to keep your eye on. Another hometown boy makes good.

Of course, pitching a no-hit, no-run game against the Senators anytime after 1930 should not have been too hard, and anybody who stays longer than five minutes in Wilmington is likely to do anything to get out, even enlist in World War II. But these are nitpicking editorial comments which detract from the classic beauty of the prose. The writing was factual but not without human interest. Indeed, Buddy Rosar caught 102 games in 1947, but "off season, he's a policeman."

And so what if there was a little redundancy in the writing? So what if Snuffy Stirnweiss's history seemed faintly reminiscent of McCahan's, when his paragraph began with "Another hometown boy makes good," or Buddy Kerr's opening line, "A boy who's made good in his hometown."

In those years, the writers were generally kind to their subjects. Unproven players were always "someone to watch." If you weren't sure somebody was going to do as well in 1948 as he had in 1943, you could blame the Axis powers—"the war caught up with him in 1944."

Occasionally, Bowman might note that a ballplayer had not yet lived up to his potential. Sometimes the point was made with factual finality in the last sentence, "Now on West Coast, subject to 24-hour recall by Pirates." That pretty much said it. If you couldn't make the 1950 Pittsburgh Pirates, your face would probably not appear in the 1951 series of cards.

No, baseball-card writing was always superior to most of the stuff in the baseball magazines, which are really movie magazines with shin guards. *They* represent the worst of America's literature. They make reading *Hustler* like spending a day in the Library of Congress. The realities of life altered my dream of appearing on a baseball card, and I began thinking of perhaps writing for the card companies. Well, even in America, you can't have everything, right? But I would have been good. I would have written:

> Flungo Brevelnick did not quite live up to everyone's expectations last season when, at bat, he kept facing the umpire instead of the pitcher, but word is some seasoning in Triple-D Sonesta Valley club has given Flungo the maturing he needed. Flungo is tall, married, has six children, suffered measles as a child, and loves toads. Off season, he pimps and takes a course in auto mechanics. Ask for Blony Bubble Gum.

Caryl

Drek the Halls

SUMMER IS Alan's big season for ritual. When the crocuses bloom he gets out his shoeboxes full of baseball cards and mutters strange incantations: "RBI—MVP—ERA—designated hitter—reserve clause." His version of ancestor worship is to stare prayerfully, as he sits with legs folded up, at a 1948 sepia portrait of Stan Musial on a bubble gum card and recite in a sing-song chant the years Stan the Man won the batting championship.

For me, however, summer always seemed ritual-free. Lent was over, and along with it the quaint tradition we parochial school kids had of giving up movies for the duration. We had a break from the Baltimore Catechism and rote memorization of the corporal works of mercy and the seven deadly sins. God let up on us in the summertime. Winter, however, was another story. From the time the first leaf turned brown, the rituals, civic and godly, came in a rush, with Pilgrims and pumpkins and a parade of saints to celebrate. This all led up, however, to the Big One, the holiday that put all others to shame, Christmas day.

In the parish church I attended as a child, the pastor had the Midas touch, especially at Christmastime. Under his stewardship, even the poor box turned a profit. Christmas was an important time of year in terms of the balance sheet, and he made no bones about it.

He would stand in the pulpit, his portly frame ablaze with vestments that could make disco dresses look as drab as nuns' habits, and give his pre-Christmas sermon:

"Now, I don't want any White Christmas around here. I want a Green Christmas. *Green.* When the collection basket goes around today, I don't want to hear any jingling. I want *rustling.*"

I found his attitude refreshing. No mealy-mouthed humility, no talk of the widow's mite. He had a job to do—a school to run, two basketball teams to outfit with blue and gold warm-up jackets, bingo games to run. God's work on earth doesn't come cheap.

My own approach to Christmas runs along these lines. Let others decry the commercialization of Christmas, the desecration of the real meaning of the day. Not me. All the cultural deficiencies I suppress during the rest of the year hang out in December, particularly a weakness for kitsch and bourgeois sentimentality. I *like* the Muzak version of "O, Little Town of Bethlehem," electric guitar and all, wafting across the parking lots in shopping malls. I watch, voluntarily, the endless kiddie TV specials about reindeer whose noses light up and talking snowmen. My eyes glaze like the frosting on a Christmas cookie as I sing along with the musical scores of these productions, mouthing lyrics that in other seasons would make me want to throw up. Even my kids get disgusted at the excess. Steven said to me last year, "You're not gonna put all that crap all over the tree again, are you? It spoils the beauty of the tree."

I stood firm as the mighty oak. I consider myself a superior decorator of Christmas trees. "Only God can make a tree," I said to Steven, "but if He had any imagination He'd grow 'em with little red and green balls."

During the rest of the year, I worship at the Bauhaus altar. Less is more, and one perfect chair made out of a steel tube is *class.* In December I throw out *The Atlantic Monthly* and buy the *Good Housekeeping* Christmas issue which shows you how to make 407 different decorations out of old socks. I hang so much green and red *drek* around the house that it resembles nothing so much as a turn-of-the-century brothel during Christmas week. My latest passion is homemade Christmas ornaments, a family project that I thought could get us all into the spirit of the season.

"Let's make Christmas ornaments!" I announced in my Mary Poppins voice, which sets everyone's teeth on edge.

"Yeccccchhhh!" said Steven.

"Do we *have* to?" said Alyssa.

After dismissing notions of infanticide, I considered forced labor. It worked for Stalin. However, I guessed that the resulting mood would be more Triangle Shirtwaist Factory than Goodwill to Men.

"You don't know what you're missing," I said to them. "A chance for a happy childhood memory, right down the old tubes. Stab your dear mother in the heart, see if I care."

"Can it, Ma," Steven said as he went out to play street hockey.

"I'm going to the movies. Can I have four dollars?" Alyssa said.

"OK for you guys," I yelled. "I will have all the fun." And I sat there, making bunnies, angels and wreaths, happy as a clam.

Of course, the whole question of decor gets a little complicated at this time of year, because we are an ecumenical family. We have Chanukah as well as Christmas to contend with, though the paucity of Chanukah images is a problem. There's not a hell of a lot you can do with a *dreidel*. I once tried some Israeli Uzi submachine guns in a cunning shade of pink felt, but Alan didn't think they fit in with the message of the holiday. I broached the idea of a patchwork Torah bedecked with holly, but withdrew the offer when I saw the expression of sheer horror—or perhaps it was awe—on his face.

Christmas gives me an excuse for indulging my newfound passion for patchwork. It was all Gloria Vanderbilt's fault. She declared patchwork was chic and let *House Beautiful* take pictures of the way she used patchwork quilts for tablecloths. I was hooked—a new art form. I gave up the Sunday *Times* for *Quilter's Handbook*. I began to wander around mumbling "Sunshine and Shadow" and "Flying Geese." I bought a sewing machine, and since I can't sew during the day when I am working, I create at night. The drone of the machine drowns out the last act of "Kojak." It makes Alan uneasy. Who wants to be married to Madame Defarge? He wonders if I am stitching his name in the corners of the blocks. I do go overboard on my hobbies. In one week of frenzied sewing I turned out more quilts than a platoon of Amish women could have whipped up locked in a sweatshop. I hang them on the wall, on the beds, on the dog. One day I may quilt a Christmas tree. I do not, however, lower myself to mundane pursuits where sewing is concerned.

Steven came up to me one day when I was hunched over the sewing machine and tapped me on the shoulder.

"Hey, Ma, could you sew a button on my jacket?"

I cast him a cold, Defarge-like glance.

"I don't do buttons."

"My neck gets cold."

"Wear a scarf."

But then, I had a thought. My face brightened.

"How about I quilt you a whole new coat? I could do it in two hours, tops. I'll make it in purple, green, and red, in the Lone Star pattern.

You'll be the only kid in the junior high with real country chic. Let's see, where did I put that calico?"

Steven backed away, fear in his eyes, and tiptoed back to his father, who was straining to hear the final minutes of "Kojak."

"Dad, I got this button . . ."

Last year at Christmas I did patchwork cows, beavers, and owls. I hung them about the windows. Alan claimed the house looked like the hallucination of a vice-president of the ASPCA after he had dropped acid. I ignore such jibes and go on with my decorating. One day right before Christmas I was walking by a local florist's shop and saw a beautiful arrangement of dried flowers, berries, and pinecones in a rough-hewn planter. My heart leapt with greed. I *had* to have it. I walked in and said to the florist, "That would be great for my table Christmas day."

He looked at me with sheer horror—or perhaps it was awe. "But that's a cemetery planter," he said.

"Well, maybe people wouldn't know. It sure would make a great centerpiece."

"You can't put that on the table," he said, his voice getting tense. "That's for a gravesite."

"Well, my kids always say you could drop dead from my cooking. Heh-heh." I thought he would appreciate a little mortuary humor. He didn't.

"Lady, you really don't want to buy this!" he implored.

I did, I really did, but I watched him as he hugged the planter and glared at me as if I were a grave robber who got $15.75 a head from the Harvard Medical School and lost my nerve. I didn't buy it because of superstition. It would be an omen. I would strangle on a strand of tinsel trying to get the gilt-encrusted star to the top of the tree, and there I would lie, on the floor, quietly decomposing amid the discarded wrappings, presents, and patchwork ornaments, not to be discovered until the January cleanup.

I did, however, purchase a dozen pinecones, three sprigs of berries, and a genuine small spruce for the coffee table. I named the spruce Gilbert and told the kids to be sure to water him. They did, with a vengeance. Gilbert drowned on Christmas Eve, going down for the third time in a sea of watery mud as the radio blared "Jingle Bell Rock." We tried to save him, but mouth-to-mouth does not work on a spruce.

Clearly, I am afflicted with a bad case of excess where Christmas is concerned. It comes from my childhood. Mine was a sober, sensible, middle-class family, and my parents were given to pronouncements about cleaning one's plate and saving one's allowance. We vacationed in modest wooden cottages in Ocean City, Maryland, ate meat loaf once a week, and never owned a vehicle flashier than a Chevy sedan. But at Christmastime, all stops were pulled out. Our tree was not so much decorated as burdened, groaning under the layers of tinseled glop. It was as dazzling to me as the sight of the Almighty Himself would have been. The lights blazed, the presents were piled under the tree, and the stocking bulged with fruit and candy. It was opulence worthy of a sultan, about which my mother always felt a bit guilty. "We've got to stop going overboard on Christmas," she would mutter. But they never did, of course.

I see this season as my own winter solstice, that old pagan fete in which the Bronze Age folks whooped it up and danced and sang so the sun god wouldn't forget to come back, or something like that. Don't preach to me about materialism, or bad taste, or use any of those rational arguments. Take away my patchwork and my tinsel and my shiny ornaments and I might wind up painting myself blue and running around in the backyard baying at the moon. Just play me another chorus of "Rudolph" while I finish wrapping a piece of plastic junk that I had to wrestle away from a little old lady in a discount store. She went down like a rock under a karate chop but she came to in a minute or so. I went home feeling nothing but goodwill towards my fellow men. "Have yourself a merry little Christmas. . . ."

Alan

Victory at Sea

I DON'T mind the Christmas tree, and, in fact, I sort of like looking at it.
I like looking at it the whole week before Christmas. I like looking at it
on Christmas Eve and Christmas Day. I like looking at it on New
Year's Eve and even the first couple of days of the new year. It starts to
lose a little of its luster during January. By mid-February, I don't like it
so much. By early March, I yell a lot about said tree. By mid-March,
the brown, droopy thing with the strange quilted decorations on it actually scares me. One night, when alone in the room with it, the thing
walked over to where I was reading and threatened that it would get me
before I would get it. By April, even Caryl agrees to help throw the
thing out over the back porch. Who says Caryl doesn't clean? I suppose
I say it. One day, she announced she was needed in Maryland. I
couldn't get away, so she would take the kids. I could run the house the
way I wanted for a couple of days.

So, when I heard the thump, thump, thumping, I was the only
human in the house. I knew I was not thumping, because I am very
alert from about 4 A.M. to 6 A.M. Those are my most productive hours.
Those are my only productive hours. Jane, capable of such stupid things
as thumping her head against a wall, was not yet part of our lives. The
mice were not up to thumping; they were losing weight and looking
frail, for with Caryl away, there wasn't any garbage on the floor or on
the counters.

"It must be the shotgun," I thought. The airport has a crew of guys who go around firing a shotgun to scare away seagulls and other birds that might get sucked into the jet engines. In those days, that was about the only socially progressive thing the airport was doing. Every morning, you'd hear a few thumps and see sudden rushes of birds and gulls going off in one direction or another. "It must be the shotgun."

Thump. Whomp. Thump. Whomp.

"But if it's the shotgun," I reasoned, now talking out loud to myself, "how come it doesn't stop, and how come it is louder than usual, and what the hell is a whomp instead of a thump, hah? A whomp? Shotguns don't go whomp." I thought for a while about what goes whomp. Somebody thrown to the mat in a wrestling match goes whomp; I knew this first hand. Some early back-up rock 'n' roll singers went whomp, as in "Whomp bomp a doo daa de whomp whomp whomp." What else went whomp?

Oy vay.

Guns. Guns go whomp. Big guns. My vast military career was not for naught. I knew a big gun when I heard one. First, I had grown up in this community, when our coastal defense systems used to whomp expensive government shells out into the Atlantic so that if the bad guys showed up, the town of Winthrop would not keel over without at least a whomp. Second, I had been in tanks.

"Tanks?" my father had said, when I announced one day on the phone that the University of Massachusetts offered two military programs, both for the totally insane—one for guys who wanted to fly jets and the other for guys who wanted to crawl into tanks and go to the Black Forest in Germany or the Thirty-eighth Parallel in Korea.

"Tanks," I had answered.

"You're velcome," said my father, laughing hysterically. I believe it was on that day that burlesque officially died.

At UMass, we drove tanks with 75-millimeter cannon up and down a farmer's field. The United States, through the state university, paid the farmer for the right to do this. He undoubtedly made more money getting his field torn up than he ever made for growing anything. There's no such thing as a dumb farmer. There was, however, such a thing as a dumb tanker. I know this the way I know about going whomp when you're losing a wrestling match.

A check with the Department of the Treasury records undoubtedly will show that for six weeks in 1958 and for six months in 1960–61, the value of America's defense bonds dipped decisively. Those were major moments in our nation's military history, for America proved just how liberal it could be by allowing me onto the Fort Knox reservation and near its weapons. I may have been the only person who was asked to burn his draft card in the interest of national security. I could not then, nor can I now, read a compass. I could not then, nor can I now, read a map. I could not then, nor can I now, walk into a patch of woods— defined as an area with fewer than four tenements on one acre of land —and find my own way out. The only thing that I did then that I don't do now is lose tanks. I lost a tank. I had left it in perfectly good shape and then I returned (to the woods, of course) to find it was gone. You can't leave anything alone in this country anymore. My only joy was in trying to figure out how the guy who hooked it was going to fence it.

My military incompetence was not unexpected, for I had actually failed my first ROTC interview. This is hard to do. You have to jump over the desk and kiss an officer full on the mouth before you flunk. I didn't. I just got confused. One officer got the feeling I didn't know much or care much about the outdoors. Given that most of the wars America has fought have been outdoors, this lack of sensitivity on my part could be a problem. With some disgust, the colonel asked me, "Cadet Lupo, were you ever in the Boy Scouts?"

"Boy Scouts?" I answered, as if I had never heard of them.

He seemed impatient. "You must have heard of the Boy Scouts."

"Yessir. I have heard of the Boy Scouts, but I never joined the Boy Scouts. I probably would have enjoyed the Boy Scouts, but we didn't have them. We had Cub Scouts once in the Jewish Community Center, and we put on a play, and one kid got his foot stuck in the spit-toon," I explained, assuming a jocular air, which he and the other officers declined to share. One of them, in fact, was staring at me with his mouth open; he would remain, motionless, like that for the rest of the interview, which went like this:

"Excuse me, Cadet Lupo, but I never heard of an American community that didn't have Boy Scouts. You did grow up in America, didn't you?"

I not only had grown up in America, but I had never belonged to any of those strange organizations listed on the paper the officers made me sign. I couldn't have belonged, even if I had wanted to, because most of them had gone out of business or were located somewhere in the Balkans.

"We had Brownies, sir."

"What's that?"

"Brownies. We had Brownies, where I grew up. And I think when the Brownies grew up, they turned into Girl Scouts. I remember that because they sold cookies. Vanilla ones and mints."

The captain who wasn't paralyzed turned to the colonel to ask him what he thought might be going on at this point.

"What cookies?" the colonel thundered. "Why are we talking about cookies?"

"No, sir. We're not talking about cookies. We're talking about Brownies."

"Are you telling me you ran around selling Brownies?"

"No, sir. I got the cookies from the Brownies who later became the Girl Scouts as best as I can trace it. Actually, my mother bought the cookies."

"What cookies?" the colonel screamed.

"Ah, sir," the captain able to talk interjected, "Ah believe the training group for the Girl Scouts are the Cookies, and Ah believe to make money, they sell Brownies."

By then, the colonel was looking at him the way the other captain was looking at me.

I smiled and leaned forward. "Not to be too forward, captain, sir, but the Brownies sold the cookies. The cookies didn't sell the Brownies, because that would be white slavery. Brownies sell cookies to make money, so that when they grow up . . ."

"Enough, dammit!" the colonel ordered.

He stayed away from my second interview, and I was admitted. I promised that even though I was about twenty at the time I'd consider getting in some Boy Scout experience, and what's more, I'd stay away from cookies and Brownies and Girl Scouts. My career moved steadily downward from that point.

But even a checkered career in the service of my country had not deadened me to the sounds of war, the drama of combat and the meaning of whomp. Whomp meant big guns. And the whomping on this particular morning was clearly coming from the harbor. I looked out my window to the left of my bed and saw two ships bristling with guns moving up the ship channel into the inner harbor. I saw flashes, then smoke, and heard whomp, thump, whomp, thump. Then I quickly reviewed the options: (A) A local lobsterman got a good buy on some Navy surplus and, instead of the drudgery of putting pots in the water, he was shooting the hell out of them. I discounted this, because most lobstermen would have been out and back before this hour. (B) Immigrants who had previously been refused entrance to the U.S. were now forcing their way in. This too I discounted, because I couldn't see anyone wearing shawls or eating pickled herring in steerage. (C) The United States was being invaded.

I settled on C. The United States was being invaded cleverly by sea, when for all these years we had dismantled our coastal defenses and sent guys to war rooms in Nebraska somewhere to look for radar blips in the air. Furthermore, we did not appear to be defending ourselves.

I would waste no more time. I crawled across the bed and got information for the Coast Guard and called them. "UnitedStatesCoast-Guard. OfficeroftheDayBurnsidesirmayIhelpyou?" Military people answer their phones the way law firms do. If you're not used to what they're saying, you have no idea what it is. Thank God for America's sake that I knew.

"Look, I know this is gonna sound stupid, but I just want to tell you I'm not fooling around, and I'm not drunk. I live in Winthrop, right near the harbor. Outside my window are two big ships coming into the harbor, and they're firing guns. Why is that?"

"You say they're in the harbor, sir?"

"Yes, and they're firing guns."

"Well, sir, that's not in our jurisdiction."

"You're kidding me!"

"Pardon me, sir."

"I'm sorry, we have a bad connection, just skip it. If I don't call the Coast Guard when two big ships come into the harbor firing guns, who do I call, the cops?"

"No, sir," he said without losing his polite bearing or enthusiasm. "You call the Navy and I'll get you that number and you ask for the officer of the day."

He did, and I did. I told the Navy, "Look, I know this is gonna sound stupid, but I just want to tell you I'm not fooling around, and I'm not drunk. I live in Winthrop, right near the harbor. Outside my window are two big ships coming into the harbor, and they're firing guns. They are firing guns generally in the direction of where I live, and I don't see anybody firing back. I have three questions. Question number one is—Are we at war? Number two—If so, with whom? Number three—Have we surrendered, and if not, why the hell don't we shoot back? I mean, I'm not a hawk or anything, but I don't know how to say 'I surrender' in Russian."

"Sir," he interrupted, "for this question, you have the wrong office. The officer in charge who could handle that question is not in yet. If you care to call back in an hour . . ."

"Call back!" I interrupted this time. "In an hour, kid, you and I will be in a boiler room, manacled and singing 'The Volga Boatman.' In an hour, Boston is gone. Three hundred years of history down the tubes, for Chrissakes!"

"Sir," he said, without losing his polite bearing or enthusiasm, "I'll try to connect you with another office." He did. This time I got a lady operator, the kind of lady operator I grew up listening to on the phone, the friendly ones with the flat Boston accents. No disrespect, but the United States is under attack, and they hand me to a lady operator.

I had lost any command presence in my voice. I was breathing a bit too quickly, hyperventilating to a background of increasingly louder whomps and thumps. "Ma'am, I have been transferred all over the place," I said. "Whatever you do, don't transfer me. Hang up on me, swear at me, but don't transfer me. I live in Winthrop. Outside my window is the harbor. In the harbor are two big ships. On the ships are guns, lots of guns. They are firing the guns. We are not firing back. Lady, are we at war, and if so, who is the enemy?"

She laughed. Well, what the hell, I told her she could laugh, as long as she didn't transfer what I by now presumed would be a high-priority call. She had a very hard time stopping the laughing.

"I'm sorry," she said. "I'm not really laughing at you. It's just you're gonna die when I tell you."

"From here, I'm gonna die anyway. Better I should die laughing."

"It's the Japanese!" she said, before being convulsed with hysterical laughter.

"Why are you joking?" I asked.

"I'm not!" she screamed, guffawing.

"The Japanese? I thought we beat them already."

"Ohhh, Margaret," she said, apparently to another operator manning America's front line of defense, "this gentleman is really funny. When I told him the Japanese, he said, 'I thought we beat them already.' Isn't he funny, Margaret?"

It took awhile, but she explained that the Japanese Navy was making its first formal call on the United States since before World War II. There was going to be a big ceremony and, if I wanted, I could go down to the docks and get a guided tour of the ships. The guns, she said, were just the Japanese way of saying hello.

"The last time they said hello this way was at Pearl Harbor."

"Oh, Margaret, this fella just said that the last time . . ."

When Caryl and the kids came home a few days later, she asked what, if anything, had happened while they were away.

"The Japanese Navy came by to say hello. They shelled the neighborhood."

Caryl made a face. "I asked a reasonable question. You don't have to get sarcastic."

"I called the Coast Guard, and they told me to call the Navy, and the Navy guy shifted me to the operator, and . . ."

Caryl walked out of the room.

Since then, I've had sporadic dreams of being awakened by some whomping and thumping. In the dream, I look out the window, and they're back. In the crow's nest is a young Japanese sailor with a megaphone. He's yelling, "You're probably wondering, Margaret, why I speak English so well. I went to your University of Southern California."

Printed in the United States
by Baker & Taylor Publisher Services